Flanagan's Dolls

WARREN ADLER

Chapter One

"Chaos reigns," Joshua Flanagan thought, "and all's well with the world." It was his repetitive homily, rarely spoken, more often whispered, especially now as he arrived from his morning jog with Caesar, his Rottweiler companion, friend and nudnik at the front entrance of Flanagan's Antique Emporium on 7 North Pratt Street.

"I declare thee open for business," he muttered, unhitching Caesar's umbilical cord and by a jiggle and twist of an oversized key opening the shop's front door.

Not that this act made much of an impression on the already stirring morning world of Lakeland Falls, which, according to Flanagan's personal gospel, was ground zero for the dotty, the eccentric and the whimsical and therefore the perfect place to nest for the latter fourth of his life. Or so he hoped.

Flanagan, buffeted impolitely by Caesar, entered into the eclectic clutter of the large front room of the shop. The room housed his seven tall clocks as guardians of Emily's hodgepodge of Victorian furniture, their oval backs and faded floral patterns set in helter-skelter disarray, much to the stoic disapproval of a trio of solid oak Dutch armoires. They, in turn, could take some satisfaction in their obstruction of the view of early American primitives, mostly of stiff-faced somber children posed with absurd looking animals.

Before entering into the living quarters in the rear where he and Emily nested, Flanagan scrupulously followed the ritual of the lighting of the lamps, twenty-two in all, including peacock lamps, brass-carriage side lamps, an opalescent Gone with the Wind lamp and an assortment of Art Deco bronze lamps of young ladies with hands raised to the shades, Flanagan was certain, begging to be released from this prison of wacky antiquity.

The tall clocks, now known as Flanagan's folly, hadn't attracted a single buyer in a year. So much for his marketing skills. Emily was far better. She knew what merchandize moved. Her latest exhibit contained three full sets of dining tables and chairs, one a valuable Victorian walnut loo table. The tables supported a forest of silver candlesticks, epergnes, vegetable dishes, pedestal dessert stands, vases, vinaigrettes, trays, salvers, toast racks, teapots and tureens presided over by dark varnished floral paintings.

Emily had given Flanagan license to create a dark paneled library in a corner of the store, which, he thought, offered a private lesson in logical clutter, with neatly standing leather-bound sets of English and American authors, most his favorites, on the high shelves and with the lowers set aside for smaller objects like paperweights, scent bottles, glass goblets and drinking sets, Staffordshire figures, Ralph Wood Toby jugs, terra-cotta busts, cane handles, car mascots, carved wood, small bronzes and a couple of china dolls.

Lamps lit, he proceeded to walk the long hall to the so-called living part of the house deliberately done by Emily in minimalist modern, mostly with built-ins and lots of shiny chrome. The back part of the house had been extended and redone with a glass facade that looked out on Emily's garden, half formal English, halfvegetable, and a screened-in bandstand gazebo where she did her pottery and breeze block carving.

From the front, the modern rehabbed rear could not be seen

and a screen of evergreens, bought already tall, protected the sides and rear from nosy tourists who roamed Lakeside Falls spring, summer and fall seeking country serenity far enough from big city life to recognize the purity of oxygen that swept in over the giant lakes from Canada. According to Flanagan's self-created rumor, a scientist who had turned to real estate for a living had once suggested, based on a genuine research project, that Lakeside Falls was the least polluted spot in the United States, which brought an end to tranquility and hoards of tourists seeking life extension through better breathing.

Small hotels and clutters of bed-and-breakfasts had proliferated at Lakeside Falls and were spotted throughout the town. When the tourists descended in the summer months, one realized, from the display of broad beams, thick thighs and distended stomachs, that the obesity pandemic was still in flood stage.

Flanagan's steaming coffee was waiting on the glass table in the children's mug, exclusively his own, with the inscription: "Keep Thy Shop and Thy Shop Will Keep Thee." Emily was already dipping her unfrozen water bagels in her Queen Victoria Commemoration mug, an anomaly if ever there was one, but he had long ceased to offer any puns or sallies on this point. In the background the ever present polishing tumbler tumbled. Emily was polishing stones for the jewel tree she was crafting, one of many that she had created.

The shop, which they had opened two years ago, represented a life change of sorts since they had chosen to reverse the pattern of full-time Manhattan life in a West Side apartment with a second home in Lakeside Falls, where they both had grown up by making the town their full-time residence and Manhattan an increasingly part-time sojourn, especially now that their twenty-something offspring had absconded with most of the space.

Joshua still continued to consult as a freelance insurance adjuster and Emily, who had worked full time at Christie's where she diligently applied her degree in decorative arts as an appraiser, was often called by her ex-employer to eyeball various entries to the auction world of antiques and collectibles.

Now in their late forties, they had chosen this less frenetic life to concentrate on Emily's lifetime dream of operating an antique store. They had done all the traditional preliminaries, raising their children in the Big Apple. Both of their offspring, who visited infrequently, characterized Lakeside Falls as a place for one's last lap after a disorderly and dissolute life, when better breathing was an absolute necessity.

Joshua, his name a compromise moniker agreed to by his Irish dad and Jewish mother, parlayed his degree in criminology into a lucrative freelance practice as an insurance investigator, a legacy of his father, an insurance agent whose stories of fraud and duplicity at the dinner table had turned him on to the profession. For years his father trudged up and down the streets of Lakeside Falls and all its rural appendages selling insurance on the installment plan, mostly at a dollar or two a week, which he collected and recorded in his long black insurance book.

Emily was the descendent of storekeepers who ran what was once the only general store in town. Her own father was still a storekeeper of sorts, running the only family-run pharmacy in town. It was hard to believe, but growing up there was a hierarchy of so-called class in Lakeside Falls and although Josh had watched Emily from afar throughout his early life, he had never felt a return of interest, which he had attributed to his own father's humble profession.

"I loved you from the moment I saw you," Josh had once confessed.

"When was that?"

"I saw your mother dry your little naked tush at the beach on the lake. That did it for me."

"How old was I?"

"Five, give or take."

"You were a pervert, even then."

The miracle was that they passed each other in Lakeside Falls with nary a blink of recognition until they met again in Manhattan at the Metropolitan Museum. His opening line was the cliché of clichés.

"Don't I know you from somewhere?"

"I have never been somewhere," she had responded.

Then as they say, fate intervened.

"I'm Josh Flanagan."

"Flanagan, Flanagan. Flanagan." Then came the oh my Gods. "The gawky string bean with pimples."

"The flaming redhead nose-in-the-air snob."

That was it, as they both recalled. Josh dubbed it "the moment of the joining of the hips."

The fact was that both Josh and Emily truly loved their child-hood home and Josh and she summered there for most of their married life. Emily had early on discovered in herself an esthetic sensibility which brought her a scholarship to Yale. There she excelled in history and enhanced her knowledge of old objects and the decorative arts. His work dovetailed with hers, another miracle of sorts.

As he began the ritual of breakfast with Emily, Caesar laid his heavy head on his right Nike.

"Rottweiler, will you remove your heavy-heartedness?" he said, trying to extract his foot.

"Can't you call him by his name?" Emily mumbled, flipping a well-soaked clump of bagel between her lips, and dripping dark stains on The Lakeside Falls Herald which lay open on the table.

"That is his name."

"That's his breed. His name is Caesar."

"Another Roman dog," Flanagan muttered.

"But he loves you. He's entitled to your respect."

"He is entitled only to my services, which include such items as maintaining my life according to his erratic schedule of waste disposal."

"You should have paid more attention to the way he was housebroken."

"It's him who's breaking me. I'm now on his schedule. Last night he had the urge before dawn. I didn't see you stirring."

"He sleeps on your side."

"Bedding with him is not an inducement to sexual congress."

"It doesn't seem to interfere with frequency."

"It is sinful," he smirked, "for him to watch with those doleful brown eyes. He is learning bad habits. He is, after all, only nine."

"Sixty-three in man years," Emily said.

"Mighty Caesar continues to stand fast."

"A bit too frequently."

"His ancestors are legion."

"A bit too legion. The vet wants him fixed."

"What is not broken must not be fixed."

She nodded, at times more adamant than he, a great supporter of the natural.

He took his Swiss chronograph from his flannel shirt's vest pocket and peered at its enamel dial. "Dawn of a new error," he said.

Emily smiled and shook her head in mock exasperation as they waited out the ten seconds until the tall clocks struck. They both listened, obviously counting off the strikes as the familiar cacophony vibrated through the house like the knell of church bells calling the faithful of diverse persuasions. Then suddenly only one clock was striking.

"Accept it," Emily said. "It will only drive you mad."

"It has already," Flanagan said. They had tried the best craftsman in the country. None dared to even try to eliminate the extra strike.

"The clock is accurate. It's only the beats that are screwed up."

"We could always ship it to Holland," Flanagan sighed. It was an eighteenth century Dutch marquetry longcase built by the great Rotterdam clockmaker, Steven Hoogendyk.

"Hoogendyk is a bit on the dead side."

"May he turn in his grave at every extra strike," Flanagan murmured.

"Why can't someone fix it?"

"That word again. You are fixated on fix. Some things are beyond such mundane chores. It is Hoogendyk's voice from the grave."

The clock had just been shipped back by still another craftsman. None of them wanted to take the chance of ruining the mechanism. The result was a ten thousand dollar white elephant. Still, the workmanship was miraculous. But no one wanted a tall clock with an extra strike. It made people crazy. Besides, it was a giant, one hundred and ten inches, too tall for most ceiling heights. And more than a foot higher than its nearest brother, a George III mahogany longcase by Lawson.

"Accept it, Flanagan," Emily said. "It's a white elephant."

"Not at all," he replied defensively. "It's a one-of-kind. Like a stamp printed upside down."

"It needs a special customer, someone one beat off."

"In that case, it should be a best seller. Everybody in Lakeside Falls is one beat off."

She looked up at him pointedly.

"I'm not one beat off." He lifted her hand with the bagel and bit off a piece. "I'm two."

"Hosannas for a man who knows himself."

"It will sell. I will not be daunted," he protested.

"Even the others are laggards. Problem is, Flanagan, you go for the big guys. They're all well over eight feet. Most ceilings are that size. I wish you hadn't...."

"None of that. You promised. Besides, I'm over my tall period."

"Let's hope." She emphasized an air of finality by pinching his cheek.

"I still say they're all gorgeous. People have lost their taste. Especially the summer people."

Since it was the beginning of October, most had left. Perhaps they might sell to the winter people due to arrive in a few weeks to ski the nearby slopes. Or the smattering of tourists who will come by to breathe better in the thin air of icy winters.

"They'll move," he mumbled. "Time marches on."

"Like my armoires," Emily snickered. As she talked, she had been taking a cursory interest in the newspaper. She was squinting, having trouble with the smaller print.

"Face it. You need specs."

"I'm only 43."

"Seven."

"That's what I said. Four and three is seven."

Josh snickered.

He watched her sly smile, which showed her double dimples and ocean green eyes peering under her reddish bangs, still radiant even as her once-flaming red curly hair was somewhat tempered with age. Seeing her like this every morning was a special treat, a celebration of the dumb luck of the mating game. He knew, too, that when he appeared for morning inspection, he felt certain that she exhibited the same thrill of recognition. Of course, such emotional content could never be insulted with words. Some things do not require verbalization.

To keep this illusion verdant, he took great care with his own physical grooming. Workouts kept his stomach flat and his muscles firm. He had turned gray prematurely and thanks to his late mother's genes he had not lost his hair, and the little wrinkles that had popped up beside his hazel eyes were giving him an air of gravitas, or so he believed. He was tall and enjoyed his height advantage, especially in viewing spectacles like parades and pageants. People always remarked that they were an attractive couple. He believed implicitly in such observation.

Suddenly, Emily's eyebrows rose. "Looks like our hopes for more winter people are down the tubes. They've stopped work on that new ski slope and condo project. The one that Jessie Shanks has been building." She read snippets from the story. "Apparently they've run out of money."

"Those fellows don't run out of money. The banks just stop throwing it at them."

She shrugged and continued to read, but with effort.

"Eyes," she said, conscious of his observation. "My eyes no longer see the glory," she said, aping his pun pretensions. It sparked in him a tiny tug of alarm. He was not very good dealing with her pain or defects, or, for that matter, any hint of her unhappiness. She knew it, too. "I think I need eye aid. I've already made an appointment with that new Dr. Blandings. Here three months and making quite a stir. He's a specialist in contacts."

"Blandings? What's wrong with Dr. Grant?"

"Dr. Blandings is younger, probably more progressive. Grant is way behind, especially on contacts. Besides, Audrey knows what's good."

"Case closed," Flanagan sighed. "The guru has spoken."

Audrey Hazeltine was more than Emily's best friend, confidante, and all-around advisor. They had been friends since first grade. She had married Sam Hazeltine, who had become county sheriff, a post he had acquired, by Flanagan's reckoning, through some inherent flaw in the system.

The two men, thrown together by the irrevocable sisterhood of their wives, were pugilists locked in a life-and-death competitive struggle for—Flanagan always faltered at an all-encompassing definition—ascendancy, ego satisfaction, stubborn pride.

Neither could resist the opportunity to taunt the other, although it all took place just beneath the surface of civilized respectability. The arena, naturally, was criminology, in which they had each spent a great deal of time, Sam as a cop, Flanagan as an insurance investigator.

Thrown together at closer proximity since the Flanagan's full-time return to Lakeside Falls, both had, by mutual and silent consent, resumed the taunt and torment, the play and counter-play, the warp and woof of their relationship. For them it was the spice of life, as necessary for their well-being as water and oxygen.

"Audrey is up on the latest in everything," Emily said, barely missing a beat. "Dr. Blandings, being younger and comparatively new to the area, would naturally know more about the latest developments in vision improvement. Yes, I'm going to try contact lenses. He's supposed to be marvelous at that."

"Vanity of vanities. All is vanity."

"Remember those old black-and-white movies, when the girl takes off her glasses and the man suddenly falls in love?"

"Now there's a good eye-dear," he said, aiming the pun to light up her smile. It did. She offered him a look of mock deprecation and, shaking her head, began to turn the pages of the newspaper again. She came to the last page and grimaced.

"Not one mention of Sam's testimonial dinner," she said with disgust. The sheriff was to star at a dinner in Traverse Park glorifying their "Clean County," since it had one of the best records on all forms of pollution including crime. Sam, being the best, most popular and obvious symbol of the county's well-being was to be given an award and would be making a speech. "When Mr. Sanford owned the paper, a story like that would never have been missed. He never should have sold the paper to strangers."

"A barbarian has entered our gates," Flanagan mused. "But business is business."

"And that man that runs it—what is his name?" She pursed her lips until her mind found the answer. "Herb Braker. He just doesn't know Lakeside Falls. Audrey is convinced he's loaded for bear against Sam."

"Sam could use a bit of criticism occasionally. All public officials can." He paused. "Especially dear old Sam."

At that point the front bell tinkled and the Flanagans exchanged puzzled glances. An eight o'clock customer was as unusual as snow in July.

Emily patted her hair, but Flanagan was swifter, having slapped away Caesar's heavy head and padded through the long hall. At that hour, he knew, serious business was afoot. It was not the time for browsers, not in October. At first, he saw no one, until he heard the squeak of the main room floor. An older man turned abruptly, offering a startled, slightly annoyed look through thick spectacles.

In one hand, the man held a brown slouch felt hat. In the other was a doll with a china head. Flanagan, responding to habit, dated the man as circa 1930s, with a polka-dot bow tie that could not hide a wattled neck, striped shirt, blue serge double-breasted suit with wide lapels, a gold signet ring on his pinky. Frozen in time-period, Flanagan concluded, probably retired for twenty or thirty years. He had well-shaved shiny red jowls which shivered as he spoke.

"I'm looking for a certain doll," the man said, gazing down at the object in his hand. "Not this." He was holding one with a long-sleeved taffeta dress with buttoned bodice and white laced-trimmed petticoat. She was wearing a hairdo with a wraparound braid.

"That's a shiny finish, porcelain," Flanagan said, mostly to establish his authority on the subject of dolls, which was hardly awesome.

"Doesn't matter. She doesn't want it. I'm not a collector," the man said grumpily. "But I know what I'm looking for."

"A man with a mission. Good starting point," Flanagan said. The man leveled magnified steel blue eyes on Flanagan, whose attempt at ingratiation fell flat, prompting the strictly business approach.

"I'm looking for Bonnie Babe. 'Bout twenty inches high. Brown hair. Brown eyes that close and a mouth that opens."

"Bonnie Babe, is it?" Flanagan asked. He could vaguely recall the item from his insurance days. People often made claims for antique dolls stolen or destroyed by fire.

"Bonnie Babe," the man repeated, lips tight. "For a child." There was a brief flicker of alarm in his eyes, an excess of sudden blinking. Flanagan was on the verge of saying something facetious, but seeing the brief pain, held back. "Bonnie Babe, you said." He had said it twice.

"Remember the box. Bought it for my daughter when she was

a child. Middle twenties, I'd say. Millie was photographed with it, you see. Now Charlotte wants it and I promised I'd find it."

"Have you got the picture?"

"Back in Flint. If I saw it, I'd know it." The man shook his head. "I promised it."

His determination was as real as his apparent frustration. Still the man did not smile and gave off unpleasant vibrations, which considerably sparked Flanagan's disinterest. He was about to shrug the customer away.

"It's my granddaughter. She's at Lakeside General for a heart operation. Leaky valve. Fair chance. Tricky." His last remark seemed unsure and his eyes could not hide their worry. "She's being prepped for an operation. I told her I'd try to find it. Not try, exactly. I said I'd find it. You know what a promise means to a little girl?"

"Let me check my inventory," Flanagan said, ignoring the answer. The oldest mush in the world, a doll for a little ailing girl. He felt that tug of storekeeper greed. Manna from heaven. The perfect customer. No browser, he. "Be back in a jiff."

Flanagan went back to the kitchen where Emily was rifling through the catalogues.

"Live one?" she asked.

"To die for." He chuckled. "Dolls. He wants a Bonnie Babe. Brown eyes that close. Mouth that opens."

She tapped her teeth and her green eyes grew dreamy, which was her usual thinking mode, followed by running her fingers through her hair.

"Not Bye-Lo?"

"Bonnie Babe," he repeated. "For his sick grandchild. She's going to be getting a heart operation. Call it a desperate need."

Emily got up from the chair and headed up the winding metal staircase which led to their office, gathering speed as she ascended. He went back to the store, where the man still stood essentially in the exact same place. Nothing else interested him.

"My wife's looking it up," Flanagan said, rubbing his chin. "Nothing else will do it?" It was a stupid question, he knew.

When there was a want, a specific identifiable need, no substitute would ever do. He had learned that long ago and it had made his reputation as an insurance investigator. A missing object had a life of its own. Dollars could never compensate for its loss. He never understood what made people attach themselves to things, but then it wasn't necessary to understand why the earth was round, either. He was not surprised when the man did not answer the question.

Emily came into the display space with an illustrated book of doll collectibles, laying the open book on the checkerboard surface of a Victorian walnut games table.

"That's the one," the man said, pointing a roughened finger.

"Designed by Georgene Averill for the Averill Manufacturing Company in 1920. It was a biggie." She thumbed through the back of the book and whistled. "Pricey."

"Cost me twenty bucks. Bought it for my oldest daughter. Handed down to my youngest, Millie. That's Charlotte's mother. Pretty beat up after five girls. Threw it away finally. It's in a lot of snaps, though. I want one good as new and I don't give a damn about the price. People in your business are a bunch of robbers. Selling old junk for such high prices."

"Even so, we can still be friends," Flanagan muttered.

"Not now, Flanagan," Emily admonished. "Obviously the man is upset."

"I'd pay it, though," the man said, unrepentant. "Pay more. You name it. Especially if I got it fast."

"We'd have to do a search," Emily said. "There are sources."

"I need it fast and I'll pay."

"We'll do the best we can." Again she tapped her teeth. "Maybe we can find one around town."

"We're really good at poking around," Flanagan said brightly. It was strictly a placebo.

"Remember. Bring me the real thing and I'll pay whatever you ask," the man growled.

"It's the fund thing in this business," Flanagan said, knowing that the tiny barb would barely prick the man's hard old hide.

"We'll try," Emily said, bowing to pragmatism. They were so heavily invested in inventory they could not sell, being a middleman without risk was balm for her antique dealer's heart. And Emily was not one to let a lucrative sale go by the boards. The man pulled out an engraved card and wrote a telephone number on the back of it with an old ink-filled Waterman and handed it to Emily.

"That's the telephone number of her hospital room. Her mother and me are there most of the time. Faster the better," the man said. Flanagan looked at the card. "T. Richard Ingersoll."

The bell was already tinkling before Flanagan could offer his good-byes. He followed Emily back to the kitchen where she poured two more coffees.

"Aside from giving the girl a boost, we sure could use the do re mi. The time frame's a bummer—unless."

"—unless we can find some old lady with self-indulgent parents who had the temerity to buy the little apple of their eye a nearly two-foot-tall Bonnie Babe." He looked at the open book, turned it around. "Even a voice box in the lower back, a lace cap with satin ribbon and crocheted cotton booties."

"So who in town might have had one of these back eons ago?"

All her little thought tics came into play now, the teeth tapping, fingers brushing through her hair, to which she added the soft shoe tap under the table. Her green eyes grew vague and fixed and her cupid's bow upper lip curled in under itself.

He knew better than to intrude, urging his own concentration on the matter of collecting dolls, looking over pictures of Baby Grumpy, Patsy Baby in Hamper, Lil Darlin, Bubbles, Tantrum Baby, Kaiser Baby, Dream Baby, although none could boast the heft, size and sweetness of dear old Bonnie Babe.

As he expected, Emily began to verbalize her thought

processes. What her mind's computer was turning over, he knew, was the directory of old Lakeside Falls families, descendants of those who came to the great lake region to earn a living from the waters, either as boatman, woodsman, and traders, fruit farmers and, much later, as health nuts. As often happens to the converted, Josh had taken to the lore and history of his town and had made it his business to know everything he could about its origins and mores. Emily, too, had surrendered to the same urge. Her dictum was: If you don't know where you come from, you'll never truly know where you're going.

Familiar names of streets, storefronts, orchards, joined the listings. The Pratts, the MacPhersons, the Pettigrews, the Foxstones, the Downses, the Larsons, the Honnigers, the Goldmans, names that he, too, recognized from childhood days and their summer sojourns.

But the Foxstones, Emily's family tree, went back five generations, six if you counted Big Jim Foxstone who arrived in Lakeside Falls by getting drunk and falling off a coal barge on its way to Canada. Lord knows how many Foxstone seeds were sprinkled around Lakeside Falls before Big Jim got religion and sobriety from Emily's great great grandmother, whose life and legend made today's women's libbers seem like shrinking violets.

"It wouldn't have been the Pratts, who lost their timber business back during World War I according to Dad. The Goldmans, on the other hand, were great child indulgers. Sarah Goldman got a pony with solid silver harness for her fifth birthday. Of course, Lizzie Honniger got a dollhouse for her tenth that took up an entire room and was furnished with genuine antique doll furniture." She grew silent, sipped the last of her coffee and tapped the table with her knuckles.

"Lucy Downs. If anyone got a doll like that it was Lucy Downs. Of course, she was a few years older than me...."

"Still is, as a matter of fact," Flanagan agreed. His historical recollections of Lucy Downs were far less photographic, although he did remember her father and the vague celebrity of Lucy's marriage to a something Farnsworth from over in Battle Creek, who was a pilot killed in Vietnam. "You mean Lucy Farnsworth," he corrected. Flanagan himself had been a Marine lieutenant in Vietnam.

As a confirmed born-and-bred Lakeside Faller, Emily snobbishly persisted in not counting "outsiders," which on occasion included Flanagan having arrived in town three years after he was born. Even their own twenty-odd-year absence in Manhattan had been put down by her as a "brief interlude," like a tour of duty with the Foreign Service.

"William Downs had to get the largest of everything," Emily continued, his mildly defiant interruption barely noticed. "He would have gotten her the largest doll. Later he gave her the largest car when she was sixteen and, of course, she did inherit the largest cherry orchard."

Lucy Downs was, as all the antique dealers in the region had learned, one of the great local sources for Art Deco and Art Nouveau—the period of Bill Downs' most blatant acquisitions. Such folderol was considered gauche at the time by Lakeside Fallers, despite the fact that it was the rage of London, Paris and New York. In those days, circa 1920, Lakeside Fallers were probably still suffering from the ravages of Victorian esthetics.

"I'll give her a call," Emily said, marking a note in her appointment book. "More than likely she would have handed it down to her daughter Kay. Actually they're more like sisters these days. Inseparable. Poor Kay. Never married. Lucy hadn't much luck with her kids."

"They say Tony is a gambling addict. In debt up the kazoo and Lucy as the grapevine avers is finished staking him," Flanagan said. "And that creepy brother-in-law Jessie Shanks of hers. I read they shut down that ski area he's building. Ran out of dough and Lucy's run out of patience with sister Amy. With a son like Tony and a brother-in-law like Jessie Shanks." He shook his head. "Ah, the travails of the super rich. My heart goes out to them."

"Anyway, if she does have a Bonnie Babe, we know the old man will pay. So we can afford to buy higher."

"And she knows what it means to have a sick little girl."

As everyone knew, Lucy Farnsworth and her daughter Kay were devoted and inseparable. The Kay and Lucy Show was the way the townsfolk characterized them behind their backs, as if there was something slightly unsavory in such mother-daughter devotion.

The fact was that Kay had been an asthma sufferer since birth, which explained a great deal about Lucy's motherly protectiveness. Some said possession, but Flanagan always attributed that kind of mean-spiritedness to small-town insularity. An unmarried maiden like Kay was still an object of curiosity and speculation in the boonies.

"Worth a try," Emily mused. "I'll give her a ring."

"And may you live happily ever after."

"But I already do that." She pecked him a kiss on the forehead.

Emily got up from the table and climbed the circular metal stairs to the office while Flanagan read more about the culture of old dolls and tried to memorize the fine points of Bonnie Babe's picture. Suddenly, he took out his pocket watch and braced himself for the nine o'clock striking of the tall clocks. He waited, listened, his ear discerning the count, satisfied, once again, that they were, with the exception of the Hoogendyk, in good working order.

Under cover of the striking, Emily had slipped down the stairs. He was aware of her humming behind him, although he did not turn until he had identified the tune.

"You did it."

"...it's so nice to have you back where you belong," she sang.

"I played it cool. She said she had lots and lots of dolls in the attic somewhere. Saved them all for Kay who wasn't much for them."

"And Bonnie Babe?"

"She thinks there was one like that. You'll have to pop over there and see for yourself."

"I've always been pretty good at chasing dolls."

"News to me."

"I caught you, didn't I?"

"You make it sound like a cold."

"A hot. Not a cold."

He winked, remembering the routine of their awakening.

Chapter Two

Flanagan drove the Chevy SUV along the state road toward Lucy Farnsworth's place. As always, when he drove through the countryside, he would marvel at the proximity of such exquisite natural beauty to the town itself. Within a stone's throw were lakes and mountains and deep valleys of rich soil which nourished the local crop, the cherry, which was the symbol of the town's earlier bounty.

As a boy, he had both picked and gorged himself on the fruit on summer weekend hegiras to the inland lakes. Memories of winter treks through mountain trails white with snow would sustain him through Manhattan's mushier days when he would long for the clear sweetness of Michigan's winter mountain air. Of course, there was the big lake itself, Lake Michigan, which was Lakeside Falls' ultimate backdrop, playground and lifeline and the magnetizing image that kept its sons and daughters emotionally rooted to its shores. In the near distance, he could see the humps of the low mountain range, looking, as always, like a herd of charging buffaloes. Even through the mist, he could see the swaths being cut through the pines to make still more ski trails for the burgeoning army of winter sportsmen.

On his left, he could see Jessie Shanks' ill-fated project. It had been started with great fanfare with plans for three lifts, many trails along the slopes, and a motel and condominiums at the foot of the range.

Farther along on the same road, he passed a big sign announcing the property line of the Downs Cherry Orchard spread, Bill Downs' legacy, which stretched for nearly a mile along the state highway. The cherry trees were barren now, suggesting to Flanagan a perfectly symmetrical military cemetery for some exotic race of giants marked with a strangely twisted and alien religious symbol.

Ahead, on the opposite side of the road was Jack's gas station. A quick glance at his fuel gauge told him that he was getting low. For a moment, he considered pulling into the station. A big black car was filling up beside the single island. Do it after, he decided, as the turnoff to the Farnsworth place came into view.

The light mist had turned into fine rain, creating condensation on the inside of the windshield. Slowing down as he turned into the gravel road that led to the Farnsworth main house, he bent over and wiped it away with the palm of his hand. Suddenly through the clouded surface, he saw a car speeding toward him at a clip that indicated that the driver was oblivious to his coming in the opposite direction of the narrow road.

"Damned fool," he muttered, reaching for the headlight knob, then realizing suddenly that it was even too late for that. With both hands he swung the wheel to the right, hit the gas and careened off the road onto a muddy shoulder, which quickly mired down his rear wheels. By the time he had rolled the window down in order to fire off some well-chosen words, the offending car was a faint blip on the horizon.

His SUV had stalled, but he allowed himself to calm down, an act that met with momentary success, until he flicked the ignition key again and discovered that he couldn't rock his wheels out of the mud. To Flanagan, the whole adventure seemed no longer worth the candle until he summoned up a sense of nobility about all this hardship being in the service of bringing joy to some young child badly in need of it.

He was, he knew, a sentimental sucker, especially when it came to the helpless unfortunate—kids. As a doting father, he knew the drill. A sick kid was a parent's nightmare.

Puffed up with this worthy sense of purpose, he got out of the car, squished his Reeboks up to their laces in the mud and began a run up the gravel road until he realized that the distance to the house meant he would get thoroughly soaked no matter how fast he ran. Slowing down to a spiteful walk, he arrived at the front door of the rambling stone house hardly surprised at his moist and ratty reflection in the glass storm door.

It took what seemed an inordinate amount of time for someone to answer the buzzer, which brought back the full fury of his irritation. It was Kay Farnsworth, Lucy's daughter, who finally let him in. Wearing slacks and a blue turtleneck, which set off her moist Wedgwood blue eyes, she showed frown lines of confusion on a high forehead under tightly pulled-back black hair, already powdered lightly with gray. Her oval face showed pique and uncertainty and her demeanor was one of tentativeness, as if she wasn't at all sure why she had opened the door.

As she stood framed in the doorway, Flanagan stepped through the only available space, the hallway, where he puddled the floor.

"Some jackass ran me off the road," he blurted, unbuttoning his orange plaid mackinaw which the water had made three shades darker.

"I'm sorry," she sighed, as if she were taking the blame.

"Not your fault," he mumbled.

"Sometimes Tony gets self-absorbed."

"Tony, was it?"

She nodded.

"I think your mother was expecting me," he said.

She shrugged and took his coat, holding it cautiously by the collar, not sure what to do with it. She opened the closet door, took out a hanger which she inserted in the coat and carried it to the bathroom under the stairs. Then she led him into the living room. He had been there before, he remembered. Time had added to the general tackiness which, even the first time, had puzzled him, since Lucy Farnsworth was reputed to be very rich. That's why the rich were rich, he thought.

"It's about the dolls, isn't it?" she asked. He had deliberately sat on a straight-backed wooden chair to keep the upholstery from getting soaked while Kay settled into a leather wing chair.

In a glance he had already taken in the room. Unchanging old world, period mixtures. Lots of photographs in fancy gold frames. Naturally. The rich were into ancestor worship, reminders of who buttered their bred. He smiled at the silent pun. Dominating the room was a large, rather bad painting of a middle-aged man wearing jodhpurs, leather jacket, white scarf, and slouch hat with the brim down all around. He was looking appropriately heroic before a stand of cherry trees in full bloom. Bill Downs at the height of his powers, Flanagan thought, with a touch of sarcasm.

"A particular doll," Flanagan said to Kay. "One called a Bonnie Babe."

"Yes, I remember they had names," Kay said. "I think we had a whole box full in the attic. Are they valuable?"

"For collectors they are treasure."

Kay's eyes looked up suddenly beyond his shoulder and when he turned he saw Lucy Farnsworth at the tail end of a severe look at her daughter. Seeing Flanagan staring at her, she offered a tight, tense smile. He saw a slight tic in her cheek and her lashes blinked nervously. As he stood up, he felt suddenly more like an intruder than an expected visitor.

"I guess my memory was faulty when I spoke to your wife," she said, trying to maintain a facade of amiability. She stood imperiously in the center of the room, shoulders squared, wearing a cardigan, woolen skirt and sensible shoes.

She vaguely resembled her daughter except that she was bulkier. Her face was round and fleshy and folds of skin wattled under her chin. She struck him as a woman trying to appear normal while bearing heavy interior burdens. She also seemed to be hiding some annoyance, and when he had taken her hand, it was cold, although her handshake was firm.

There was something else about her that made her seem different in some way. He had seen her many times at various local functions or on the street, but she simply did not seem the same. He wondered if it was a flaw in his own memory.

"My father gave me lots of dolls. I think I saved some. I'm not really sure," she said, settling slowly down on the couch.

She seemed oddly vague and unconvincing and when he looked at Kay, she deliberately averted her eyes.

"We thought it might be worth a try. This old duffer wanted this one particular kind for his granddaughter. She's about to have an operation."

He felt uncomfortable with the explanation, as if he were awkwardly looking for ways to fill a conversational gap and find an appropriate way to end the interview. Worse, he resented the fact that his moist feet and stuck car were unwelcome rewards for his compassion.

"I hope it didn't cause you any inconvenience," Lucy Farnsworth said, looking at him with a squinting intensity. He wondered if there was something especially curious in his own face that made her want to inspect it so thoroughly.

He was about to say "not at all" until he realized how moist and chilly his bottom had become against the hard wooden seat. Which again reminded him that this combined effort of mercy and business had been a needless bust.

"Actually, I've got a bit of a problem. My car is stuck in the mud at the top of your road." He looked toward Kay for help, but again she averted her eyes. He decided there was something conspiratorial in the way he was being treated and plunged ahead. "I think it was your son that ran me off the road."

He saw the despairing look in Lucy Farnsworth's eyes and the flimsy effort at cover-up. That's it, he thought, as he watched her. Something about the eyes. They seemed glazed.

"I'm terribly sorry," she said. "As long as no one was hurt. I'll call Sam Blatsford, my neighbor, to get one of the men to pull you out." Blatsford had the huge contiguous orchard. Vaguely, Flanagan remembered hearing that the Blatsfords and Downses had a partnership of some sort going between them.

"No trouble," Flanagan said. "I'll just call Jack's across the road."

"Believe it or not, he'll take hours," Lucy Farnsworth said. "And charge you triple what it's worth."

She had not sat down. Now she walked slowly to a telephone which lay on a corner table. But she seemed to have great trouble dialing.

"I'll do it, Mother," Kay said. She quickly dialed the number while her mother clutched the handset. Someone answered at the other end and she explained about Flanagan's car. But it didn't end the conversation. He saw Lucy's face turn ashen as she listened, her eyes rising despairingly to the ceiling.

"Not now, Sam, please. Yes, Tony has discussed it with me and the answer is still the same," she said with a flash of anger, hanging up the phone, turning her face away. He watched her hunched shoulders ease as she got herself under control.

"He's sending one of the trucks," she said. Flanagan wasn't sure whether or not this was meant as a dismissal, but when his eyes drifted to the window, he saw the rain coming down in great sheets and he stayed planted in the chair. He half expected to be offered coffee or a drink, something warming to take away the chill, but neither mother nor daughter offered any, increasing his feeling of intrusion. For some reason, he had arrived at a particularly tense time and the two women were obviously anxious for him to leave.

"I never thought you people would be so interested in old dolls," Kay said suddenly, looking at her mother, who shrugged as if it hardly mattered now what she said.

"You'd be surprised what people are into these days. Matter of fact this morning I learned an awful lot about old dolls. We had a kind of a heyday in doll making and design in the twenties."

Lucy Farnsworth nodded and her lips folded into a tiny smile.

"I loved my dolls. Daddy bought me so many of them. They were so beautiful," Lucy Farnsworth said with a flash of what he believed was heartfelt nostalgia, that strange longing for happier days. In the strange light which filtered into the room through the heavy sheets of rain, he imagined he could see a moistness coating the glaze of the older woman's eyes. "Remember your dolls, Kay?"

"I was never much for them," Kay said, looking at her mother. "I do remember the Dy-Dee doll you got me. I think I decapitated it."

"It needed a certain kind of imagination to enjoy them," Lucy said, ignoring her daughter's remark. "You could invent an entire life for them."

"Yes, I suppose you could," Kay said cryptically.

"Then you grow up," Lucy sighed.

"And you have live dolls to play with," Kay said. "Only it's not as easy to invent lives for them."

The silence that followed increased his discomfort and he slapped his thighs and stood up.

"If by chance those old dolls do turn up, I'd appreciate your giving me a ring."

"I doubt it. Of course you never know," Lucy Farnsworth said. Too quickly, Flanagan noted, looking toward the window. He heard the sound of a truck rumbling in the distance. Lucy moved closer to the window and squinted outside.

"I'll wait under the portico," Flanagan said. "No sense disrupting your morning." At that point, he wanted to flee.

"No more than it has been already," Kay whispered.

They both followed him out to the hall and waited as he retrieved his coat, which felt clammy and smelled rather gamey with moisture.

"I do apologize once again, Mr. Flanagan," Lucy Farnsworth

said with no let-up in her gaze's intensity. It was then that he realized why she seemed so different. She wasn't wearing glasses. The fact that he had missed the detail added to his annoyance. With a cold and hasty good-bye, he let himself out and stood in the chill of the portico. In the distance, he heard the thrust of the truck's wheels as it gripped the gravel roadway, obviously straining to pull his car out of the mud.

After awhile, he saw the truck coming toward him. The driver waved him on and he jumped into the cab, but not before getting thoroughly drenched once again. The driver of the truck was a sour-faced man with a stubble of beard and the smell and look of an old rummy.

"How'd you get into that jam?" the man asked.

"I was run off," Flanagan said with some resentment. "Near killed me. I think it was Tony."

"That one," the man snickered, opening a mouth of sparse brown teeth. "No-good sombitch."

"My point of view exactly. What was his rush?"

"Always running from somethin'. Maybe someone's chasin' after him tryin' to get a bill paid. Goes through money like a hot knife through butter. Lives in Chicago. Comes home only when he has to con the old biddy out of bucks to bail him out of gambling debts. Hear she won't give him another dime. Tough old broad. Real tough seeing as she won't sell out to Sam. Not 'till she croaks, or so they say."

"Why sell?" Flanagan said casually. He felt the old compulsion, the nudge of blind curiosity, that affliction with a mind of its own.

"Get the dough while she's still alive and kickin', 'stead of waiting till she's boxed and buried. Old man Downs made a will that puts her in charge a the whole shebang. Old sombitch was no dummy, makin' her the boss 'stead of that flaky sister and sombitch husband a hers—and those two kids a hers ain't worth a damn."

"Kids? They must both be around forty."

"Kids is kids. No matter what age. I got two in the fifties. To me, they's still kids." He rasped a laugh, showing a row of rotted or missing teeth.

"Point taken," Flanagan said, reminded of his own two kids. Kids forever, he thought.

"Was me, I'd take Sam's offer and split it with them hogs, then run off to some place down South where it was warm. And the hell with them."

"People are different," Flanagan said, getting the picture. By then, the truck was abreast of his SUV which now sat on the gravel road.

"Thanks a jillion."

The man nodded, then parted his mouth in a sneering smile.

"All the world loves a shover," Flanagan said, waving.

From his rearview mirror, Flanagan watched as the truck disappeared down the road toward the neighboring property.

Before heading back to town, he pulled into the gas station and filled his tank.

As always, when he was confronted by other people's messed-up children, he thought of his own and the luck of the draw. Judy and Paul were on their own, off in the Big Apple to make their fame and fortune. Paul was a budding investment banker, training to be super rich. Judy was an actress going through the hard luck period for the beginner. He hated the idea of her facing perpetual rejection but he admired her spunk and persistence.

He wished they would come to visit more frequently. The big world beckoned, the magic lure. He had seen it, savored it and put it behind him. But when he saw how badly other kids had turned out, he was seized with an irrational dread and he missed his twice as much. He'd have to call them when he got home, concocting a ruse of some sort just to hear their voices, to know they were all right, to touch them in some way.

The brief anxiety took the edge off his frustration regarding the doll. They seemed a sad lot, these Farnsworths, full of dark and dingy secret animosities. He could feel it in their presence. He recalled his discomfort, the awkwardness. They were people hiding things. He could smell it on them like stale perfume. As he reached the outskirts of town, he made a conscious effort to put them out of his mind, partially succeeding.

He parked the car behind the house, walked through the garden, passed the gazebo and entered the house by the rear entrance. From the kitchen, he heard voices in the front rooms, mostly Emily's as she explained the mysteries of a Victorian walnut stool. Rottweiler came down the long hall to greet him with a lick on his hands, which was strangely welcome after the unloving atmosphere of the Farnsworth house.

"You're home," Emily said, announcing the obvious, coming back from the display rooms.

"Where the heart is," he said, meaning it.

"And Bonnie Babe?"

"Flew the coop. She said she hadn't any dolls to show. She did say she might keep looking."

"That's odd," Emily said, tapping her teeth. Then she shrugged and smiled. "No matter. One's come up."

"You're kidding." He felt his entire face crinkle into a smile.

"Pat Lacey called from Tucker. Said there was a rumor we were in the market for a Bonnie Babe. Had one in mint condition. I said I'd call him as soon as I spoke to you."

"Did you call him earlier?"

She gave him a puzzled look and shook her head vigorously.

"How do you suppose he got the word?"

"Does it matter?"

"Maybe the old man got to him," Flanagan mused.

"No, he didn't."

"How can you be so sure?"

"I spoke to him. Called him at the hospital. Thought it might cheer up the little girl if she knew." Emily hesitated for a moment. "Didn't matter if Lucy Farnsworth had one."

"Logical."

"Now we have a choice of one. A stroke of luck."

"Did he quote a price?"

"Right out of the catalogue, less twenty. Which means almost $900 for us. He said he'd pay double."

"You quoted him?"

"Oh, he moaned for a second or two. The point was that he was happy and he was going to make his granddaughter happy." She smiled. "And we're happy. Happy all around."

But Flanagan's mind was running on another track.

"If the old man hadn't told Lacey that he was in the market for a Bonnie Babe, who did?"

"Could have been Lucy," Emily speculated with a shrug. "But why would she say she thought she had one?"

"She did seem slightly out of it. Glazed look. She did talk about dolls and how she loved them as a kid."

"Didn't we all," Emily sighed. "Anyway, who cares who told who? Lacey has the real thing. That's all that matters."

"Aren't you curious about how he got the word?"

"Mildly. Bottom line, he has the doll. Old man Ingersoll wouldn't care. Charlene wouldn't care." She looked at him and shook her head. "Why is it important who told who?"

"Did he mention Lucy?"

"Not a peep."

"How long has he had it?"

"Didn't say."

Flanagan looked at his watch and calculated the driving distance from Lucy Farnsworth's house to Tucker.

"I'd put his length of possession at no more than a half hour."

"Even that is irrelevant." But her comment had less conviction than her earlier remarks.

"Is it? Do you know the penalty for being an accessory to doll napping?"

She cocked her head and looked at him peripherally, unsure about his meaning, perhaps expecting one of his puns.

"Don't say it."

"This is a much too fencey deal for me," Flanagan said, not disappointing her. She caught his drift instantly.

"Are you sure?"

"Does Carter make liver pills?"

"Who?"

"Tony Farnsworth. In his haste, he nearly made you a widow." He explained about the car and watched her complexion grow ashen. Chucking her chin, he kissed her forehead and color rose again in her cheeks.

"And I've opened my big mouth to Mr. Ingersoll," she said.

"All is not lost."

"We can't sell him stolen goods."

"That my dear... as the Burberry said to the trench coat... may be reversible."

$$Chapter\ Three$$

Flanagan arrived at Pat Lacey's antique store just outside of Tucker at noon. It was a rectangular cinder block building with a wooden wagon wheel on the front lawn and a huge cloth sign on the building bearing the words "Sale Today." He had never seen Lacey's store without the sign. Lacey was a former advertising man on Madison Avenue which, Flanagan had concluded, explained his ethical standards.

He made his way through aisles of heavy oak American furniture, cowboy bronzes, wallpaper-covered bandboxes, a forest of historical flasks and floor-to-ceiling walls of hunting scenes and ornamental paintings. A section of the store was filled with old brass, iron and copper cooking utensils, which, like Flanagan's tall clocks, never seemed to move out of the store. But the pride of Lacey's inventory were, judging from the care which he lavished on displaying them, his Meissen and Royal Worcester figurines.

"Bloodhound's got a scent," Lacey's voice boomed from a cluttered corner where he sat behind a rolltop desk.

"I get scents. You get bucks, Lacey," Flanagan said, grasping Lacey's pudgy hand, ringed on five fingers with gold signets. Lacey stood up to his six-and-a-half feet and what seemed like matching girth. He was bald as a billiard ball and wore a mustache waxed to points. When he smiled he looked like the Cheshire cat, the face high enough to make it seem like it peered from the lofty branch of a tree. He was a man to be enjoyed, Flanagan knew, but never trusted.

They exchanged the usual joshing pleasantries between competitors who relished the conflict as half the fun of business. Lacey poured out two mugs of steaming coffee without asking Flanagan's preference and put them down precariously on the slant of a Victorian walnut davenport.

"Didn't know you played with dolls, Flanagan," Lacey said, jowls shivering with chuckles.

"Case of arrested development," Flanagan said. "And here is ground zero."

Lacey looked askance, shook his head, sipped his coffee and returned the mug to the davenport. Flanagan's remark had confused him and he was searching for a proper retort.

"Well, you better get the kid out of here before she catches it," Lacey said with unmistakable pride.

"Not bad for an old advertising hack," Flanagan said. Lacey went behind a beaded curtain and brought out a doll which he carried as one would carry a baby. "A real cry-baby, this one." He jiggled the doll and activated the voice box and they heard a reasonable imitation of a modest tantrum. Then he cradled the doll in his arms and the brown eyes closed. The crying also stopped.

"I'd call it mint."

Flanagan took the doll, inspected it and lifted the pink cotton gown.

"Dirty old man," Lacey mumbled, adding, "You'll find the imprint on the back of the neck."

Flanagan found it, read the copyright imprint and nodded.

"As you said. The real McCoy."

He turned the doll casually, inspecting the craftsmanship, then, almost in a stage whisper he asked: "How did you know we were in the market?"

"Tom-toms, Flanagan."

"Seriously."

"There are no secrets in this business, Flanagan. It gets around."

"I think what we have here is a provenance problem."

As Flanagan knew, such words could strike terror in the hearts of antique dealers.

"Come on, Flanagan. No cryptic puns, mixed metaphors and bad jokes." Lacey's face flushed. "Are you saying this is hot goods?"

"Practically still in the oven," Flanagan said. "Unless you got a call from me. I never made one. From Emily? She never made one. From my potential customer? Doubtful. How about a cherry heiress?"

"You chasing insurance claims again, Flanagan? Or just playing amateur detective?"

If Flanagan found insult in the remark it was in Lacey's reference to his amateur status.

"I've got a scenario for you, Lacey. Want to hear it?"

"Must I?"

Flanagan plunged ahead.

"Man comes in with a box full of dolls." Flanagan looked at his watch. "Maybe three, four hours ago. Says he'll sell you the lot. You rush for the books. Check the marks. The prices. Play it low key. He says the Flanagans are looking for a Bonnie Babe. He got that from dear old Mom, who may have sent the boy up to the attic to fetch the little ladies. The guy is always hot for dough, always in trouble. You put lucre in his hot little hands. Then you call Emily to confirm. Bingo."

Lacey had been listening with his mouth open. His face flushed. Flanagan watched him swallow, then clear his throat.

"That a crime?"

"Doesn't belong to him. It's his mother's. Lucy Farnsworth."

The flush on Lacey's face faded. He blew air out of his mouth in a sigh of relief.

"You scared the hell out of me, Flanagan. It's family stuff, then."

"But it doesn't belong to the son. It belongs to the mother."

"Maybe the mother approved it. Who knows what goes on in families?"

"How many were there?"

"Seven." Lacey moved his big frame to his rolltop desk, put on his half-glasses and read from an index card. "A Bye-Lo Baby, Century Doll, a Jumeau Bebe, a Thuillier, Tynie Baby, a Patsy Baby in a Hamper and the Bonnie Babe." He took off his glasses and studied Flanagan. For some reason, Flanagan got the feeling there was something tentative about Lacey, an air of expectation, as if Lacey expected some kind of rebuttal. "Not exactly a killing, but a quick buck. Your spouse accepted a grand. I thought you were here to pick it up and give me a check."

"The thing is, Lacey, it's a theft." He gave Lacey a credible account of Emily's earlier phone call to Lucy Farnsworth and his visit, including his encounter with Tony's car. He did, of course, leave out the specifics of the old man and his granddaughter. Instinctive professional caution, he assured himself. Never reveal a potential customer.

"You think she'll go after them? Call the cops on her son?"

"No, I don't."

"So why are you sweating it?"

"Because... as Sherlock Holmes was wont to remark... the plot sickens."

"All right, Flanagan, don't get morally superior. I'm out five Gs for the lot. I figure the lot's worth fifteen, maybe twenty. They're perfect and rare. Maybe I can sell them back to the lady. Some bucks for my time."

"Better chance of that than getting it from the lovely Tony. It's probably either, already spent." He hesitated for a moment, thinking of the two men in the black Cadillac. "The point is, Lacey, I do want the Bonnie Babe. I want it now."

"The pot calls the kettle," Lacey said. "You practically accused me of fencing hot goods."

"I want the Bonnie Babe," Flanagan insisted. "I'll try to get Lucy to sign something that makes it legal."

"And the others?"

"Your problem."

"No way," Lacy said. "If its so important, clear them all."

"I'll certainly try," Flanagan began.

"Good. Then come back and I'll give you the Bonnie Babe."

"I want it now," Flanagan insisted.

"Give me five thousand and you got it."

"The lot?"

"The Bonnie Babe."

"That's highway robbery."

"Now I'm a thief. The five is just collateral. Get me the legal paper and I'll give you back half."

"Twenty-five hundred for the Bonnie Babe. That's probably triple the catalogue price."

"Hell, Flanagan. You know this business. When you find someone with an overwhelming need, strike hard. Like sex. When you gotta have it, you gotta have it."

"And if I don't get her to sign?"

"Tough nooky."

Emily, he knew, would be furious. In this case, time was more important than money.

"This is a business, Flanagan. Not a hobby."

For a brief moment, he wondered if he should tell Lacey about the little girl in the hospital, then decided against it, as if somehow the revelation might jinx the poor child.

"Okay, then. Show me the doll."

"Smart dude," Lacey said. He lumbered his way to a back room and brought out the Bonnie Babe. It was still in the box in which it came. Flanagan opened it and checked its markings.

"Absolutely authentic. Do you think I cheat?" Lacey said, smiling.

"Yes. As a matter of fact."

"Getoutahere, Flanagan. We both spent time in New York."

Flanagan shrugged and wrote out a check for five thousand dollars, feeling the hot breath of Emily's impending wrath. Then he had Lacey gift wrap Bonnie Babe and, shoving it under one arm, used the other to shake the hand of the big man who offered Flanagan an ironic smile. Flanagan strode out of the store thinking, "Heart over head, schmuck, the fatal flaw."

* * *

THE RAIN HAD STOPPED, but a sharp breeze swept over the landscape and clouds swirled overhead, offering occasional patches of deep blue and unencumbered bright sunlight. Before turning off into the gravel driveway that led to the Farnsworth house, he glanced casually toward the gas station across the road. A large black Cadillac was still parked alongside the garage. It might have been the same one he saw before gassing up.

Two men sat in the front seat, stoic and unmoving. For some reason, he had the impression that they were watching him. He shrugged away the idea and headed his SUV toward the house. He saw clearly the mud tracks of his vehicle and the place where it had bogged down.

Pulling up in the parking lot beside the house, he noted that there were a number of cars parked there, including the one that had run him off the road earlier that day. One of the cars, he observed, was a current model Cadillac with a caduceus on its license plates. Carrying the box with the doll under his arm, he approached the house and pressed the door buzzer.

Kay opened the door. She seemed tense and concerned. Also a bit confused by Flanagan's presence.

"I was hoping I could see your mother."

"She's in with Dr. Mowbray," she replied. He noted a slight trembling in her speech.

"Nothing serious?" The inquiry was reflexive. It was, after all, none of his business. Kay did not evade the question.

"An upset of some sort. I hope it's nothing. She's not a well woman." She was quite clearly distressed, which made him feel awkward for having come at the wrong moment.

"I'm sorry. I had just wanted to see her for a moment and explain...."

She did not seem to be listening.

"A diabetic with a heart condition has to be very carefully watched. I thought it best she see the doctor."

"Of course," he nodded, once again experiencing the feeling of intrusion. He had held the box with the doll under his arm, but it did not seem to attract her attention. The brief exchange had taken place in the hallway at the foot of the stairs. As they stood there, a short, florid-faced man in an immaculately tailored expensive suit came into the hallway. He had a full head of gray wavy hair and carried an alligator-skin medical bag. Dr. Mowbray was no stranger to Flanagan. Wedgwood, Flanagan remembered. Dr. Mowbray had bought a piece from them once. He had one of the largest medical practices in Lakeside Falls.

Flanagan felt caught between politeness and propriety. Apparently Dr. Mowbray did not notice him immediately, directing his attention to Kay, whose anxiety-ridden face must have clearly indicated a need for immediate attention.

"Not an attack. More like an upset stomach," he said cheerfully. "I've increased both her diuretic and potassium. Probably overdoing it a bit. She's also complaining about her eyes. When the lenses are out, she says she's blind as a bat. I'd have her eyes checked when she's up and about."

"So there's nothing to be alarmed about?" Kay asked.

"I don't think so. Sometimes a chemical imbalance occurs. Who knows why?" He gave Kay's arm a fatherly pat.

"She had a very aggravating morning."

"Stress is something to be avoided. Let her rest all day. Keep her away from stress. I think she's over-tired. Rather drowsy. I'm sure she'll be up and around by tomorrow."

"You didn't increase her insulin?"

"Just a mite," he said cheerfully, with typical paternalistic superiority and charming evasion. Obviously, he did not wish to provide technical medical details to the unschooled, especially concerned family members.

At that point, he directed his attention to Flanagan.

"Flanagan—what are you doing here?"

"Hello, Doctor." Flanagan welcomed the opportunity to be noticed enough to take polite leave. "Just a little business I had with Mrs. Farnsworth. It can easily wait. Maybe tomorrow...." He nodded in Kay's direction, received a noncommittal response, waved to Dr. Mowbray and eased out of the door.

In the driver's seat of his SUV he contemplated his dilemma. Should he give the doll to Ingersoll today and put his faith in Lucy Farnsworth's understanding and potential good intentions? He'd have to talk that one over with Emily, he decided. In the meantime, he ruled out further contemplation on an empty stomach.

Reaching the main road, he could not resist another side glance toward the gas station. The black car was still parked there and once again he had to shrug away the idea that it was watching something. He noted that it had Illinois plates.

He did not need the golden arches to remind him of his hunger. It reminded him instead of Emily's admonitions against junk food, of which she decided McDonald's was the prime offender. "All air, sugar, salt and filler." It was like a repetitive lyric and, in the end, it had cured his craving. Instead, he headed toward the interstate, picked up the parallel road and turned into Jerry's Diner, which catered mostly to the big long-distance semis.

Taking a booth in the rear, he ordered a tuna on rye, which made him briefly nostalgic for New York, that is until the sandwich came. This is not rye, he told himself, this is a lie. But a locally made cherry pie and coffee gave him back to his comfortable sense of place. As he was about to take his last bite, he glanced out the window and saw Dr. Mowbray get out of his Cadillac and stride into the diner. For some reason, Flanagan slid around the three-sided booth and hid his face from view. It was an instinctive maneuver. Nor was he sure why he made it. Perhaps it was the incongruity of seeing the prosperous doctor with his elegant clothes in the unlikely atmosphere of Jerry's Diner. Or was it purely a symptom of investigator's syndrome, wherein the brain picks up mysterious signals of intrigue and suspicion?

Flanagan hunched over his coffee while truckers came in and out on a steady basis. He ordered a second pie just to hold his moral right to the booth and promised himself to give the impatient waitress a larger tip. Why Jerry's Diner, he wondered? A clandestine meeting with a woman? Or perhaps nothing more deceptive than reasons similar to his own? Finally, curiosity overflowed and he turned his face for a quick glance to see who, if anyone, the doctor was with. He was surprised to see him with Jessie Shanks, Lucy Farnsworth's brother-in-law, her sister's husband. He was vaguely disappointed, which prompted him to get up, pay the check and leave.

He did not look in their direction. Not that it would have mattered. They were hunched over the table, deep in conversation, and he quickly dismissed the incident from his mind.

Getting into his SUV, he drove back to the store.

Emily, having seen him carrying the package from the office window, was down the circular stairs by the time he reached the kitchen.

"You got it."

"More or less."

It was one of his most frequent warning phrases. As always, Emily's first response was to search his face for clues. He suffered the inspection, keeping his eyes level with hers, smoothing the frown lines under his cap of salt and pepper hair.

"Bottom line. As you see, I got the doll. The real thing."

He fully explained the transaction and his failure in getting a release from Lucy Farnsworth. In retrospect the whole story was too painful to recall.

"Leaves us with a problem. Do we sell Ingersoll the doll without having unencumbered rights to sell it?" By shifting the focus from the material to the moral, he presumed he might get her to avoid the subject of money.

Yet, in the final analysis, he knew, he would trust her business instincts. He could always depend on that. In his years as an insurance investigator, she had been his confirming mechanism.

"When I spoke to her," Emily said, "she showed no inclination not to go along, providing she had the right doll."

"That's a double negative," he shrugged, weakening his resolve.

"I said I would buy it, but gave no price."

"Well, we've already invested $2,500. Without the signed paper we'll be five thousand in the hole."

He could tell from her glazed look that she was calculating in her head.

"If we gave Lucy the catalogue price, give or take it would amount to, say, $1,500."

"The dollars involved are minuscule as far as she's concerned."

"As for Mr. Ingersoll," she explained, "he did say money was no object."

"Well then, would it be fair to charge him five thousand? We'd be near even, except for what we would pay Lucy. And if Lucy signed that paper we will refund him twenty-five hundred that we would get back from Lacey."

Suddenly, she looked at him severely. He braced himself. "It's so much like blood money. I can't stand it." She tapped her teeth. "Money aside," she paused, looked at him and raised her eyebrows.

"The hard part of being broke is watching the rest of the world go buy," he whispered, kissing her earlobe.

"Good things happen to good people," she winked.

"And your faith seems familiar."

"Let's hurry before the posse from the Harvard Business School finds us with a rope."

"Hang it all. Let's do it."

Lifting Emily from the chair, he embraced her, breathing the sweetness and warmth of her. He felt the stir of emotion, the magic trigger of attraction that twenty-five years of marriage had not blunted. It was one of the special joys of their soft-paced life in Lakeside Falls. After all, they had comparative freedom, control over their own destiny, good healthy libidos and, most important, unlimited access to each other.

"Shall I flick the sign?" he whispered into her ear. She offered no response, which meant affirmative, but before he released her the tall clocks began their maddening ritual.

"If we're going to do it, we better do it," Emily said.

"Exactly my thoughts."

"I mean, get Bonnie Babe to the hospital."

"We're miscommunicating," Flanagan said, an element of pleading creeping into his tone.

"You give rainchecks?" she asked, stroking the back of his neck.

"Better to have love and lust, than never to have love at all."

"That did it," Emily said, disengaging.

He bowed ceremoniously.

"I yield to the lady in this new age of chivalry."

She snickered coyly, pursed her lips, and put on her coat. He went to the front door, flicked the sign from "Open" to "Closed," then locked up and let himself out the rear door, leaving Caesar who guarded as he slept. Emily was already seated in the SUV, the package on her lap.

"I'm sure Lucy will understand. You'll tell her tomorrow."

Like him, he knew, she could not totally dismiss a tiny twinge of guilt. But even that quickly dissipated when they arrived at the little girl's hospital room. It was a private room and Mr. Ingersoll himself came down to the reception area to escort them up. In the harsh light of the hospital corridor, he seemed older, his walk slower. But his manner, as he clutched the doll, was less gruff than during their first meeting.

"You come on up," he said hoarsely. "Say hello to my little Charlotte."

They followed him to his granddaughter's room where a wan-faced, fragile child of about nine or ten lay in a hospital bed, her skin as white as the pillow on which her head rested. She seemed to have difficulty in raising her eyelids.

The old man whispered an introduction to a woman, whose moist puffy eyes marked her as the child's mother.

"Look what I got, darlin'," the old man whispered. "Would you like me to unwrap it?"

The little girl made a valiant effort to nod her head and the old man, with elaborate movements, unwrapped Bonnie Babe. They watched the little girl's eyes widen as she saw the doll. Flanagan had to swallow to hold the lump down. Peripherally, he saw Emily blink, forcing tears to run down her cheeks.

With tender care, as if the doll were alive, Mr. Ingersoll placed it gently beside the little girl, slipping it under the coverlet and resting its head on the pillow beside her. The little girl turned her head and kissed the closed eyes of Bonnie Babe. Beside them, they heard the mother's choking sobs.

"She was lost," the old man said, "and these kind people found her for you, Charley." The little girl turned her head to see them and offered a thin smile of gratitude.

"Now you've just got to get better to take care of her, child," the old man said. The little girl nestled her head close to that of the doll's and kissed her on the cheek, then closed her own eyes. The four adults watched her for a long time. She barely stirred, her breathing shallow. Then Mr. Ingersoll roused himself and they followed him out to the corridor. Emily wiped her cheeks with tissues.

"See what it meant to her?" Mr. Ingersoll said.

Flanagan glanced toward the red-eyed Emily. They both nodded agreement.

"Who knows, maybe it'll turn the trick. Operation is first thing in the morning," Mr. Ingersoll said.

Flanagan wanted to inquire after the little girl's chances, but could not bring himself to ask. It did not look promising.

"Now what do I owe you?" the old man said. He took a checkbook from an inner pocket. "I said I'd pay whatever you asked and I meant it."

Emily looked at Flanagan and curled her cupid bow lips.

"On the house," Emily mumbled.

"Nonsense," the old man said. "You delivered. You're entitled."

Emily shook her head. Her cheeks were flushed and her eyes still moist.

"Call it a gift," she said. Flanagan held his tongue, resisting any comment, forcing his mind not to do the obvious calculation of the day's losses.

"As long as you're not out-of-pocket," Mr. Ingersoll said.

"Not us," Emily said, avoiding Flanagan's eyes.

"Are you sure?" the old man said with considerable skepticism.

"We're in business, Mr. Ingersoll. It'll balance out a great year. We could use the write-offs," Emily said, deliberately avoiding Flanagan's eyes.

"All right, then." Ingersoll squinted through his thick glasses. "You don't look like fools."

Looks lie, Flanagan thought. He shook hands and started back to his granddaughter's room.

"We'll pray for her," Emily said, her voice too tremulous to carry.

Hand in hand, they walked through the hospital corridors, not looking at each other or speaking. Halfway home, Emily turned to him and smiled.

"Let's call the kids."

He stepped further down on the accelerator.

"Good idea," he said.

Chapter Four

T he brief orgy of emotion, Flanagan observed the next morning, left Emily with a hangover of rampant inadequacy. She seemed withdrawn and regretful, especially since she considered herself the business brains behind their little antique business. It was she who repetitively preached the theme of business being business and the necessity of holding unyielding fealty to the proposition of buying as dear as one could and selling as high as the market would bear.

They had returned to Lakeside Falls from Manhattan three years earlier with a nest egg derived from a decade of good years in the insurance investigation business. The boom in objects d'art and antiques during the sixties and seventies and the ingenuity of a new breed of thieves had given Flanagan both a peculiar skill and an appreciation for the value of these material creations. To some this value was dictated by a love of the lost art of fine and patient craft and beauty. To others the lure of profit was paramount. In fact, the discordant elements of greed and acquisition seemed to exist in tolerant harmony in the human psyche. Still, he had come across thefts that were purely for an emotional rather than a material need.

But the bottom line of this experience was that things had an intrinsic value that, unlike people, increased rather than declined with age. Since he and Emily had spent interminable hours haunting auction houses, galleries and antique stores in the line of his duties, searching for objects stolen, copied or, as the stupendous concoction of the trade had dubbed it, "misattributed," it seemed natural for them to put this knowledge in the service of their personal business.

Prompted by Emily's inheritance of the family house on North Pratt Street through her mother's death, and their own children, Paul and Judy, off to pursue careers, the Flanagans began to notice a growing lack of identity and familiarity in their lives. Perhaps it had been the realization of a kind of "burnout" that is one of the maladies of big city life? Or was it simply a sudden urge to rediscover a sense of place? They weren't quite sure, although they understood that, whatever the reasons, they had to go home, home to Lakeside Falls.

It had changed, of course, but moved at a snail's pace compared to the big cities. Indeed, the town fathers in their shrewdness had made a conscious decision to regulate change so that even the summer and winter people could live with the illusion that they could, at least temporarily, slip back in time to "the way it was."

But the Flanagans hadn't banked on whittling away the vast chunk of their nest egg on inventory. Early in the game, they discovered that consignment, meaning taking certain goods for sale without "up-front" payment, had drawbacks, especially in terms of display space. They chose instead to pay hard cash for what they thought might move quickly, trying to ride the crest of the craze for collectibles based on their own gut instincts and experience. They were half right, just enough to eke out a respectable cash flow, which they used to remodel the back end of the house into a fit habitation for those used to modern comforts. For these reasons, they were always somewhat short financially and little emotional fits of largesse were costly reminders that earning a bigger buck took a harder heart than they possessed.

Therefore, in an obscene way, Flanagan took a bizarre pleasure in Emily's attack of mushiness, because it took the onus off his own business stupidity in giving Lacey the five thousand dollar check. But it in no way placated his own fine-tuned conscience and he left the silent breakfast table the next morning determined to square things with Lucy Farnsworth.

The icy cold, bright sunny morning lifted his spirits somewhat, although he could not keep simple arithmetic from intruding on his thoughts. Ideally, he might get her to sign a paper, which he had composed that morning, covering the full sale of what Tony had gotten from Lacey. Case closed. If she refused, he would accept his fate. To steal from the rich to give to the needy had the good ring of self-justification, although it riled him to think that Lacey would profit from the transaction.

By the time he reached Mrs. Farnsworth's property, he had worked up a good head of indignation and resolve and was fully prepared to insist she sign. Heading into the gravel driveway, he glanced at the rearview mirror. Slowing down, he studied what he saw. The same black car was parked beside the garage. Inside were two men. It was enough visual evidence to dismiss any idea of mere coincidence. The men were watching the Farnsworth house. He put it in the back of his mind and drove towards it.

The door was opened by a sallow-faced man in a silk robe with hair spiked by an obvious night of unhappy sleep.

"...'bout time," the man began, checking himself. "Who the hell are you?"

He was certain that the man facing him was Tony, although he hadn't ever seen him around town. He had a tense, surly look about him and Flanagan's nostrils seemed to pick up a sour effluvia, as if his pores had sweated the residue of some filthy substance all night long. Red veins mapped his eyes.

Flanagan did not smile, dismissing any idea to berate, lecture or argue.

"I'm Joshua Flanagan, here to see Mrs. Farnsworth."

The man inspected him from head to toe, which Flanagan resented. He glared at the man.

"Mother's out of sorts," Tony responded, pushing the door slightly forward.

"It won't take long."

"What's it about?" he asked impatiently.

"It's rather private," Flanagan said, anger rising.

"I'm her son. I'll be glad to..."

"Just with her, thank you."

"I just told you. She's not well."

"It's all right, Tony."

Her voice came from the living room and Flanagan, who had been standing just outside the open door, strode in. Tony slammed the door behind him.

"You're supposed to take it easy," he called into the living room, looking impatiently at his wristwatch.

Flanagan saw the woman lying on the couch. She looked awful, a radical change from yesterday. Her skin was the color of ivory, her eyes moist and sunken, her hands trembling. Beside her on a table was a carafe of water and various medications.

"Just for a minute, Mrs. Farnsworth," Flanagan said. She had given him her hand. It was cold. Tony had followed him in and had sat down on a chair in the corner of the room.

"As you see, I'm a bit under the weather," she said weakly.

"I told him that, Mother," Tony said with a surly snicker.

"It's rather private," Flanagan began hesitantly, acknowledging Tony with a movement of his head. Lucy Farnsworth nodded understanding. He was certain she knew what he had come about.

"Would you please leave us, Tony," Lucy said in a strained whisper.

"The hell I will," Tony said, flushing. "I've been out of things too much lately."

Flanagan turned to him.

"This is a private matter," he said coldly.

"Please, Tony," his mother pleaded.

"I have a right to know everything that happens around here...," Tony began.

"Please...." Her eyes closed for an inordinately long time.

"A matter of simple courtesy," Flanagan said. "And your mother's wishes."

"I insist," Lucy Farnsworth said with effort. She raised her head from the pillow. The act seemed further debilitating. She looked very ill, indeed. Shockingly so. A far cry from the woman he had seen only yesterday. Was it possible for deterioration to take place so rapidly, he wondered?

"You shouldn't be seeing anybody. And Kay had no right to leave," he said testily.

"She'll be back shortly," Lucy said weakly. "Went to Dr. Blandings to pick up my drops. I need my drops."

But he did rise from his chair and angrily stormed out of the living room. When he had gone, Flanagan turned to her and cleared his throat. He did not feel that sense of intrusion that he had felt yesterday. Lucy closed her eyes and for a long moment he debated with himself whether to speak or not. Her hand reached for a bottle on a table beside her. Her fingers plucked out a pill.

"It's about the dolls, isn't it?" she asked weakly.

"Yes. It is."

"I'm so sorry about that." He wasn't sure whether or not she was keeping up pretenses or was prepared to acknowledge the truth. His investigator's mind dredged up an old ploy.

"You know, then?"

"It's my cross to bear." She put the pill in her mouth.

"Well, you see...," he stumbled. The woman's pallor was alarming. He decided to blurt it out as quickly as he could. "He got Pat Lacey over in Tucker to give him five thousand dollars for the dolls. I was only after the Bonnie Babe." He faltered briefly as she lifted a hand to her breast. "Are you all right?" he asked, realizing that the exercise of response was beyond her strength.

"I don't understand," she said weakly.

"What don't you understand?"

"This feeling. Like I'm sinking."

"Has Dr. Mowbray seen you today?" His questions seemed incongruous, as if he had ordained himself as a family member.

"I did speak to him. He said it will pass." She was silent for a moment. "Kay." It came out as a weak cry of frustration.

"I—I think your son said she had gone somewhere."

"Oh yes. I forgot. Yes. Amy was supposed to be here."

"Amy?"

"My sister."

She opened rheumy eyes and squinted at him with curiosity. Looking into them, he saw the rim of contact lenses. Despite her debilitation, he sensed a flicker of a question. Debating whether to move ahead, he opted to keep her involved. It was a tactic that he used when he used to visit his father at the nursing home.

"About the dolls. I did get the Bonnie Babe. But you see, I gave it to the sick little girl. Emily said she told you about that."

"Yes, she did."

"Legitimately, it was your property. I'm here to pay for it."

Her eyes closed and her breathing became labored. She lifted her arm, then let it fall helplessly. It was futile to continue. He gave up all hope of getting her to sign the paper that Lacey had asked for and which he carried now in his back pocket. Somehow it seemed crass and unfeeling to put such a paper before her.

"Is there anything I can do?"

She sighed and seemed to sink further. Flanagan got up and went to the hall where he found Tony sitting on the stairs, sulking. Obviously, he had heard much of the conversation with his mother.

"You bastard. You told her."

"I think you better get the doctor on the phone."

"None of your damned business," he muttered. He was sitting on the third step. Suddenly he rose and, holding the banister, moved menacingly toward Flanagan. In good shape, Flanagan braced himself, secretly hoping for the opportunity of tangling with the man. Somewhere between the steps and the landing, reason must have gripped him and he pulled out a cell phone. He squinted into a mirror rimmed with calling cards and punched in a number. Then he turned and sneered at Flanagan.

"Will you get the hell out of here?"

"I was just going."

He passed Tony, whose concentration was now deflected by his conversation. Then he peeked in again at Lucy Farnsworth. Her eyes were open, but she looked yellow and sickly in the bright morning light.

"We'll talk about it when you're feeling better," he said. She managed a weak wave and closed her eyes.

Outside, he shielded his eyes from the bright sunlight, and got into his SUV. He did not feel very good about leaving Lucy Farnsworth with her miserable son, although the admonition of its being none of his business could brook no argument.

His natural bent to investigate things had already given him the reputation of something of a snoop in Lakeside Falls and, more than once, Sam Hazeltine had dismissed his various suspicions as "fantasies," although he had acted on many of them, just in case. He wondered if it was time to spar with Sam over the events in Lucy Farnsworth's life. With a shrug, he postponed the idea and reached for the ignition key.

At that moment a big Lincoln lumbered off the highway. Not wanting to risk another driving problem, he waited until the car came through and reached the lot. Through the rearview mirror, he saw a woman get out of the car and walk toward the front door. She was impeccably dressed in what seemed rather high fashion for Lakeside Falls and he assumed she was the tardy Amy. When she had disappeared into the house, he started the car.

Coming out of the gravel road, he drove slowly, directing his attention toward the big black car which still sat parked next to the garage. He noted that the two men in the front seat watched him as he came down the road. The car in which they were seated was a late model Cadillac, but its body was dusty, as if it had come from a long distance away. He looked at the plates, and memorized the numbers. It was, he supposed, something to be filed away for future reference.

Driving toward town, he realized that this was actually the third time in two days that he had come back from the Farnsworths' empty-handed. Worse, he had a vivid sense of frustration about Tony, whose presence in the house seemed almost lethal as far as Lucy Farnsworth was concerned.

But there was another tug of emotion that could not be ignored. Perhaps his own experience at "sonhood" had conditioned his reactions. The road ahead misted as the loving, saintly wonder of his own mother materialized in his memory. Little Esther, his father had called her, although she was little only compared to his six-foot-five stature. Beyond that she was a giant of loving tenderness, self-sacrifice and support. She was the rock on which their family had been built and when she died, the sense of loss in him was profound and eternal.

He pulled the car over on a shoulder of gravel, overcome, not simply by the sorrow of it, but also by the vividness and joy he felt in her memory. It was unthinkable to Flanagan, against nature, for families not to be bound by love and affection. Indeed, he felt reverence about parenthood and it offended him deeply to see parents abused by their children.

He remembered, not with sorrow, how he and his father had taken turns holding their dying mother in their embrace in the last month of her life. It was not a duty for them. Indeed, they had to be torn away. Nor was it, by a long shot, a fair recompense for what she had given them.

In an odd way, the brief interlude of memory restored him and settled him, although it did not fully chase his anger at Tony. Turning the ignition, he gunned the motor and headed home.

Passing the gingerbread facade of Seven North Pratt, he was surprised to note that the "Closed" sign was posted on the door. He couldn't imagine why, although he did remember that at breakfast there had been little communication. Letting himself in, he suffered Caesar's affectionate and moist greeting. He wondered whether the Rottweiler's physical displays of excessive devotion were, well, normal. He chucked the dog under his snout and smiled, offering his politically incorrect judgment. "Long as you don't bark with a lisp." The words and gesture calmed Caesar, who ceased slobbering on Flanagan's hand. In the kitchen, he found a number of notes magnetized to their bulletin board.

"Forgot. Went to optometrist. Dr. Blandings," read one.

"Charlotte touch and go. Please call," read another.

"Lacey called," read another.

"Defrost three steaks. Dad coming for din-din," read still another.

He walked to the front rooms, unlocked the door and flicked the sign to "Open," then went back to the phone and called Lacey.

"I got the sweats last night," he growled into the phone. "Have you got the Farnsworth lady to sign the paper?"

"Not really," Flanagan said.

"I was afraid of that. I checked around. She once pressed charges against her darling son and heir. A bit of a do about a bronze mounted in glass by Lalique. She made a big fuss, about five years ago. One dealer got her tit in the wringer. Got listed for selling hot goods. Very messy and costly."

"Just protecting the family coffers. I met the darling, by the way."

"Never mind that. What about the paper? I want a clean bill of health."

"She's in no condition to sign anything," Flanagan said. "Believe me, I tried." He knew he wasn't being convincing.

"Dammit. You're the one who stirred things up."

"Worried, Lacey?"

"I've got three more of the dolls sold. I need that paper."

"Then try getting it yourself. I'm sure Tony will oblige."

"You said you could get the clearance."

"I said I'd try."

"Okay, then give me back the Bonnie Babe."

"Too late. It's gone."

"Bet you got more than your money back, Flanagan. Sold stolen goods, did you?"

"I want that signed paper, Flanagan. You hear? Or…"

"Or what?"

The telephone went silent.

Then he called the hospital and asked for the condition of Ingersoll's grandchild. "Very critical," the voice on the other end said. Damn, he thought, surprised at his own sudden burst of unfocused anger. "After all this hassle, little lady, you better make it."

Chapter Five

"You don't notice anything different?" Emily asked. She had been acting strangely since she got home. Now she was reading aloud a recipe for Bearnaise sauce out of a cookbook, another sudden and unusual eccentricity. He had just filled the ice bucket with cubes and put out the George III three-bottle cruet stand with three decanters, one filled with Doc Foxstone's favorite twelve-year-old scotch whisky, another with white wine for Emily and a third with water.

"Haircut?" he asked rhetorically, knowing that it couldn't possibly be that. She turned to look at him full face and he noted, for the first time, that her eyes seemed irritated, slightly moist.

"Dilated pupils?"

"Well, you are warm," she said with some disappointment.

"I give up."

"Am I squinting?"

"Not that I noticed."

"Contacts, dummy."

"Be damned," he said, manipulating her head with two hands so that the light caught her eyes.

"They're soft. Won't be half bad getting used to. Want to see how easy they are to put in and out?" She took out a pocket mirror from her purse and showed him the process.

"Doesn't hurt?"

"According to Dr. Blandings, the eyeball is a tough little hombre."

"That's exactly why we're having them before dinner." When she looked puzzled, he pointed to the cruet stand. "Eyeballs."

"Deliver me," she said, blinking and testing her focus. She took out a bottle of drops and squeezed some liquid into the eyes. With a flourish, Flanagan patted his reading glasses, which he kept in the breast pocket of his shirt.

"That's yesterday," Emily said, pointing to the case. "But never as old as your bad jokes."

"At least you won't be fiddling with damned glasses."

"Dr. Blandings did away with all that."

"A miracle man."

"Good looking, too. And getting extremely popular. His office was chock full."

"Poor Dr. Grant."

"The march of progress. Proving once again the wisdom and good judgment of Audrey Hazeltine."

"Lakeside Falls' great pacesetter."

"She keeps up. She has flair."

"My flair lady."

She shook her head and dipped her finger into the Bearnaise sauce, tasted it, savored it a moment and then with a nod of her head, signaled her approval.

"Which reminds me," Emily said. "I saw Kay Farnsworth with Dr. Blandings. Very chummy. Deep in conversation."

"Yes, she was there to pick up drops for her mother. Poor woman."

"Looked like there was more to it than a simple pickup."

"Gossip monger."

"Power of money."

"Or love."

"Or both."

He had told her about his visit to Lucy Farnsworth and the call from Pat Lacey.

"He wants that paper. Seems the dolls were a bonanza. She was too sick to sign. And I met the darling Tony."

"Life's too short," she sighed, her mind elsewhere. "Should we call the hospital again?"

He looked at his watch.

"Give it an hour or two."

He had called in mid-afternoon and the report was still critical.

"That poor child," Emily sighed. At that moment, they heard Doc Foxstone's familiar tread on the back steps.

"There's Daddy," Emily said. Flanagan opened the door to let him in. It had started to rain again and Doc closed his umbrella on the landing before coming through the door. Flanagan relieved his father-in-law of his umbrella and coat and hat and stowed them in the closet.

Doc Foxstone was a rather sturdy man in his mid-seventies, with a fringe of white hair around a shiny bald pate. His skin was ruddy and when he smiled, his entire face crinkled. Doc had run the same drug store on South and Main for half a century. Foxstone's was an institution in Lakeside Falls and its circa-1930s design and fixtures, including the soda fountain, were now considered trendy by the summer and winter people. The natives revered the place as the symbolic heart of the town and Doc Foxstone was celebrated as its guru of health and remedy.

They settled in the den. Flanagan poured out two scotches and water for Doc and himself and a glass of white wine for Emily, who went through her "notice something different" routine. It was as puzzling to Doc as it had been to Flanagan.

"Thank you all for your small attention to my physical presence."

"My eye," Flanagan said. "Where is her heart-shaped beauty mark?"

"On her butt. Right cheek."

"Daddy!"

"Haven't seen it for years, Darlin," Doc said.

"I was looking for it only this morning," Flanagan said.

"Gross," Emily harrumphed, shaking her head. "Comedians. What an affliction to be sandwiched between two of them." They sipped their drinks.

"She's been rhapsodizing on the glories of the new optometrist, Dr. Blandings."

"Seems to be developing quite a practice. Had to stock lots of new products for lenses. Another practitioner on the make."

"Now, that's unfair," Emily said. "He is simply responding to the latest in medical technology. He's modern." She looked at her father, who raised his heavy white eyebrows.

"I do dig the implication, young lady."

"No you don't. Your fixtures may be behind the times, but not your pharmacopoeia. And I'm not a young lady. I'm forty-five."

"Seven," Flanagan whispered. Emily stuck out her tongue.

"Who's counting?" Doc Foxstone said. "It's not medical technology I'm knocking, it's medical greed."

"Now that's an accusation."

"I have nothing against Blandings. He's entitled to make a buck."

"I saw him and Lucy Farnsworth in deep conversation."

"There," Doc said. "Case closed."

"How about Mowbray?" Flanagan asked. The image of the doctor in his Cadillac and snazzy clothes surfaced in his mind.

"Right on the money," Doc said, his complexion getting ruddier. "That's the prime example."

"I only know that he's got an eye for a good thing," Emily said. "We sold him some Wedgwood about a year ago that really escalated in value. What was it?" She thought for a moment, tapping her teeth. "An octagonal bowl, Fairyland luster."

"Are you sure?" Flanagan asked. "I thought it was the round bowl with the woodland bridge pattern."

"Of course, I'm sure. Problem is, he's always running up to the New York auctions. He makes some good deals, though. At least that's the scuttlebutt."

"The man does have a sharp eye for a buck," Doc Foxstone muttered, sipping his drink.

"I'm sure he's a good doctor. He has some of the best people in town as patients."

"As in rich," Foxstone said somberly.

"Is rich now a dirty word?" Emily prodded.

"If so," Flanagan smirked, "find me a mud puddle and I'll go for a swim."

Emily looked at him severely with pursed lips. Her Dad was not exactly a fan of their antique emporium.

"Lives high off the hog," Foxstone continued along his thought line. "Big house up there with the best view of the lake, swimming pool, tennis courts, latest cars, tailor-made clothes. No. It doesn't all come from an internist's practice. Maybe a surgeon. But not an internist. No matter how fancy his patients."

"Well, it doesn't matter to us," Emily said. "He has exquisite taste."

"I saw him with Jessie Shanks yesterday," Flanagan said, popping off the last of his own scotch. He poured refills all around. "Slumming at Jerry's. Conspiring with Jessie Shanks."

"That Jessie," Doc Foxstone sighed. "That ski deal he's put together looks like it's going belly up." He shook his head. "He's a crafty devil, though. Up and down like a jack-in-the-box. Only his sister-in-law won't invest with him."

"Who can blame her?" Flanagan said, winking at Emily. "Some say she's a tightwad." They hadn't filled Doc in on the incident of the dolls.

"I wouldn't put it in those terms. She's thrifty, all right. But considering the leeches she has surrounding her, she has to be. Old Bill Downs knew what he was doing when he put her in charge. Amy is more like Betty, her late mom. Very spendy. And of all people, she marries Jessie Shanks, who can charm the fuzz off a peach. Not that he hasn't had one or two good ones. I'm not saying he's dishonest. Let's say he sometimes exaggerates. But in real estate when things go sour, they go sour. He taught me a lesson." He looked into his glass and shook his head.

"Not you, Daddy?" Emily said.

"A little flyer, a few years back. Not his fault, though. Recession hit at the wrong time, is all." He looked up, his face brightening. "He came at me with his ski resort deal. Looked good, too. I said no."

"Old iron-willed Foxstone? You were lucky," Emily said, sipping her wine.

"You never know about these things. Too chancy for me. You have to be at the mercy of weather." Doc shrugged. "Anyway, not my worry." He drank a good slug of the scotch.

"Lucy Farnsworth's not in good shape," Flanagan said, trying to bring the conversation back on track.

"Diabetes. Rough disease. She also has congestive heart disease. Has to be watched."

"Too bad," Flanagan said.

"In more ways than one," Emily said pointedly. She had been disappointed that he had not been able to settle the matter of the dolls.

"What happens to all that Downs dough when she checks out?" Flanagan asked.

"Don't know how she has it figured," Doc said. "Bulk should go to Kay and Tony, and, of course, dear sister Amy gets a chunk and that means her hubby. End of a fortune. The kids sure didn't amount to much. Kay not married. No marketable skills. I will say though that the two of them, Lucy and Kay, sure have stuck together over the years. Really devoted to each other. That's something, I suppose. Which is more than I can say for Tony. They say he's already run through a bundle. Gambling. Rarely comes back to town, except, of course, when he has to hit on

Emily for do re me. Lives in Chicago." He sighed and became lost in thought for a moment. Flanagan did not interrupt. "What is it they say? Shirtsleeves to shirtsleeves in three generations." Doc looked up suddenly, confronting his son-in-law.

"What's all this interest in the Farnsworths, Flanagan?"

"Learning the language," Flanagan said.

Emily and her father exchanged glances.

"I'm trying to understand how money talks." He chuckled. "And now I shall illustrate how bullshit walks and see about the steaks."

After Doc had left, Emily called Lakeside Falls General. Her expression registered disappointment.

"Still very critical," she said when she hung up.

Flanagan shook his head, thinking suddenly of the Farnsworth offspring.

"Life's unfair," he whispered then, gazing at Emily.

The plight of the little girl depressed them both into silence and as they undressed for bed, Emily stopped suddenly and called the hospital again. This time she asked for the floor nurse.

"Do you happen to know where Mr. Ingersoll, the grandfather of Charlotte...." Flanagan put his ear to the phone.

"I'm sorry," the nurse said, "...unless you're a very close relative, I'd leave them be."

"That bad?"

"Touch and go. He's been with her in intensive care ever since she came in after the operation."

"Just tell him that the Flanagans called, that we're rooting for the child."

"Of course."

She put on her nightgown and got into bed beside him. As always, like two spoons, she cuddled her back against him. Then, suddenly she sprang out of bed and rushed to the bathroom.

"What is it?" he called to her in alarm.

"The contacts. You're not supposed to go to sleep wearing them."

"That all?"

He lay back, hands under his head waiting for her to return. Tomorrow, he decided, he'd try again at the Farnsworths'. He hoped Lucy would be feeling better. Emily flicked off the bathroom light and he heard her cautiously making her way back to bed in the dark. Slipping between the sheets, they assumed their regular position. He kissed the back of her neck and she kissed his hand.

"Talk about devotion," she whispered. He waited, knowing that she needed to articulate the thought. "If Lucy Farnsworth was so ill, what was Kay Farnsworth doing at Dr. Blandings'?"

Chapter Six

Flanagan had had this terrible dream in which a woman clung to the bars of a cell, screaming her innocence. The woman looked vaguely like Lucy Farnsworth. Then he saw himself in the dream, being held back by unidentifiable people, also screaming that the woman was innocent, that he was the guilty party. Worse, when he woke up, he had total recall, including the sharp nudge from Emily which dissolved the images.

"Was it really that awful?" she asked. "You even woke Caesar." They were sharing the bathroom mirror. He was shaving and she was cautiously putting in her lenses.

"Very," he answered.

"Dope it out?"

"Last night's Camembert."

He did not wish to relive the experience. Thankfully, her concentration was deflected by trying to squirt the drops into the target of her blinking eye. A few hit her cheeks before she zeroed in. He watched her curiously.

"Crocodile tears," she said. "Keeps the lens moist."

Yet, try as he could, he could not quite get the dream out of his mind. He had, he decided, apparently offended his own sense of morality and ethics and it was giving his conscience a fit. The woman, most certainly, was his substitute image, and his own was that dastardly conscience of his. He had given away—it would not have been a greater crime to his conscience if he had sold it—something that was not his to give—or sell. Strike one. He had not told Emily about the five-thousand dollar check to Lacey. Strike two. And worse, although it only struck his subconscious sometime in the wee hours, he had aggravated a very sick woman by revealing his knowledge about her son's theft.

At times he wished that his parents hadn't imbued him with such high-minded ethical standards. To them a lie was a lie was a lie. Or, as they would more often express it, the truth was the truth was the truth.

What such parental conditioning had done was to make him sensitive to other people's lies. That was a virtue, of course, and probably accounted for what ultimately was the secret of his investigative prowess. It had even given him the ability, as if his psyche was a water wand, to spot a fake painting or object d'art, to ferret out the real truth, to sense those three brothers of evil: sham, hypocrisy and cant.

By the time he had performed his morning routine, gone for the mail, opened the store and had his coffee, he had resolved to see Lucy Farnsworth and this time get her to sign a release. Perhaps the closure might ward off any further bad dreams.

He waved a goodbye to Emily, who had gotten busy with an early customer who showed profound interest in one of the Victorian dining tables. She would never brook interference during such delicate negotiations and he could see from the interest of the woman customer that she was a real Victoriana aficionado. Once hooked on the table, Emily just might steer her toward the tall clocks, especially Mr. Hoogendyk's creation. Considering his bad night, he decided to layer his thoughts with optimism for the rest of the day.

Odd, he reflected as he drove, how what to others might seem trivial and inconsequential had assumed a monumental importance in his mind. Yet throughout his life, all his acts and decisions seemed measured against his parents' approval. Was it strange that a man who was on the verge of a half century of living should be anchored to such a concept?

He wondered if his own children were imbued with the same set of constrictions. There is the right and wrong of things, Esther had taught with Mike Flanagan's blessings. Such verities were impressed upon him not by rote but by example. If it felt right, it had to be right. If it felt wrong, it had to be wrong. Like now. What he was doing felt right.

* * *

THE DAY WAS COLD, clear and bright and he had to drop the windshield visor against the blinding light of the morning sun. Again, he saw the black Cadillac parked, not far away, at Jack's gas station across the road. As before, he made out the two men in the front seat.

Because the sun shone on their faces, he was able to see their features clearly. One was dark, the other blond. Both appeared to be in their thirties. They were squinting into the sun, somber looking and unsmiling. They must have sensed his surveillance, and, as he watched, they flicked down their sun visors, hiding their faces.

Up ahead, at the Farnsworth house, he could see sunbeams reflected on numerous cars, some in the parking lot beside the house, some parked helter-skelter in front of it. Besides simple curiosity, although his was rarely simple, the ominous message seemed quite clear. He noted, among the group of cars, three that were familiar: the doctor's Cadillac, the wine-colored Lincoln in which he has seen Lucy's sister drive up to the house yesterday and Tony's convertible which had driven him off the road.

Stopping a few yards from where the driveway began its sweep to the front of the house, he deduced what quickly became obvious. Behind him he heard the sound of another vehicle. In his rearview mirror, he saw an unmarked beige Dodge van. It was, of course, familiar to anyone whoever used the services of Mason's Funeral Home.

The van left him in the awkward position of having to move his car forward toward the house, a situation further complicated when the van backed into the front door and blocked any access for his return to the main road. It was, of course, no time for intrusion and he was left to wait it out.

He did not have long to wait. Soon two men were backing out of the open front door, carrying a black zippered body bag. A woman's scream rent the air. "Mama, Mama!" It was Kay, her hair askew, being held back by Dr. Mowbray and a man he vaguely recognized as Jessie Shanks. Kay was showing inordinate strength as she clutched at the bag, her screams carrying in the sharp morning air. To Flanagan, the bright serenity of the weather made the scene even more poignant and pitiful than it might have been on a gloomier day.

Tony, looking gaunt and more bleary eyed than when Flanagan had last seen him, sulked, watching his sister's violent grief. Amy, still elegantly dressed and coiffured, her makeup blurred under a puffy face, sniffled into a handkerchief. It was a pathetic scene. Kay finally fell to her knees on the gravel driveway while the men expertly slid the body bag into the back of the van. It struck Flanagan, despite the efficiency of the operation, as somehow inhumane and disrespectful, although he did remember that when his mother's body was removed from the house, he had stood off in the corner, too distraught to observe the process.

The slam of the van's door put an air of finality on the scene and he half expected a totally different shot, as in a movie. Only it didn't quite happen that way. The men simply got into the van as if they had picked up a piece of furniture and, almost in deliberate slow motion, backed out of the driveway, pointing the snout of the van toward the main road, where cars continued to pass, oblivious to this scene of personal tragedy.

Shanks and Dr. Mowbray lifted the rag doll form of Kay to her feet. Her shoulders trembled with hysteria. Tears ran down her cheeks and she reached out toward the departing car. Flanagan noted that her stockings had torn at the knee where the sharp gravel had opened a cut.

Gently, the two men, one of whom he recognized as Dr. Blandings, supported Kay's limp form and began half dragging, half cajoling her back into the house. Then suddenly, in a mad burst of wild energy, she broke away and began running toward Flanagan's car. Reflexively, Flanagan got out to intercept her, which he did momentarily, but it was Blandings who had quickly caught up to her and she dissolved into their arms. Another man joined him. This time they took no chances and forcefully dragged her back into the house.

Flanagan had wished to remain anonymous. Now he regretted his sudden appearance in the family scene. He had reason to regret it still further, for as he bent to get into his car, he felt an arm grab his shoulder. It spun him around and he found himself suddenly confronting the twisted features of Tony Farnsworth. There wasn't much time to contemplate them as a fist bashed into his nose, setting off fireworks in his head. Vaguely, he heard a woman's scream and soon Jessie Shanks had come running out of the house and was holding Tony in a viselike grip. Flanagan's vision cleared, although he could taste the familiar metallic backlash of blood.

Tony struggled for a moment, his eyes alive with the glint of hatred. Then, obviously spent, he quieted down. Flanagan searched for a handkerchief in his pocket. Finding none, he used the sleeve of his jacket.

"Have you gone crazy, Tony?" Jessie Shanks shouted to Tony.

"He had to come and aggravate her yesterday. Had to...," Tony said, shaking his head. Then his voice trailed off. His eyes had already lost their fury and were beginning to glaze over. Flanagan lifted his free hand, palm outward.

"It's all right," he said hoarsely, feeling the metallic taste of blood in his mouth.

"Couldn't resist telling her about the bad seed," Tony hissed, but the force had gone out of him.

"What the hell is he talking about?" Jessie Shanks asked.

"He's just distraught," Flanagan said, holding back the urge to pay his respects in kind to the tethered Tony.

"As you can see, we've had a bit of a family problem here today," Shanks muttered, turning to Tony. "Will you behave?"

Tony shrugged a form of consent and Shanks released him.

"He deserved it," Tony mumbled. "Mother might still be alive if it wasn't..."

"Pay no attention to him," Shanks said to Flanagan.

"Believe me, I'm trying."

"Will you please see to your sister," Shanks ordered. Tony glared at him a moment, then turned and ran into the house. "I don't understand any of that," he said when Tony had gone.

"In a way, he's got a point," Flanagan said. It was obvious that his sleeve was not doing the job of stopping the blood coming from his wounded nose.

"Better let the Doc see you," Shanks said, shaking his head.

Reluctantly, he followed Shanks into the house just as Dr. Mowbray was coming down the stairs.

"Amy is with her. I've given her a sedative—what's this?" He had seen Flanagan, who confirmed his condition with a quick glance in the hall mirror.

"Tony let go a haymaker," Shanks said. He was a tall handsome man with what could be called an advertising model's face. High cheekbones, deep-set eyes, strong square chin, brown hair with a perfect straight part. Even in his present condition, Flanagan could detect the dye job on his hair. He could also detect the man's aura, the salesman's instinct for charm and ingratiation.

"People show their grief in odd ways," Flanagan said.

"Better let me take a look at that," Dr. Mowbray said, leading Flanagan to the hall bathroom. He directed him to sit on the closed toilet seat and, wiping the blood away with a towel, inspected the nose.

"Not broken. That's something."

"Will I need a transfusion?" Flanagan joked as the blood poured over his lips and chin.

"Bend over and put your head between your knees."

He did as he was told, putting a towel over his nose.

"I thought it was the other way. Head back."

"Who's the doctor here? I don't second guess you about the authenticity of your antiques."

"The position just seems a bit silly."

"Why did that idiot slug you?" Dr. Mowbray asked.

"Long story."

"He filched some objects of value from the house. Tried to sell them to you. Right?"

"Right disease. Wrong diagnosis."

"Listen. You don't have to say. It's not my business, either."

An idea occurred to him. Despite the awkwardness of his position, he had not been able to stifle his compelling curiosity about the death of Lucy Farnsworth, which seemed to have occurred with odd speed. In a kind of intimate potential trade-off, he briefly told the doctor about the dolls, although he heavily edited the business portion of the story. He wasn't sure whether it was because of his own sense of shame about his faulty business acumen or simply a desire to see the episode dead and buried once and for all.

"That's been the problem she's had all along with him. He can't hold on to money. A compulsive gambler. Whatever he gets out of her will, I'm afraid, will quickly disappear into the hands of the bookmakers."

He wondered if the moment had come, but since he was growing exceedingly uncomfortable, he accelerated his time table.

"Tell you the truth, I was concerned that I had aggravated her condition by talking with her about it. These skeletons are family matters. One really doesn't want them bandied about by outsiders. Perhaps Tony had a point. I probably did upset her."

"Can't blame yourself. Maybe so. Maybe not. Look at it this way. If he hadn't taken the dolls there would be no cause for your worrying her. Anyway, nobody likes to be accused of inadvertently injuring other people. I'd say a lifetime of aggravation beats anything you might have done by accident."

"Thanks for the small comfort," Flanagan said, feeling that the moment had come. "What exactly did she die from?"

He could not, of course, assess the doctor's reaction from his features, which he could not see in that position. There was a long pause and he cautioned himself on jumping to the wrong conclusion. After all, he had heard the doctor tell Mrs. Farnsworth that she might be all right in a day or so. Malpractice was a menacing specter these days and doctors were understandably cautious, he assured himself.

"Heart failure," he said, clearing his throat. "She was a diabetic, you know, with a history of a heart condition."

"She seemed to have faded rather fast."

He wondered if his casual remark had engendered any undue suspicion in the doctor's mind. Indeed, why exactly was he asking the question in the first place? Precisely because she had faded so fast. He wondered if it also puzzled the doctor.

"Happens sometimes," the doctor said. He could detect a shallow sigh. "I did increase her medication. She simply didn't react to it."

"Tricky disease, diabetes," Flanagan said, pressing the towel against his nose and lifting his head. The doctor's face came into focus.

"Thought we had it under control," he said, offering a puzzled look. It was difficult for Flanagan to assess whether or not it was genuine. "Never know."

Flanagan dabbed at his nose with the towel. Then he felt it with his fingers. The blood seemed to have crusted.

"Looks like you'll make it," Dr. Mowbray said with a gentle

pat on Flanagan's back. They went out of the bathroom and the doctor accompanied Flanagan to the door. Flanagan thanked him.

"Next time watch where you put your nose," the doctor said. Fortunately, he did not see Flanagan's flush of embarrassment.

He got into his SUV and headed toward the highway.

Chapter Seven

T he blood had caked inside of his nostrils and he felt closed in, slightly isolated trapped inside an airtight container. But despite the physical discomfort, he detected certain internal signs that were familiar, the heightened awareness that came with the triggering of instinct. He wondered if this sense of isolation exaggerated the condition, like sounds which deepen in an echo chamber.

At first, reason dictated that he dismiss the condition, a hangover from a previous incarnation. He was no longer in the business of tracking down objects or people. Dismiss it then, he urged himself, forcing away the tidal wave of suspicion. He turned the radio dial, searching for the soothing strains of the golden oldies, but he seemed to have hit an avalanche of inane talk instead, none of which was capable of engaging his attention and soon his mind was inevitably back to its well-rutted track.

As he drove away from the Farnsworth house he looked pointedly and deliberately toward the two men sitting stoically in the black Cadillac. He puzzled over it for another moment, then dismissed it from his mind as he pondered the strange and sudden death of Lucy Farnsworth.

On the surface, the simple demise of an ailing woman would

seem a natural consequence of the human condition. Disease inevitably hastened death. Why then the sudden emergence in his mind of red flags? It helped always, he knew, to analyze the roots of suspicion. Of course, that meant that he had given in to his instincts, surrendering to the animal force of it.

Hadn't he heard Lucy Farnsworth complain about her sinking condition? It did not necessarily follow that it was a prelude to death. Even Dr. Mowbray had assured Kay that her mother would be better in a day or so. He had increased her medication. Flanagan wasn't sure exactly what that meant. He'd have to ask Doc. He had detected a tiny note of confusion in Mowbray's assessment. Perhaps even slight tremors of guilt.

But a major puzzle had been Tony, who would, it seemed, be likely to welcome his mother's death. He detested the thought, although Tony's violent reaction might be either a deliberate sham or some kind of reflexive reaction to the biological imperative. Guilt, after all, was a powerful instinctive force. He touched his nose which still smarted, wishing that Tony might have worked out either his genuine anger or dramatic illustration elsewhere.

Kay, on the other hand, provoked his sympathy. On the occasion of his previous visits she had seemed tense, concerned and irritable, even with her mother. Indeed, she might have resented her mother's indisposition. Who knows? It had to be devastating for her to lose her life's companion. He thought suddenly of his father, whose life seemed to dead-end after his mother's death, but whose body simply resisted his desire to join her.

Some people are irrevocably twosomes, he thought, incomplete on their own. He had seen it in all human relationships. Husbands and wives. Siblings in all combinations. Parents and children. Even friends. It was as if mysterious bonding forces were at work or, on the supernatural side, as if people were created in halves and ordained to forever search for that piece which would make them whole. Having found Emily, Flanagan counted himself among the lucky ones.

For some reason, equally mysterious, his concentration was suddenly deflected and he found himself looking upward at the clear view of the browning ski slopes running down the nearby mountainside like some giant circulatory system. Go with it, he told himself, swinging the station wagon off the road and heading upward to the low foothills. He came to the construction site where half-made superstructures sprouted from the ground, which had in parts been swept clean of the evergreens that once held total control of the earth.

Flanagan parked his car in front of a trailer which was obviously the construction office. Beside the trailer was a parking lot filled with idle earth-moving equipment.

He hesitated for a moment, waiting for his mind to rationalize his impetuosity. Then he got out of the car and headed toward the trailer. It was, he supposed, a typical construction trailer with offices and large desks laden with open plans. A young girl sat at a computer looking myopically into the screen's type display, then peering over at her handiwork and mumbling incoherently with frustration. There appeared to be no one else in the trailer.

"Composition problems?" he asked pleasantly. The girl turned quickly, slightly embarrassed.

"Me problems," she said, apparently relieved to be interrupted.

"Where is everybody?" he asked with a broad smile. She studied his face and frowned. It occurred to him that perhaps his red nose and puffed face might suggest to her a man who lived the rougher life of a construction worker. Her next remark confirmed the idea.

"If it's work you're looking for, we're not hiring." She hesitated. "Not at the moment. Didn't you see the papers this morning?"

"Never read 'em."

So she had assigned him a stereotypical role. Relieved suddenly of creative responsibility, he accepted the casting.

"How soon before you might be taking people on?" he asked.

"No way of knowing—although—" A thought had come to her, but she rejected any further articulation. "I'd say try in a week or two."

"Thought you were pushing to get the slopes ready for the season?"

"We are—I mean, we were."

"Usual delays, I suppose," he said.

"That, too," she shrugged. "As I say, give it a week or two."

"Sure could use the work," Flanagan said, relishing the role. He had played odd parts often as an insurance investigator, noting that it was not unusual for the role to be created by the person being interrogated.

"What's your trade?"

"Run that equipment out there." Momentarily confused, he had looked out of the window at the idle earth moving equipment.

"Could be an opening there. One of the men couldn't wait. Had another job down in Flint. Lucky. Not easy to find work downstate these days."

"Wait for what?" he said, offering a puzzled look.

"Until it started again. Let's face it, I was a little worried myself."

"Tough to be without work," Flanagan said. "Never know about these projects. Sometimes they run out of dough. And the banks just close the tap."

"They never care about people like us."

"Never."

"Anyway, it could be starting again soon. Mr. Thurmont just called." She checked herself, perhaps confused as to why she was telling all this to a stranger.

"He the boss?"

"My boss," she said. "Not the real big boss."

"Mr. Shanks?"

She lifted her eyebrows. He had expected surprise.

"You know him?"

"Just by name," Flanagan shrugged. "So you just heard that things will be starting again?"

"Not exactly. Mr. Shanks' sister-in-law died. She was the money bags and Mrs. Shanks, the sister, is supposed to come in for a bundle."

"That means things will start up?"

"Thurmont think so. Says the inheritance could influence the lenders, or something like that. It's not my area."

"So there's hope?"

"I'll see it when I believe it," she mumbled, marking the end of her interest. He shifted his weight uncomfortably from one foot to another, acting the working rube.

"Should I call later? Or leave my name?"

"You call," she said, abruptly turning back to her computer.

He walked out of the trailer, observed the half-finished building skeletons, calculated the enormous investment lying fallow as easily into the multimillions, then got back into his station wagon. His nose still throbbed, but the discomfort was blunted by at least one satisfaction. The answer to the fundamental investigatory question: "Who benefits?" was already a given. That was science. As to the question: "How badly was the benefit needed?" That was art. And the ecstasy was always in the art.

The car radio was already trumpeting Lucy Farnsworth's death as a major loss for Lakeside Falls. The announcer went into a long and glowing account of the contribution her father, William Downs, made to Lakeside Falls, Pike County and the State of Michigan by developing the cherry orchards that made the area the cherry capital of the world. His daughter, the eulogy went on, had carried out many of his benefactions.

There wasn't, after all, much to say about Lucy Farnsworth. Married to a pilot who served in Vietnam, widowed early, never remarried, two children and a speculation on the woman's net worth, always a titillating bell ringer. Multimillions, the announcer said. Lotta bread, Flanagan told himself, wondering why she had allowed Tony to be reduced to selling her old dolls for pin money. It only made Tony's violent reaction more puzzling.

By the time he had arrived back at his house, he had gotten too absorbed in suspicious speculation to remember that he had planned to dissolve the caked blood around his nostrils before Emily saw him. He heard her determined footsteps coming down the long hall from the front rooms as he let himself in the rear door. "My God, Flanagan," she cried, worry lines deepening on her forehead.

"Don't say it."

"Say what?"

"That I finally put it where it didn't belong."

"Are you all right and is it broken?"

"Yes and no."

She took him by the hand and gently guided him to a chair by the kitchen table. Then she got a wash cloth, soaked it in warm water from the tap and slowly dissolved the caked blood in his nostrils while he explained what had happened.

"Poor woman," she sighed. "Had everything and nothing. But Tony had no right to take it out on you."

"Maybe he was taking it out on himself," Flanagan speculated.

"Then he should have hit himself in the nose." She held him by the cheeks, tilted his head toward her and kissed him lightly on his swollen nose.

"Aside from the nose, my mission was aborted by fate. No Lucy. No clearance letter."

"Lucy's death changes everything," Emily said. "The dolls belong to the estate and Tony obviously has at least some owner-ship rights. It seems so trivial now."

She was right, of course. He had been a stickler for legality and it hardly mattered now. He would have to talk to Lacey, settle up properly.

"Wouldn't have mattered," she said. "I still would have given the doll away." She shook her head.

"The child?"

"Very bad. Still critical."

"Not a very good day for nice people," Flanagan said. He still retained an instinctive positive feeling about Lucy Farnsworth. She must have had good reason to keep Tony on a tight financial leash. "Matter of fact, I'm not really satisfied with the way Lucy died."

"Not again, Flanagan." Under her bangs, he caught her exasperated look. Also the note of curious expectancy. As it had been during his insurance days, he had always shared with her the tosses and turns of his investigations.

But, lately, the real frosting on the cake was to confront Sam Hazeltine with his suspicions, paying out the line until Sam could no longer resist the bait. In the game they played, the object was—there could be no other word for it—humiliation. Not that Sam was a pushover, which added the a la mode.

Sometimes, Flanagan knew, he'd push the game at the wrong time and place. After all, Sam was not retired. He was an active, conscientious servant of the public. Harassed by a thousand other demons of his job, he was always operating with a full plate on his desk. Flanagan and he had been schoolmates together, albeit always competitors. The fact that he had married Emily's best friend made the rivalry even keener.

Flanagan also knew that the sheriff resented his quarter-of-a-century hiatus in the big outside world. It made matters particularly sticky when Sam reluctantly sought out Flanagan on some investigatory point. Actually, he had done so with Mike Flanagan for years. Still did on occasion. But, of course, Mike had never deserted the local ship.

The fact was that, since the two wives were as close as peas in a pod, Sam and Flanagan had been forced to keep their warfare, if not friendly, civil. The price of peace at home was dear, very dear. He looked at Emily.

"For one thing, Dr. Mowbray didn't think she would go off that fast," Flanagan said after a long pause.

"What do doctors know?"

"And Jessie Shanks' ski deal was going down the tubes. Apparently, Lucy's death is about to crank up the works. I hear there's ten million to pass around."

Emily whistled.

"Still only coincidental. That nose bash has you hallucinating."

"I just said I wasn't satisfied. I didn't say I was sure."

He knew, of course, that she could be right in terms of coincidence. Too many years of living with suspicion caused a hair-trigger reaction in his mind.

The throbbing in his head seemed to have gotten worse.

"We have any aspirin?" he asked.

She looked in the kitchen cupboards without success. Then she went into the hall bathroom. Not finding any there, she went upstairs. He heard her poking around, then coming down again into the kitchen.

"Would you believe? Nada."

"She was only a pharmacist's daughter, but all the horse manure."

"On that note, I'll pop over to Dad's." At that moment the entry bell tinkled.

"I'll go to Dad's," Flanagan said. "I'm not hardly in sales mode."

"I'm not so sure I am," Emily sighed. "I nearly had Grandma's Victorian table sold. Came this close." She lifted her hand and showed her thumb and forefinger almost, but not, touching.

"We all have our tall clocks to bear."

She shook her head, smiled and kissed him on the cheek.

Doc Foxstone's Drug Store was on the corner of South and Main, just four blocks away. He lived over the premises, as he had for most of his life. He walked to the rear of the old-fashioned store where Doc worked behind a counter of carved wood, using vials and bottles and pestles that looked like they hadn't been changed since the day he opened. Actually, he had had to make them up to order when the old ones wore out, to keep up the image of the old remedies being the best remedies. He was no dummy, this sweet, shrewd old father-in-law of Flanagan.

"Walk into a truck?" Doc said when he saw him.

"Just aspirin, Doc. I've had about all the treatment I can stand today." Knowing he couldn't get off scot-free, he told Doc about his altercation with Tony. Doc, of course, had already heard about Lucy Farnsworth's death. Tom-toms, Flanagan thought. He scrupulously avoided hinting at any of his private suspicions and doubts. In the parlance of his sainted mother, his beloved father-in-law was a bit of a yenta. Doc handed over the aspirin and got a paper cone of water from the fountain. He looked out the door of the store as Flanagan popped the tablets and washed them down.

"Not much traffic. Snow season'll take care of that," Doc said.

The remark put an idea into Flanagan's head, although, he decided, it had probably been there all along.

"Be great if they got that new ski slope working."

"Doesn't look like it."

A customer came into the store and walked back to the prescription counter. Doc got up, talked briefly to the woman and went back to his work counter. Flanagan followed and stood for a while watching his father-in-law at his work. He was squeezing some kind of white cream into the back end of a tube.

"Lucky you didn't get into that deal," Flanagan said, casually feigning some interest in a jar's label.

"Win some. Lose some," Doc shrugged, wiping off the metal tool against the large brown jar from which he had taken the substance.

"Jessie Shanks the only general partner?"

He stopped for a moment, looked out toward the store, then squinted upward toward the ceiling.

"Not on that deal. I think Mowbray was a general on that one."

Flanagan felt a sudden rush of adrenaline.

"What is that stuff?" he asked the old pharmacist, pointing to the tube. His father-in-law bent over and pressed his mouth to Flanagan's ear.

"A little remedy for the last part over the fence."

Flanagan chuckled, but his mind was already far away.

Chapter Eight

"Pat Lacey called for you and I gave him what for," Emily said when Flanagan got home, shattering his concentration.

"For what?"

"Taking that money. Making it difficult for you."

"And what did he give you?" Flanagan asked cautiously.

"Contrition."

"Him?"

"Believe in your fellow man, Flanagan. They are capable of enormous change. He was all unctuous with apologies and charm."

"Actions speak louder than words," Flanagan said, after mulling things over. "Lacey gives nothing back." He was afflicted with an outpouring of doubts. With Mrs. Farnsworth dead, Lacey would have no incentive to give back the dolls.

"I suspect that even Lacey has a heart. I told him about Charlotte and giving the doll away."

"How is she doing?"

Her sudden downcast expression told him the answer.

"Maybe we'll all get back what we gave," she sighed.

"Maybe," Flanagan said. "I'd rather test the waters around dear old Lacey. Mind if I go out there?"

"Where is your sense of trust in our fellow creatures?" Emily said. But he could see beyond the words. She was having second thoughts.

It really was out of character for Lacey to give anything back, he thought, anxious now to dissect his incongruous act of generosity. He also knew he had to chase the thread of his uncertainties over the circumstances surrounding the death of Lucy Farnsworth. Suddenly, his mind was swarming with possibilities.

He got to Lacey's antique shop in early afternoon. Pat Lacey was dealing with a lady customer who showed some interest in a small carved music box showing the Three Bears. When the box was opened, the music played and one of the bear's arms moved as if he were playing what looked like a cello.

"I'm losing money at $850," he said, grimacing in pain and shaking his head.

"It's darling, but it seems so high," the woman said, mulling the purchase, opening and closing the box. Flanagan could see that she was hooked on the purchase. As near as he could judge, the box, based on other recent sales of similar ones, should go for no more than $300.

"It's a rare one," Lacey prodded. "Actually, I've turned down $600." He shook his head. "You really want it, don't you?" He opened the box and watched as the woman listened to the music.

"Don't you just love that sound?"

"It's lovely."

"Problem is purely ethical. I can't let you have it and turn down that $600 bid." He watched the woman's fingers as they touched the bear's head.

"If only we could simply enjoy these things and not even think about money," the woman said.

"That's the one thing that hurts the most about this business. I love being around these beautiful things—especially these astonishing music boxes. How many have you?

"About ten now," the woman said.

"Thing is, they're going up at a rate that absolutely flabbergasts. Sold one last year. Almost the same as this one. I couldn't buy it back for double. Not today."

"What would you say if I offered $650?" the woman said, looking up with a bright smile. She's playing her game, too, Flanagan observed, but she wasn't a match for Lacey, who scratched his head and pursed his lips in mock agony.

"You're making it very difficult for me." He touched the woman's arm. "Actually I'm torn. I got this stupid idea that I'm finding foster homes for worthy kids."

"You are selling things that give pleasure," the woman said.

His nostrils quivered as he took a deep breath that expanded his rib cage and seemed to double his girth. He frowned as if the pain was too unbearable to endure.

"I'll go $700. But I just can't see my way clear beyond that. I mean, there's still the question of my own self-respect. I can't keep things going by losing money."

The woman hesitated and rubbed her chin. Flanagan knew he had her and she shook her head with mock reluctance as she dipped quickly into her bag for her checkbook. Flanagan caught her eye for a moment. The woman actually thought she had gotten the better of the deal.

"Gotta keep the economy going," he said after the woman had gone. Flanagan withheld his comment, but not his hand, which Lacey pumped warmly.

Flanagan nodded.

"Your wife told me about the little girl."

"I know. I'm here to settle up. Its obvious with Lucy Farnsworth dead, a release from her is impossible."

"No kidding."

"I guess it's now the property of the estate."

"Au contraire, Flanagan. Follow me."

Flanagan followed him to the back of the store. He had lined the six remaining dolls on a shelf. Little girls all in a row. Flanagan picked one up.

"A Jumeau Bébé," Lacey said, lifting the doll and showing its marks. He gently removed the wig and pointed out the stamp behind the head, reading it aloud: "Déposé/Téte Jumeau/Bte. Then he turned over the doll and showed the stamp on the leather shoes: "Bebe/Jumeau/Med D'Or 1878."

It was only vaguely familiar to Flanagan.

"Jumeau was famous for their dolls in France in the 1860s to the 1880s. Made the heads out of bisque. Look at that face. And the eyes. Blown glass. Made to represent a girl between six and twelve. Look at that craftsmanship. It was the clothes that really gave them value. Krauts came in by the end of the century and the French faded. This is the real McCoy. And worth bucks to a passionate collector."

"No argument. But its provenance is still suspect."

Ignoring the statement, Lacey pulled another doll from the shelf, this one seated in a wooden chair. It was wearing a blonde wig with bangs and corkscrew curls and was dressed in a white dress with elaborate embroidery on the skirt and a pink sash. "Look at this." He lifted the doll's dress, showing three under-skirts, white socks, brown leather shoes and metal buckles. Lifting the wig, he read out the mark. "A 10 T ... meaning A. Thuillier, a firm operating in France in the 1880s."

"Still...," Flanagan began, then demurred. At this stage, it seemed pointless to protest. Money would almost always trump ethics.

"Come on, Flanagan. It's junk in the attic. Eventually it gets tossed or under the hammer somewhere. Come down to people like us anyway. With the old lady gone, so is the emotional value. There really is no one to give them back to."

"Look. Quid pro quo. You took the Bonnie Babe. Gave it away." He held up a pudgy hand. "I'm not casting aspersions. I admire you for that. You people are compassionate. Good for you.

Money isn't everything. But the fact was that it wasn't yours to give away."

Flanagan felt Lacey's eyes boring into his face.

"You can't be serious."

"Dead."

Lacey considered his answer and moistened his lips with his tongue.

"Here's the emmis. I gave Tony five large for the bunch. You gave me five. When I sell the lot, I'll figure it in, less what I lost on the Bonnie Babe. You have my word."

"Your word? Since when do you have a word?"

"Maybe not. But I do have your five grand. I told you. You get it back when I sell the lot. Way I figure, there's maybe fifteen, twenty K in it. I've checked and have interest. There's lots of interest in these old dolls. When I get mine, you'll get yours. Emmis. Less what I lost on the Bonnie Babe."

"The ownership is still questionable," Flanagan said. It was a weaker argument than a few days ago, but it was all he could think of.

"Well then," Lacey shot back, "if you cling to that argument, you gave away stolen goods."

He felt speechless with rage.

"Okay, then discount what the Bonnie Babe would have fetched and reimburse us for the remainder. As of now."

"How many times must I explain, when I get mine, you'll get yours?"

"Looks like I fell into the wrong mud hole," Flanagan sighed.

Lacey threw him a puzzled look.

"Hell, the Farnsworths had no idea of the value. That's the way we get inventory in this business, or have you forgotten? It don't get manufactured, buddy, it gets discovered. The antique dealer's golden rule. You get what you can get."

"If there is one thing I've learned in life, Lacey," Flanagan said, clearing his throat, "it is that if you don't feel comfortable with a situation and can avoid it, you avoid it. I don't feel comfortable with what you propose and I don't feel comfortable with your keeping the dolls. So I'm in a double bind. On the one hand I can avoid an involvement. On the other hand, I can't."

"You're out of your gourd. I said you'd get the money back. That's the biz, Flanagan. We buy for peanuts. Then they morph into gold nuggets and that becomes our margin." Lacey offered a benign smile. "You're in the wrong business, friend."

"Not at all. The heart of this business is provenance. And provenance is sacrosanct." He had, after all, spent years tracing the legality of ownership. Lacey was typical of the crooks who infested this business.

"No one will be the wiser," Lacey pressed.

"I would."

"You self-righteous bastard. You superior, self-righteous son-of-a-bitch. This business is a bullshit business. Half the stuff we sell has been ripped off from somewhere in one way or another. You know it and I know it." He seemed to be gaining steam and venom as he talked. "I say screw you. I'm going to do it anyhow. I don't give a rat's ass what you do about it. In fact, I don't think you can do a damned thing. Hell, you got rid of what you knew did not belong to you. So where's your argument? You're not going to be able to stop me."

Flanagan let him rant. There was really no point in arguing. Greed had taken over and Flanagan knew that there was little to be done in the face of that. Of all things, he understood the power of greed. In his years as an insurance investigator he had wallowed in it, dogged it to its source, found its blue flame of passion. Sex and greed. It was the kind of power that had to be respected... and resisted when twisted into an instrument of harm.

He had also learned that the only way to deal with other people's anger was to remove himself from it. Which he did. Besides, he needed time to think.

He drove slowly, using back roads that snaked through orchards, then curled off into narrow mountain roads which circled around lakes dotted with shuttered summer cottages.

Lacey had thrown one dart that came very close to the heart of his private target. Self-righteous! He hated that term. Others had used it as an epithet against him. An insult. And always it would pierce the armor of his self-esteem. He was a moral man, dammit, not a rigid and unbending fanatic. He had never demanded perfection in others, but, by God, he could smell chicanery at a hundred paces. And when it came close enough to him to be offensive, he simply could not ignore it.

While his conscious mind railed at Lacey and his schemes, he knew that his unconscious was at work trying to unravel the knot that held together the double bind. When it finally reached the surface of consciousness, he got back on the main road and drove as if by rote to the Farnsworth house. As to finding a specific reason for going in that direction, he wasn't sure, but the manner of Lucy Farnsworth's death had begun to obsess him.

It was already dark when he reached the turnoff to the Farnsworth place. The gas station was bathed in harsh light and he noted that the black car was nowhere to be seen. Instead of swinging right into the gravel road he hung a left and pulled up next to a pump. He noted that the fat man who had waited on him before could be seen talking on the phone in the little office next to the garage. A young man with a crew cut and oil smudges on his face leaned close to the open window on the driver's side.

"Just a topper," Flanagan said pleasantly. The young man put the nozzle in the tank and came back to the window.

"Check your oil and water?"

"Not just yet, son. Got a question."

The boy nodded. There was a bored and surly look about him and Flanagan was sure he would rather be elsewhere. No amount of ingratiation would ever work on that type. Flanagan knew that from experience.

"Looking for my buddies," Flanagan said, watching the boy's impassive face. "Couple of guys in a black Cadillac. Said they'd be here."

"Them two," the boy said, scratching his head.

"They were supposed to be here," Flanagan repeated.

"They been here. Three days now."

"They were supposed to wait."

"Probably be back. Crazy guys. Like they live here. Just set in that car all day long. Waitin'."

"Sure they're waitin'," Flanagan said, trying to ape the boy's idiom. "For me."

"You? Thought Jack said it was someone up at the Farnsworth place."

"That, too. But they're also waiting for me."

Flanagan searched his billfold for a ten. Finding none, he slid out a twenty.

"They gonna come back. Took off just a bit ago."

"How do you know they'll be back?"

"Shit man, they live here. Sleep in the car, one at a time. Use the john in the office. Jack's like their mama. Brings 'em stuff from the McDonald's. They leave only when that Farnsworth guy leaves. He comes back. They come back. They don't say nothin'."

The young man went to the back of the car and removed the pump from the tank.

"You were in pretty good shape. Three gallons is all."

Flanagan gave him the twenty.

"Do me a favor, kid, and you can keep the rest."

He looked again at the dollar total on the pump's register, then at the twenty. The offer made little change in his demeanor. He shrugged.

"I want to surprise them," Flanagan said. "So don't let on I been here. Okay?"

"No sweat for me. None of my damned business."

He pulled out of the station and, instead of heading right up the road to the Farnsworth house, drove down the road for a few miles, then doubled back. No sense giving the young man cause to talk about him.

Amy Shanks answered the door. The events of the day had apparently not ruffled her perfect grooming. Not a hair was out of place and her pleated skirt and bowed white silk blouse looked fresh and pressed. He noticed that her face had the unmistakably pinched look of the plastic surgeon's art.

"May I see Tony Farnsworth?" he asked, remembering with some degree of relief that Amy had missed the earlier episode between Tony and himself. She stayed framed in the doorway, not inviting him in.

"I'm terribly sorry, Mr.—" She was searching her mind for some name to pin on the vaguely familiar face. The Shanks were not very interested in antiques and their social set was more trendy than the native variety. They were considerably closer to the Grosse Point set who maintained large summer homes on the choice properties around the big lake.

"Flanagan," he reminded her.

"Of course," she said with a tight smile. "Where is my mind?" She looked out toward the orchards, her eyes misting suddenly. "We've had a terrible time. Terrible. My sister Lucy died." She swallowed, tamping down a gush of tears.

"I know. I'm terribly sorry. She was a fine woman." Apparently she had not noticed that he had been there earlier.

"The most wonderful sister...." She cleared her throat and made another valiant stab at maintaining her poise. "Kay is a mess. She's under sedation."

"I came to see Tony."

She grimaced and shrugged. He was obviously not her favorite.

"He said he was going to Sam Blatsford's place." She made a vague gesture toward Blatsford's adjacent property. He followed it and saw the lights from what was apparently the Blatsford's house, built on a high knoll at the other end of the orchard. "When he comes back, I'll tell him you wanted to see him." He noted that her nostrils twitched as if the mere reference to her nephew generated a foul odor. It reminded him of the irrational tangle he had had with him earlier.

"It's all right," he said. "Sorry to have troubled you."

She nodded and began to close the door. A jumble of questions crowded into his mind. Personal matters. He decided on an oblique approach.

"Must have come as a shock?" he asked in a casual, semi-rhetorical way.

"Very much so."

"Unexpected?"

"I'm afraid so."

"Guess Tony must be taking it badly."

The overhead light on the portico above the door reflected the kind of light that etched deep frown lines in her forehead for which she would not be grateful. A sigh of contempt escaped from her. He wasn't sure if it was meant for him and his prying or for Tony. Before he could find out for sure, she closed the door. As if to emphasize the withdrawal of her welcome, the light went off above the portico.

Now a canopy of stars provided the only light. Looking up, he could barely see the crescent of the moon which was just on the verge of shedding its new moon phase. Across the wide expanse of orchard, he could still see the lighted windows of Blatsford's house. Starting toward his car, he hesitated a moment, then changed direction and cut across the orchard path on foot, walking swiftly, his heart pounding. He could not deny to himself the thrill of danger, the sense of expectation and adventure.

Besides, there was no going back from the plan which persisted in his mind. Once it had gripped him, he knew there could be no retreat. Lacey would hardly let the matter rest until morning. He'd probably already set the wheels in motion to dispose of the dolls.

Walking at a fast clip, he reached the periphery of the residential property, then slipped surreptitiously over the unfamiliar terrain, moving carefully up side steps to the porch. The house, like his own, had Victorian antecedents. But this one showed little remodeling improvement. Blatsford had the reputation of being a miserly eccentric, shrewd and unbending in business, but one of the area's best cherry orchard operators, which was undoubtedly the reason that William Downs had arranged it so that Blatsford would operate their joint properties.

Emily positively salivated over the possibility of poking through the old Blatsford house in search of Victoriana. The man was exactly the right type to hoard old items. A regular string baller, she had dubbed him—a person who couldn't bear to part with even the most inconsequential piece of string, which he knotted together to make an ever-growing ball.

He had barely climbed the porch steps when he heard loud voices. An argument was obviously in progress, a real screaming session. Ordinarily, he was not an eavesdropper unless he found the matter pertinent to an immediate investigative interest. Only that could suspend his standard for violating other people's privacy.

But when he heard Tony's strident, high-pitched voice, he had his rationale. The voices were coming from what was probably the parlor, a fact he confirmed by pressing his face against a windowpane, where he could see into the room through a crack where the draperies did not hang perfectly together. He could see no faces, only bits and pieces of clothing moving about.

The other voice was deeper, more controlled, undoubtedly that of Blatsford, which was quickly confirmed by Tony's belching out the name like an epithet. Luckily, there was no outside light and he could remain in the shadows while cocking an ear against the pane.

"...I'll just oppose it, tie you up with lawyers until they put you in your damned grave." It was Tony's voice, high strung and desperate, followed by another string of epithets.

"It's airtight, Tony. Won't do you any good to oppose it. It'll all get figured out. The price of the property will be decided at appraisal and I'll work it out. Not before."

"I'll hire my own lawyers. Hold up the deal. All I want is an advance of what will one day be rightfully mine."

"I told you. If your mother agreed, I'd play ball. That's over with now. Out of my hands."

"I need this loan. If it can't be five hundred thou, then less. Say half. Those bastards are going to blow my head off if I don't deliver."

"They'll just have to be patient. It will take time."

"I have no time."

"You never got her to agree. That was the deal."

"So she died. How the hell was I to know that would happen? I was working on it. You know I was working on it."

"Like everything you ever did. You already got twenty-five grand."

"It didn't cover what I needed."

"You pissed it away, Tony. Like everything."

"Who the fuck...."

Flanagan heard deep derisive laughter, then momentary scuffling.

"Don't you give me any of your damned tantrums, Tony. Won't work with me."

"You promised two hundred and fifty."

"If she signed."

"She would have. I swear it."

"Doesn't matter now. Besides, you and Kay come out pretty good."

"But I know what you got coming from those developers of those high tech amusement parks, you greedy bastard."

"You'll get plenty. Not right away. There's all that legal stuff, but sooner or later it will come."

"I need it now. Don't you understand what those people are capable of? The interest is one percent a day. That's 30% a month."

"Your problem, not mine."

"It's up to nearly half a million. By the time the will is probated I'll get nothing. I need it now. Now." His voice broke. "Look, you're loaded. You know it's coming. Give me an advance. An advance. I'll pay them off and you and I can work a deal."

"Wouldn't touch it with a ten-foot pole. With your habit you'll be in the hole again in days."

"I promise you...."

"I can't help you."

"I'll blow the whistle."

"On what? It's a perfectly legitimate deal."

"Not unless the appraisers know. They'll still be thinking in terms of cherries."

"That was the deal your grandfather set up. Once I get the land, I do with it what I please. I had enough of cherries. Time for me to cash in my chips."

"You could get an extra mil. And what do I get?"

"Under normal conditions, you come out pretty good. Enough to pay off your loan. Then get yourself a job."

"I'm warning you, I'll take you down."

"You damned fool," Blatsford's voice rose and fell in measured and controlled cadences. "What are you going to tell people? That you were trying to screw your mother out of money? Then when she died, you were going to screw your sister? Who the hell will ever believe you? Who'll be your character reference, Tony? You're a liar, a thief, a bum. You've gambled away your life and apparently your inheritance. Who the hell would believe you about anything? I think...." Suddenly his voice changed abruptly. "Now you're going over the wall. I'd put the knife away if I were you."

"You don't think I'm capable, do you?"

"I think you're capable of anything."

"Damned straight I am. Everyone sells old Tony short."

In the brief moment of silence, Flanagan felt his lungs grow heavy, as if suddenly cut off from the oxygen supply. He couldn't stand by, do nothing. He bounded toward the door, then stopped suddenly as he heard Tony's high-pitched scream.

"You're hurting me."

"I should bust your goddamned arm."

Tony screamed again.

"You come in here and threaten me again, I'll have you locked up, put away—"

"Pleeze...."

Blatsford's voice grew lower, as if his words were coming through clamped teeth. Flanagan had to press his ear against the window to hear.

"I'll tell them what you said you could do to your mother, if she refused to go along."

"I would never do that. You know I could never do that."

"Not unless you figured out how to get away with it."

"It was just talk," Tony whined. He began to whimper. "I couldn't do that."

"Just don't let me see your sleazy face around here, ever. You understand? Ever."

Flanagan heard a thump, then what sounded like hysterical animal sounds. He was certain that the immediate danger was over. He sensed that Tony was heading for the front door. He heard it open and sank further back into the shadows.

By then, his eyes had become completely accustomed to the darkness. He could see Tony Farnsworth storm down the front steps and start toward his car, muttering under his breath. But before he reached the car, he stopped, or was stopped. He heard an unfamiliar angry voice speaking in a harsh whisper. Moving forward under the porch, sticking deep in the shadows, he took a few cautious steps to get a better view.

He saw Tony talking to a figure that looked much larger.

"I'll get it. It may take time, but I'll get it." Tony was pleading.

"Fuck time. You had time," a voice said.

"But it's coming. You know that."

"Sure we know that. But you said you'd get some from him. Like now. Damn welsher."

The whispers became harsher, less audible. Then suddenly he saw the larger man lurch, an arm move swiftly. He heard a thud and a deep groan as Tony went down on his knees. He saw a knee come up and Tony fell backwards onto the dirt surface. Flanagan resisted the impulse to run to the man's assistance. Reason intruded and he waited.

The men moved into the shadows and out of sight. Flanagan hurried forward to Tony's supine form. He bent beside him and reached out a hand.

But before he could connect with a tactile surface, he sensed that someone had come up behind him. Half turning, he saw the looming figure of a man. Then a kind of internal fireworks and a brief stab of pain. He would never be sure which came first.

Chapter Nine

Flanagan wondered if it was some aberrational eclipse in the heavens. A dark patch loomed above him, hiding the stars, then moved, revealing them again. Miraculously, the patch spoke.

"Not you again?" the voice asked.

Recognition flooded back into his mind. With it, his eyes were able to focus and he smelled sour sickly breath. A stab of pain behind his ear nudged his alertness still further and he sat up, rubbing a growing lump.

"I thought I was on an assault-free diet," Flanagan said. The test of his mental reflex made him feel better.

"What?"

"Never mind."

Tony stood up and Flanagan managed to do the same. A sudden dizziness made him grab Tony's arm, which steadied him until the vertigo dissipated.

"It's been a dangerous day," Flanagan said, brushing the seat of his pants, which was damp from the moist ground. He paused for a moment searching for the outline of Tony's features, trying to assess his mood. A lot of his earlier belligerence seemed gone, which was understandable, considering the pasting he had just received. When Tony did not continue the dialogue, Flanagan went on.

"Your aunt told me you were here. I needed to see you."

"Well, you've seen me," Tony said, offering a flash of the old antagonism.

"It was a helluva price to pay."

"How did we ever get mixed up with you? I mean, where do you fit in all this?"

His puzzlement, Flanagan thought, was perfectly reasonable.

"Doesn't seem like the most propitious atmosphere for discussion," Flanagan said. He heard Tony sigh, then turn to look at the Blatsford house, cursing under his breath. The lights were still on in the lower rooms.

"All right then, let's get away from this place," Tony said, striking out on a path through the orchards. Flanagan followed, taking deep gulps of the night air, which seemed to restore him, although the lump behind his ear had gotten bigger. Tony did not take the direct route to his house, swinging instead toward the main road, where he could get a better view of the gas station, a burst of illumination in the darkness.

The black car had returned to its accustomed spot beside the garage. He heard Tony's muttered curses, but said nothing. No sense revealing too much of his own knowledge, Flanagan decided, recalling the bedrock axiom of an investigator.

He followed Tony into the house. A television set was blaring in the living room.

"That you, Tony?" It was the voice of Amy Shanks.

"Yes," Tony replied, motioning with his head for Flanagan to follow. He took him to a small paneled room in the rear of the house, apparently used as an office. There were pictures on the wall representing the family at various ages.

"The good old days," Tony mumbled, seeing Flanagan's interest. In the light of the lamp, Tony's features were much clearer. He looked awful, his complexion ashen, his eyes bloodshot. He seemed suddenly vague, as if Flanagan's presence had little significance. For a moment, he debated whether or not to bring up the recent violence. Certainly, it was not a situation to be accepted or ignored. Better wait, he decided.

"I'm here about the dolls...."

"Jeez. That again." He shook his head. "What does it matter now?" All the old fight seemed out of him and he seemed to be slipping away. His mind was, quite obviously, elsewhere.

"The thing is—they're a lot more valuable than the five thousand you got for them."

He perked up slightly.

"What do you mean?"

"Maybe twenty thousand. Maybe more."

"You're not serious?"

"It's my business."

"That much?"

He grew thoughtful, watching Flanagan's face, waiting for him to proceed.

"So I got screwed."

"Technically it was your mother who got screwed."

Tony offered a sinister chuckle, shaking his head.

"Poor Mom," he sighed. "She got herself two losers. Fact is, they're half mine. All personal possessions go to me and my sister. That's a laugh." He sighed, suddenly looking up at Flanagan, his eyes moist. "Ever been so desperate for money, you couldn't think straight? I needed that five thousand for rent at my Chicago apartment. Back rent. Can you believe that?"

Flanagan could see that he was reaching out, trying to expel with words some deep inner hurt. He remained silent.

"Was never Mother's fault," he said, looking down at his nervous fingers. "Could've ruined the family. She was right in cutting me off, although I always gave her a bad time about it." He seemed to be drifting away. Flanagan felt his presence grow increasingly. "Odd how we turned out, Kay and me. I had a wife once, but she cut out years ago. Lucky we had no kids. My mother worried about both of us. At least Kay never gave her any trouble.

I'm grateful to her for sticking with mother all these years." His eyes grew moist. "I was a bastard to her... yet I loved her. I always loved her, even when she was turning me down, because in my heart I always knew she was right. Now the irony is we come into dough and I'm going to blow it all on those back debts."

Flanagan waited for present time to surface again in his mind. But the past was too compelling.

"You can't know what a curse it is to be provided for, protected economically, secure from the cradle to the grave. If I had kids, I'd cut 'em off without a dime at eighteen. I'd say go out there and do it on your own. What's life without risk and adventure and uncertainty? From the beginning I always knew it would be there. Grampa set it up like that and Mother carried out his wishes to the letter. I can tell you he was all wet. We've become professional dependents, Kay and me. And now we're technically free, but we never learned to fly on our own." He shook his head with disgust. "So I gambled. Tell you the truth it was the only way I felt alive. How else was I going to get my kicks in walking the edge, taking chances? What good's anything without taking chances?" He sucked in a deep breath. "So look what's ahead for me. I'll be like a middleman. The money will come down and I'll just sign it over to them. So I'll be free, right? Except for one thing. I don't know how to be free. I never learned. Kay never learned. In a way, neither did Mother. Victims. The three of us."

In the silence that followed, Flanagan speculated about Aunt Amy and how she figured in all this angst. Apparently, old Downs had put her also under Lucy's wing. Good intentions gone awry, Flanagan thought. Life's most common problem. But the man was right. What good's anything without taking chances? "You're on your own, son," Mike Flanagan, his dad, had told him, adding, "but you got one helluva rooting section."

"Above all, I don't blame my mother. No way." He shook himself like an old dog getting out of the water. "Once I get things squared away, I'm going to check myself into one of those gambling addict programs. Get rid of the impulse. Maybe even look deeper than that. A shrink to sort out all the internal garbage. Maybe even get a job. I'll need one." He smiled and a laugh gurgled up from his chest.

Flanagan could see he was desperately trying to pull himself together. "Look," Tony said, finally landing in the here and now. "Maybe the best thing would be to forget about the damned dolls. Those bums out there will get the money some way. Besides, you can't exactly accuse Lacey of ripping me off. I'm the thief."

He seemed sincere, but Flanagan suspended judgment. Despite his protestation, Tony still provided the apparent answer to the eternal question in a murder investigation: "Who benefits?"

In Tony's case the benefit was obvious.

"The reason I came here was to suggest a way to get the dolls back without undue hassle," Flanagan said cautiously, watching to see if Tony's expression registered genuine interest. It did and Flanagan continued. "Fraud is the big bugaboo in the antique business. The point is that Lacey knows he's being less than honest, however he rationalizes his method of acquisition. The fraud is in the knowledge of value. That makes him fraudulent." Tony's eyes flickered nervously. "He could, of course, contest the allegation. I came here for two reasons."

"Two?"

"To tell you that I gave away one doll. The Bonnie Babe."

"What the fuck are you talking about?"

Flanagan went through his contorted exclamation.

"Great. Good for you. Too bad I won't meet you in heaven."

"In a way its your gift as well at this point."

He looked at Flanagan and shook his head.

"You're too good to be true. I hope the kid makes it. Not that it's any bargain to cope with this life." He shook his head, lost in thought for a moment. Then he looked up.

"And the second?"

"Used to be an insurance investigator. I can get the word out to the dealers that the dolls in question are hot goods. The idea is to checkmate his sale and force him to give them back. The whole thing is crazy, I know. But the fact is that you did steal them from your mother even though just a day or so later they became half yours legally."

Tony scratched his head, pausing obviously to sort out Flanagan's explanation.

"Hell, I wouldn't give them back if I were him. He bought them from me in good faith." His odd understanding was confusing. Thieves are kindred souls, Flanagan thought.

"Then I take it you don't want to risk raking it up?"

"Haven't I done enough to hurt our good name?"

Flanagan rubbed the lump behind his ear, more to cover his confusion over Tony's puzzling behavior than to comfort the hurt. There had been a third reason and this was it, to scope him out. He tried to quickly sort out the possibilities. To Tony, his mother's death offered substantial benefit. Life itself.

Considering Tony's dilemma, there was only one logical explanation, despite the avalanche of self-pity and regret. Perhaps he didn't want anything to interfere with the swift disbursement of the will's value. And since when did Tony ever worry about his family's good name? Also, he seemed to be going overboard on personal insight and professing such a sudden burst of love and understanding of his mother's dilemma. Crocodile tears or pure subterfuge? Flanagan was thoroughly confused. He stood up, a gesture that the interview was over from his point of view.

"You say there could be twenty thousand involved?" Tony asked suddenly. True to form, Flanagan thought, somewhat relieved.

"Or more."

"And you think Lacey shafted me?"

"Give the devil his due. He might not have known of the value at the time," Flanagan said.

Tony rubbed his chin.

"And the money? How long...." His voice trailed off.

"Not long. There are lots of passionate doll collectors and they don't make these kinds of dolls any more."

"Leave it alone, Flanagan," Tony said. "I got enough on my plate."

"Your dolls. Your call."

"Let me think about it."

Flanagan nodded, gambling that enough intimacy had been established to begin a subtle interrogation. "I must tell you, Tony," Flanagan began, clearing his throat. He had deliberately walked toward the door of the den, then turned and come back to where Tony was still seated. It was a typical investigator's ploy. The afterthought maneuver. He had seen it repeated ad nauseum on the reruns of the "Columbo" television show. "I want you to know I did feel awful, aggravating your mother. I had no idea she was going downhill so rapidly." He let the idea hang in the air for a moment. "Did you?"

Tony shook his head, the gesture gaining speed as he thought about it.

"I couldn't understand it," he shrugged.

"Diabetes is a bitch."

"But she was being medicated. Dr. Mowbray was always making sure that she was getting the right amounts of insulin, digitalis, checking on her diuretic pills and her potassium. Makes you realize how fragile we all are. I mean, it was like one day she was fine, then poof. None of us expected her to die. Not that fast."

"How long had you been home?" Flanagan asked cautiously.

"About a week."

"And she was fine when you arrived?"

He grew thoughtful suddenly. Flanagan hoped he had been casual enough.

"A lot better than she was a few days later."

"Bad break. Your sister's taking it very hard, I understand."

"Can't blame her. They were very close."

"Never easy," Flanagan said. Of course, he wanted to ask more, but was afraid he'd make Tony overly suspicious.

"For her, I've decided to straighten out. I owe her that."

"You owe yourself, too. You surely don't want those two bullies on your neck forever." He made a stab at wry laughter. "Not to mention my head."

"Wasn't your fault. They watch me day and night. Nothing comes in and out of here without them knowing. They'll stop at nothing. And they get away with it. They're outside the law. The whole world is frightened of them. Including me."

Again he started toward the door. And again he executed the afterthought maneuver. "When is the funeral?"

"Tomorrow," Tony said. "Faster the better. No sense prolonging things."

"I'll pay my respects."

"I appreciate that." He grew thoughtful again.

He quietly let himself out of the front door. As he passed the living room, he noted that the television set was still on, although the lights were out.

Outside, he gulped deep draughts of the crisp cold night air. His little talk with Tony had accelerated the spin on his suspicion and for a moment or two, as he drove slowly down the gravel driveway, he forgot the throb of the lump behind his ear. But as he turned into the main road, he could see the outline of the big black car in its accustomed place beside the garage. The red glow of a cigarette flared behind its windshield, suggesting that there was a commonality of instinct between him and the men in the car. Neither he nor they trusted Tony Farnsworth.

But the real issue was not one of trust, he knew, but of murder. As always when the possibility became too compelling to resist, his mind turned to the inevitable question. What strategy was required to get Sheriff Sam Hazeltine motivated?

Chapter Ten

Thankfully, Flanagan was home before Emily. He did not want her to see him in this condition. She had left him a plate of cold cuts wrapped in plastic, which he shared with the slobbering Caesar. A quick look at his ashen face in the mirror forcefully suggested that he had better get to bed before Emily arrived.

With Caesar sprawled on his haunches on the bathroom floor, Flanagan showered. Feeling somewhat refreshed, he crawled between the sheets. Caesar lay down on the floor beside him with his usual air of total contentment. Flanagan leaned over and patted his head.

"Daddy's home, Rottweiler," Flanagan said aloud. "There's the good news and the bad news. The bad news is that there are, present company excepted, a lot of dirty dogs out there. And the good news?" Caesar sighed and closed his eyes. "And the good news is that this old dog up here is not exactly yelpless." In a brief moment, he slipped into a deep dreamless sleep.

But he wasn't the same old Flanagan in the morning. He felt shaky, and the bump on his head still ached.

"You were out like a light when I got home last night," Emily said from the bathroom where she was busy inserting her lenses.

He grunted an acknowledgment. "You'll be happy to know that there is a good chance that the governor will be down for Sam's dinner. And we've voted to raise the money for a gold watch." She hesitated and looked toward him. "I gave fifty dollars."

"That's because you have a gilt complex."

"Very hilarious." He didn't even have to spell "gilt" for her. "He is my best friend's husband. And as we all know, he is a fabulous keeper of the peace."

"We all know. He keeps a nice clean county." He sat up suddenly. Of course, he thought, chuckling. The strategy to get Sam involved had just popped into his head, which cleared it instantly. He felt surprisingly recovered.

"And if you and I do nudge him a bit on the murder question... so what? The county has one of the best records on open homicide cases in the country. Only ten percent open. That's quite an achievement."

"So it's you and I, is it?"

"I am your helpmate, aren't I?"

"And more," he said cheerfully. He knew she was expecting a mildly confrontational retort instead.

"Better than a stalemate," she muttered, with mock sarcasm. His ears perked as he got out of bed and steadied himself after a quick rush of blood to his head.

"Which is?"

He mentally braced himself for one of her rare forays into the world of puns.

"A husband who tells the same jokes all the time."

"That's one way to get rid of your wife. Joke her to death."

He bounded to the bathroom and put his arms around her just as she held the eyedropper over her left eye. The drop fell down her cheek.

"You made me drop a drop."

He kissed the nape of her neck and cupped her breasts.

"I love dealing with the same firm," he whispered. She reached behind her and caressed him.

"So do I."

"I'm rampant," he whispered.

"It is the ewe that makes the ram pant," she said, accurately squirting a drop into her eye.

"Who is the straight man on this comedy team?"

Again she reached behind her.

"You are. Very definitely."

He led her backwards toward their bed.

* * *

IT WAS, he knew, the best of all possible ways to start the day. But it did cause a reversal in procedures. Breakfast before mail call. He filled her in on all that had happened and she felt the lump on his head. A shadow of concern crossed her brow.

"It gave me a good excuse for my conversation with Tony," he said, with deep seriousness. If he had joked about it, she might have thought he was hiding something from her.

"I hope you're not going to get in too deep," Emily said. It was a comment made almost by rote. There was, of course, no stopping him now. She sipped her coffee and grew thoughtful. "I'm also concerned about Pat Lacey's reaction. You're attacking the most important asset of an antique dealer—his good name. There is no telling what he might do."

"He wheezes. I could take him before the first bell."

"I'm serious. He might be able to screw the tourists, but he does have some locals who believe in him."

"Then they're naïve."

"He could get nasty."

It was definitely something to worry about. Which reminded him about other worries.

"The little girl?" he asked.

She shook her head and put down her coffee cup.

"I stopped by before the meeting. The old man and her mother sat beside her bed. It was pitiful seeing that little lump of flesh lying there tied up to all those machines. She had the doll beside her and for a moment it was difficult to decide who was the live one." Her eyes misted and she wiped away the moisture with her napkin.

"Makes you realize how lucky lucky lucky you are."

He reached out and patted her hand.

After they finished their coffee, Flanagan helped her clear the table and put the dishes into the dishwasher. They did it silently. He was thinking now about Sam Hazeltine and how to use his new idea to approach him. Engaging Sam was always the most difficult step. Of course, once the hook was in, things went well. But Sam was an expert in evasion, a wily old fish.

His concentration was broken by Emily calling the hospital once again. From her expression, he could see that there had been no change.

"Tough little hombre," Flanagan said, chasing away images of his own children. He remembered how he had worried over them at the first sign of sniffles. She had timed her call to the second and as soon as she hung up, the tall clocks began their cacophony and his ear picked out the extra strike on the Hoogendyk. Someday, he sighed.

He walked to the post office, emptied the box and hurried back to the house. Opening the front door, he once again declared the Flanagan Antique Emporium open. Then he went through the ritual of the lighting of the lamps and walked back to the kitchen. Emily took the mail and brought it up to the office.

"Be back by lunch," he called up the winding staircase. He heard a muffled acknowledgment and let himself out the back door. It was about ten blocks up Main Street to Sam's office and he decided to walk. It would give him time to think, to dope out a strategy.

The office of the county sheriff was in a two-story rectangular brick building fronted by a stretch of manicured lawn, now gently browning in the fall chill. Flags of the country, county and state fluttered in the breeze from the highest flagpoles in town. It reminded him, once again, of Sam's sense of self-importance, which was both the man's armor and his Achilles' heel.

Sam wore his badge of office as a kind of halo and he literally basked in its glow, a perfect casting miracle. He was very tall, over six-and-a-half feet, with a ruddy complexion which crinkled like parchment when he smiled. His hair was like a gray wheat field curling in the wind and his eyes were as blue and shiny as sapphires. He was the idol of kids and dogs and little old ladies, and to his adoring public came across as a kind of benevolent coach whose inspiration and example kept the county team on the winning side.

Sam exuded infallibility. He always had. How could he have done otherwise? He had always been the best jock in school, the tallest, the handsomest. He had, of course, won the prettiest, most popular girl and most everything else he wanted in the circumscribed kingdom of Lakeside Falls and environs.

The problem was that Sam believed absolutely in his notices. There was a literal caste to it as well. The press had always been especially kind to him and he was rather an idol of Harold Sanford, who had owned The Lakeside Falls Herald and supported Sam in all his campaigns for sheriff. But Sanford had sold the paper a few months ago to a national chain which had installed an aggressive lout named, ironically, Braker, Herb Braker, who had no local ties and was thrashing around for "the story" to raise circulation and secure his reputation with his management.

Editorials had already been written that were mildly critical of the sheriff and his style of law enforcement for the county. There was, of course, much to be critical of. Sam simply ran the policing aspects of the county as if it were his personal fiefdom. But it was quite obvious to Flanagan, whose big city experience had taught him the ways of the press, that Braker had every intention of asserting the paper's power by tearing down some of Lakeside Falls' most sacred cows, of which Sam was far and away the most sacred. So far, the paper's forays had bounced off Sam's armor like rubber arrows.

To get inside the real man, Flanagan had to enter through the Achilles' heel and figuratively slosh through the bloodstream to the heart of the man. The fact was that Flanagan was getting quite adept at the maneuver.

Outside Sam's office sat Peggy Bilton, Sam's assistant and general factotum who provided the rasp and the hatchet so that Sam could maintain his ever-wonderful facade.

"The man in his lair?" Flanagan asked. Peggy scowled. Unlike Sam, she was petite with black hair and fierce dark eyes. She had been the first woman in the county to crack the sex barrier in the department and she never let anyone forget it. Sam had moved her into administration as his assistant, a wise move. Peggy had a real talent for attracting animosity, keeping it away from Sam, the guardian angel.

"You never call first, Flanagan," she snapped, scowling.

"Never know," Flanagan said. The only way to handle Peggy, Flanagan had learned, was to treat her in kind.

"He's in there with a bunch of radicals who object to our sniff dogs."

"They probably don't like them used on high school kids."

"Just like the rest of the pinkos," Peggy snorted.

"Haven't heard mention of that color in years."

She backed off.

"No place cleaner than this county and that's the way it's going to stay." The telephone rang and she hissed and fumed at whomever was on the other end.

"Bad morning?" Flanagan asked when she had hung up, adding a little deliberate sarcastic spin.

"Every morning is bad," she barked.

At that moment, the towering figure of Sam Hazeltine came out of his office with a small group of men and women. If they had been irate, they were now pussycats, and Sam sent the women off with kisses and the men with firm handshakes and his best crinkly smile, which disappeared when Flanagan offered a light finger wave.

"I got something, Sheriff," Flanagan said.

"I don't know why he doesn't call first," Peggy harrumphed.

"Couldn't wait," Flanagan said, seeing the sudden flash of alarm in Sam's sapphire eyes. He shooed him in with a nod of his head.

Flanagan followed him into his office. There wasn't a bit of wall space that was not covered with plaques and certificates of awards. The same was true for Sam's desk. His glory, Flanagan had often thought, certainly had never gone unnoticed. Sam lumbered behind his desk and stretched his long legs toward a nearby and much-worn leather hassock. Then he put his arms behind his head and leaned back in his chair.

"Why are you always so sure, Sam?" Flanagan said, staring at his armpits.

"About what?" Sam replied, puzzled.

"You never sweat under the arms. Here you are wearing this khaki uniform shirt, and nothing shows. I'd have two giant puddles there."

"We all exhibit different symptoms of stress," Sam said pompously.

"I have them all," Flanagan said.

"Just don't list them. I just had breakfast." Sam chuckled. He loved his own jokes, but never laughed at Flanagan's. "And you didn't stop by to stare at my armpits."

"You want me to come right to the point or shall we bullshit around first?"

Flanagan did detect the brief air of panic. They both knew that Flanagan wasn't going to appear in Sam's office as a social call. They saw enough of each other on that basis. This was business and both of them knew it.

"Dance around a little, Flanagan. Always fun to watch the footwork."

"All right then. Just how clean is your county?"

"As a hound's tooth," Sam replied. He winked. "Best record of homicide closings in the U S of A."

"With a little assist from your friends."

"What are friends for? Secret is to recognize natural aptitude. Although sometimes it does take one down the garden path."

"We're all human," Flanagan said, knowing that Sam was referring to the Barnes fiasco, a suicide made to look like a murder. "And just because it was conclusive didn't mean I was wrong."

"You're not suggesting it was a perfect crime?" The fact was that Sam had bested him, holding to the suicide theory to the bitter end. "I did go along like a good little boy."

"Because you wanted to prove me wrong. Get your kicks."

"And what a joy it was."

"How would you like another shot at it?"

"Would be lovely, Flanagan. By the way, how's your dad?" The fact was that Sam had always loved and admired Mike Flanagan, and their feeling toward each other was mutual.

"Aches and pains. But the mind's still sharp as a tack."

"Got to get by to see the old bird this week." He made a mark on his notebook. Sam had once berated Flanagan for putting the man in a nursing home and would only take Mike's word for it that he was there by his own insistence. Too much pride to be a burden. Flanagan hated the idea, but knew better than to disrespect his father's wishes. Sam looked at Flanagan and crinkled. "Okay, let's have your best shot."

"I've got two," Flanagan said, making a gun out of his forefinger and thumb and pointing it at the sheriff.

"Fire away."

"You're pretty proud of keeping the mob out of the county, keeping their scams out, right?"

Sam lifted his feet off the hassock and sat bolt upright. "As you know, Flanagan, we've got our local bad boys, but no branch offices. What are you trying to say?"

"Well, you missed something."

"Is there a punch line coming?"

"There are two Chicago capos in your so-called clean county at this very moment."

"No way. We've got the best intelligence team in the state for a dumb little county. This is not mob territory. Not since we cleaned them out ten years ago."

"I'm not saying they're getting a foothold. Only that they're here shaking down Tony Farnsworth."

He put his feet back up on the hassock.

"That bum."

"They don't quit hanging around, the papers will get it and make you look stupid on the eve of the Clean County testimonial." Again his legs swung around and he sat upright. He said nothing and Flanagan knew he was throwing the ball into his court. Like all knights in shining armor, Sam Hazeltine could not take ridicule, and humiliation was the ultimate enemy. Flanagan paid out the line carefully, filling Sam in on the details. He knew better than to hold too many things back. For all his ego, Sam could not be put down as a blockhead.

"I can just see Herb Braker salivating over that one," Sam mused.

"And they'll probably show up at Lucy Farnsworth's funeral," Flanagan said, still paying out the line. "They stick to Tony like glue. And they'll be there for all to see." He had put a little smidgen of fudge on the story. They'd be at the funeral all right, but probably never get out of their car. "So my best advice would be to pick them up at the gas station and roust them out of the county. Capos like that are not supposed to attract attention. And if you need a charge, I'll be happy to go for assault and battery."

"Are you crazy? Emily will kill me and, if she doesn't succeed, Audrey will get me in my own bed."

"Just trying to keep it legal."

Sam shook his head and gave Flanagan a long, steady appraisal.

"You'd do that for me?"

"A favor for a friend."

Sam crinkled his brow and blew air between his lips.

"You said there were two shots. Although I detest, above all things, to be in your debt."

"I know. It's terrible."

Flanagan took a deep breath and began the chronological tale of his suspicions. His first meeting with Lucy and his reasons for going to the house, his conversations with family members, his discovery of the deal between Dr. Mowbray and Jessie Shanks, the overheard conversations between Tony and Blatsford, Tony's desperation. Then the windup and pitch.

"I believe that Lucy Farnsworth was somehow pushed over the edge by a deliberately lethal method yet to be discovered. I'm not at all sure what that might be or if it's even provable, but the benefits to certain family members and her doctor are too substantial to be ignored. I personally saw her decline physically."

"If I remember correctly she was a diabetic. She was chairman for years of the Annual Ball for Diabetes. That's a rough disease."

"She also had a heart condition."

"People do die of natural causes, Flanagan. Except maybe in your suspicious mind."

"I just don't think it happened that way in her case."

"You remind me of a man always walking with his head down, watching the street for someone's lost money."

"And who sometimes finds some."

"Or gets hit by a car."

"Sam, it's there. I know it."

"If it is, it's only on the edge of your nostrils. There is absolutely nothing here but supposition. Now I do thank you for the tip on the two hoods. I appreciate that. You know I do. But the other is fantasy and unprovable."

"I'm not so sure," Flanagan said. "There are a number of possibilities. Poison, for example. Maybe even some manipulation of her medication. Or some other way I haven't thought of yet. But it nags at me and I believe it's there somewhere." He paused and shrugged. He seemed to have come up against a dead end. "At least I think it is."

"Do you?" Sam said with a touch of sarcasm.

Despite that, Flanagan detected the tiniest insertion of the hook's point in the sheriff's vulnerable skin. Experience had, Flanagan knew, taught the sheriff not to dismiss his hunches out of hand.

"Of course you'll have to get inside the blood and tissue of Lucy Farnsworth."

"Who is about to be buried."

"Then you'll have to find a way to stop it."

"Now how in hell can I do that?"

"You're the sheriff," Flanagan said, pointing. "I see the badge."

Chapter Eleven

Lucy Farnsworth's funeral was a Lakeside Falls event and the service in the Episcopal Church had all the cachet, despite its solemnity, of a social occasion. Emily had wanted to go, but could not get in touch with the lady who was dickering for the Victorian dining set. She had scheduled another appointment with her at the same hour of the funeral. It wasn't that she had a special emotional attachment to Lucy Farnsworth. But when Flanagan had returned home after his meeting with Sam Hazeltine and filled her in on what had transpired, her own sense of participation had become acute.

"Will Sam act?" she had asked, with controlled expectation as he dressed in shirt, tie and jacket for the funeral.

"Not sure," Flanagan answered with a shrug.

"Wouldn't hurt to use a little distaff pressure," he had muttered vaguely. "A word to the wife and all that."

"You really have your teeth in the tail on this?"

"More like into a boa constrictor. It's wiggling me along."

"Just keep it in perspective," Emily said, the warning explicit, although both of them knew it would hardly matter. When Flanagan was "on to it," priorities became garbled, perspective lost.

"I'll try."

She kissed him on the forehead.

"Of course, you will."

Little white lies, they both knew, canceling each other out.

* * *

FLANAGAN SAT in the rear pews, watching the proceedings, trying to discern from the backs of the principal mourners some corroboration for his theory.

Not being a divining rod, he was forced to rely on the logic system of the human brain. It was an idea that both amused and excited him. Gives you your jollies, Emily had commented often, ignoring his vague exterior. She knew his mind was burning with possibilities.

There was a healthy sense of gratification in seeing Sam Hazeltine among the assemblage, although he wasn't sure who deserved the full credit for that. Not in uniform, he was sitting in one of the rear pews. Since he was a fixture in the community, it was not uncommon for him to attend various family rituals. Only the murderer, if there was one, would view his presence with some anxiety and Flanagan made a mental note to carefully observe his little clutch of suspects.

Earlier, he had stood off to the side and watched them file into the church. Jessie's big car had pulled up to the curb, depositing Amy, Tony and Kay. There was a chauffeur at the wheel and Jessie, with all the air of the master of ceremonies for the event, led the heavily veiled women up the church steps while an ashen-faced Tony followed behind. A few minutes later Sam Blatsford arrived looking appropriately stoic, thin lips pursed tightly together.

Expecting to see the two hoods in their now-familiar black Cadillac parked within easy surveillance range of Tony, he was surprised when he couldn't see them either in the parking lot next to the church or on the street.

Perhaps they had reasoned that there was no way that Tony could slip through their fingers for the next few hours and they might have taken a break for sentimental reasons. He quickly rejected the idea. Their presence was to intimidate and there was no better way to illustrate ruthlessness and indifference than to put their message in front of a grieving man—if Tony was indeed grieving.

There were other surprises as well. Flanagan saw Herb Braker, the new owner of The Lakeside Falls Herald, among the somber-faced people walking into the church. A thin man with a ferret-like face and deep-set shifty eyes, he noted that the man's head swiveled in fits and starts, like a predatory bird. Since Braker's Lakeside Falls roots were not very deep, Flanagan felt it odd that he would be there.

He recognized Harry Ketchum walking beside The Herald's publisher, whose penchant for muckraking had been thwarted under the old Sanford regime at the paper and who, obviously, had finally been given his head. With him was a young and attractive dark-haired woman who made no bones about her role in the event. She carried a pad and ballpoint at the ready. A photographer from the paper, Flanagan observed, had zealously worked the curbside procession. Could they also have some doubts about the legitimacy of Lucy Farnsworth's death? No way, Flanagan assured himself. Probably just delving deeper into the ski resort fiasco. But he was not entirely satisfied with that explanation, either.

Flanagan listened to the reverend's laudatory eulogy sprinkled with references to Lucy Farnsworth's many charitable acts and contributions, her selfless devotion and goodness as a daughter, wife and mother. Flanagan's thoughts, as they always did on such occasions, drifted to his own beloved mother, and tears of loss and longing filled his eyes. He supposed that all of the participants, in some way, were touched inwardly by their own special grief.

After the eulogy, the reverend announced that the family would be at home to receive visitations from mourners after the burial. He quickly glanced across the church. Sam's eyes met his and he nodded. So the hook had made a tiny incision, he thought, although Sam had taken no action to stop the burial. Flanagan couldn't blame him for that. Can't fault a guy for trying, he thought with a chuckle.

The female mourners followed the coffin down the center aisle. Jessie Shanks, Dr. Mowbray, Sam Blatsford and Tony were the pallbearers, giving the event an ironic twist. Flanagan searched their faces for the slightest flicker of a clue—remorse, anxiety, fear. Actually, he imagined he saw them all, wondering if that were simply the natural condition of men who participated in such events. Death itself was the ultimate trauma and no one could remain indifferent in the face of it.

He could not read the expressions on the faces of the women, who were heavily veiled. Kay and her aunt followed the coffin arm in arm, obviously determined to brave the public spectacle without hysteria eliciting the least possible comment among the assemblage. At this point, there was a family image to maintain.

Flanagan watched the group assemble in cars behind the flower-bedecked cortege. There was still no sign of the black Cadillac.

"They're in custody," Sam said from behind him. Flanagan looked up, squinting into the sunlight.

"On what charge?"

"Assault. But I haven't made it official." He smiled wryly. "Actually, I'm hoping that the Detroit godfather calls them home. They're not supposed to tangle with the law. Not on a collection assignment."

"Get anything out of them?"

"It's a free country and that sort of thing. They've both got sheets as long as your arm. I'd be happy just to get them pulled out of here. Sooner or later, old Tony has to get out of town. Then it's someone else's problem."

"I wouldn't have him leave town just yet."

"He won't. Not until he cashes in and that could take awhile."

Flanagan knew the hook was in and that it was time for him to stop tugging on the line. Sam was the kind of man who liked to think he had originated ideas, all ideas. He had a clear sense of what his own next move would be. He also had the answer to his previous question of why Herb Braker and his troops had shown up. They had apparently gotten wind of the arrest of the two capos.

"Are you going to the cemetery?" Sam asked.

"No."

"The house?"

When Flanagan hesitated, the sheriff smiled.

"We can go in my car."

Flanagan followed Sam to his unmarked car, noting that both the lack of uniform and official sheriff's car made the matter seem more personal than business.

"Give us a chance to look around," Sam said as he gunned the motor and headed out of town, in the opposite direction of the funeral procession.

"Look for what?"

Flanagan knew, of course. Sam, despite his bullheadedness and devotion to his personal image, was not without good investigatory skills and instincts. Flanagan's job was to subtly inject an imaginative approach. In some ways their objectives collided. Sam certainly enjoyed the publicity and glory of solving a murder. But putting Flanagan down, especially in the case of a murder that was only speculation on Flanagan's part, was Sam's real motivation now. The game was on and both men knew it.

"You tell me."

"Poison. Medication. Stuff like that."

"You're learning, Flanagan."

"Thank you, Sheriff."

"We'll hang around for a while when they come back."

"Of course."

It would give them both an opportunity to assess the reaction of the sheriff's presence on the principal mourners. Sam, Flanagan thought happily, was going whole hog.

"And the lady being buried?" Flanagan asked.

"May she rest in peace," Sam said, clearly answering any question about imminent exhumation.

"She won't," Flanagan replied.

Sam drove with little fear of being stopped by the law, which meant he barreled down the sparsely trafficked road near ninety. They spoke little, each deep in his own thoughts. But when they neared the site of the ski resort construction, Flanagan sprang to attention.

"Slow down, Sam," he said with some agitation. Sam obeyed, following Flanagan's gaze. "They're back at work. Look at them up there."

Literally overnight, the construction site had sprung to life. Flanagan touched the sheriff's arm.

"I promise you it will be worth the visit," he said.

Earlier, he had filled Sam in on the connection between Shanks and Mowbray, and Sam's reaction was to sniff with skepticism. And with good reason, Flanagan knew, since he had often stooped to hyperbole to get Sam motivated, sometimes with mixed results. The sniff was repeated, but Sam turned in on the construction road and they bounced over the ruts to the trailer.

The scene was a lot different than it had been the day before. Most of the heavy equipment was in use above them, and carpenters were busy constructing forms for cement on the various structures. There was so much activity around them, they were barely noticed as they pulled up beside the trailer.

"Just keep an open mind," Flanagan said as he opened the car door and stepped out onto the hard ground. Sam got out and joined him as they moved toward the trailer. Inside, the same girl he had seen earlier was busy on the phone. The other offices, unlike during his previous visit, were apparently in use. When the girl saw Flanagan, she signaled with her fingers to wait a moment. Sam stood beside him, his head bent to accommodate himself to the height. Without his uniform, Flanagan hoped Sam would not be recognized.

"I know it's short notice," the girl said. "But you see we have this deadline...." She listened impatiently, shaking her head. "I'll have to check with Mr. Struthers. He's the only one that can authorize that. Yes. I will call you back in less than an hour." She banged the phone in its cradle and looked up in exasperation. "Suddenly, everything has to be done yesterday."

"Guess they want to make the snow," Flanagan said. The girl looked at him curiously, her eyes drifting to the sheriff.

"Do I know you?"

"I was here yesterday. Bulldozer operator."

"Oh yeah. Didn't recognize you all dressed up."

"I was passing by. Didn't know things had started up so fast."

"Got the word late yesterday," she said. "Mr. Shanks met with Mr. Struthers half the night."

"Guess the money's rolling again."

"Man from the Detroit bank was here when the sun came up. Unfortunately, so was I. Been on the phone all morning telling the guys to get their butts up here. Happy days are here again." She sighed and looked at the phone. "For them, anyway."

"So you think they'll meet the deadline?"

"Triple time. We're hauling lights so we can work through the night." She looked at Flanagan. "You and your buddy ready? We got the work."

Flanagan scratched his head and looked toward Sam.

"Not too sure yet," Flanagan said, shuffling his feet in a caricature of some movie hayseed.

"I haven't got time for this," the girl said, turning away and picking up the phone. At that moment, one of the office doors opened and a man walked out dressed in work clothes, but with a demeanor that definitely spelled authority. He looked curiously at the men in the trailer, then addressed Sam Hazeltine.

"No permit problems, Sheriff?" the man asked. He put out his hand and the sheriff took it. "I'm Struthers, job supervisor."

He was blond, with a ruddy, weatherworn face. "All goes well, we're gonna make it for the winter season. Should be a helluva boost for the county." He noted that the girl had blushed a deep red as she busied herself with using the phone, but not before she cast Flanagan a look of blatant contempt. Flanagan avoided her eyes. What was there to say?

"Knew you were in a little financial trouble out here," Sam said. "Just stopped by to offer our congratulations on the resurrection." As always, Sam's sense of politics was sharp. Flanagan tried by concentration and osmosis to get Sam to ask the obvious question. By some miracle, Sam was up to the mark.

"Amy Shanks' potential inheritance must have turned the trick."

"Every cloud has a silver lining," Struthers said. "Took a little maneuvering, but the bank went along. Just in time, I'd say. Life's like that. Ran into more construction problems than we thought. Guess somebody up there smiled. Equals out, I suppose." Struthers, Flanagan noted, was the philosophical type.

"This is Josh Flanagan. He's in the antique business," Sam said. Flanagan pumped Struthers' hand. He looked quickly at the girl to see if she had heard. She had and Flanagan was sure she would tell the story to Struthers after they had left.

"Well, good luck to you," Sam said. They both shook hands again and Sam stooped his way out of the trailer with Flanagan following. In the car, they bounced back to the highway.

"Big enough motive...," Sam began.

"To run a truck through," Flanagan interrupted. "And the good doctor is the partner."

"Hard to swallow, though. They're both solid citizens."

"Not so solid. Not when they have their signatures on a sour deal that turns suddenly sweet."

"Still circumstantial," Sam said, but he was obviously agitated.

Flanagan looked at his watch.

"And the chief witness lies beneath the cold, cold ground."

Sam said nothing, accelerating the car. In a few moments, they were passing the cherry orchards. Flanagan's eyes drifted toward the long rows of sleeping trees and, once again, the cemetery image surfaced. Déjà vu, he sighed to himself, confirming once again the gift—or curse—of his instincts. Sam maneuvered the car up the gravel road.

"Hold up, Sam," Flanagan cried suddenly. He was looking up a path through the trees that led toward Blatsford's contiguous property. "There."

Sam's eyes followed Flanagan's outstretched arm. On a rise, just above the orchards, a man was looking through a surveyor's instrument, motioning with his arms to someone down below. The man was not far from where the road bisected the Farnsworth property. Another man stood beside him, who Flanagan recognized as the fellow who had driven the truck that had towed him out of the mud. Both Flanagan and the sheriff got out of the car and walked toward them.

The man who had driven the tow truck looked uncomfortable.

"How are you, Jason?" the sheriff asked. Obviously, they had a professional acquaintance.

"Fine, Sheriff. Jes fine."

"Off the juice, are you?"

"No more of that stuff for me." Unfortunately, his breath denied his words.

"Just keep out of trouble," Sam said. He looked toward the hill, watching the man above wave and the man below acknowledge the signal.

"What's happening?" the sheriff asked casually.

"Whole new things, Sheriff. Place is never gonna be the same again."

"I don't understand."

"Blatsford says we may soon lose the title." The man snickered, enjoying his little joke.

"What title is that?" the sheriff asked.

"Cherry Capital of the World."

Sam looked toward Flanagan and frowned. Flanagan wondered if he was experiencing the same sense of sudden depression.

"The greedy should enter the Olympics. They move faster than any of us," Flanagan sighed. Sam batted his eyelashes in affirmation. On that point, they both agreed.

Chapter Twelve

The door to the Farnsworth house was adorned with a mourning wreath. A harried woman, carrying a basket of bread and wearing a black uniform trimmed with white lace, opened the door. Sam offered a crinkly smile and explained that they were here to pay respects to the family.

"They've not returned as yet from the cemetery. I'm from the caterer," the woman explained, opening the door wide enough for them to enter. Flanagan could see a buffet laid on the dining room table and a man stacking dishes on a sideboard.

"All right if we wait?" Sam asked politely.

"Of course," the woman said. Ignoring them, she went to the dining room to assist the man.

Flanagan and the sheriff went into the living room, where apparently all signs of Lucy Farnsworth's last infirmity had been removed. Flanagan recounted his last visit with the lady while Sam nodded without comment.

"She had her medications on a side table," Flanagan said, directing his attention to what they should be looking for. They each inspected parts of the room.

"Doesn't exactly look like your run-of-the-mill scene of the crime," Sam said. But the sarcasm lacked conviction. Sam's incredulousness had definitely been shaken by their recent experiences.

"That's exactly the point," Flanagan said. He followed Sam into the foyer. "Everything appears unlikely. Normal." It rests, Flanagan thought, solely on my instincts and private observations of the swift changes in Lucy Farnsworth's condition. But then, Sam knew that.

They heard voices in what was apparently the kitchen. Flanagan quickly ducked his head into the dining room, noting that it was deserted. He then signaled by putting a finger on his lips, and both men quickly mounted the stairs.

The bedroom floor was laid out in a traditional, somewhat old-fashioned style: a center corridor with bedrooms on either side. At one end of the corridor was a bathroom. There was only one closed bedroom door, which they opened. It was obviously Lucy Farnsworth's room, containing the large king-sized bed in which, Flanagan supposed, she had drawn her last breath.

Across the room was a dresser on whose surface was a forest of framed family pictures. Beside the bed was a small pile of hardback novels. Opening drawers, Flanagan noted that the contents had been neatly arranged. The same was true of the closets. Everything clean and tidy, including the poudre on which were makeup vials and containers, all neatly arranged.

Sam made his inspection with professional authority while Flanagan waited for him to make the one most essential move, which he did. Flanagan followed him into an adjoining bathroom, obviously added to the house much later than its original construction. It, too, had been carefully cleaned. There was nothing odd or abnormal about that. It was, Flanagan knew, the tendency of the human species to sweep all signs of death from sight as soon as possible. His nostrils also picked up the scent of a perfumed antiseptic.

Sam opened the medicine chest. Bottles and containers of

various shapes were lined up on each shelf like toy soldiers. For the first time that morning, he sensed Sam's hesitation.

"I have no legal authority for this, you understand."

"Perfectly," Flanagan responded. It was a question that Sam must have asked himself many times on other occasions. Flanagan had never heard him raise it aloud before. Press scrutiny, he supposed, was beginning to take its toll.

"Do you seriously believe that a murderer, if there was one, would be stupid enough to leave the poison of choice laying around for evidence?"

"All drugs are lethal one way or another," Flanagan said cautiously, almost tentatively. "Depends on how they're used." He noted that most of the prescription medicines came from his father-in-law's store. There were also a number of bottles of vitamins and other familiar toiletries and nonprescription drugs. Flanagan took a mental inventory of the various prescription drugs, squinting at the dates on the labels.

"May I make a suggestion?" Flanagan said, exuding humility.

"You know I'm not a hardhead, Flanagan." This was Sam's usual retort at precisely such a moment. They had their vaudeville act down pat.

"Take the most recent prescription drugs. Have them analyzed."

When Sam frowned, Flanagan said:

"Doc will check them. No need to make it official." Flanagan paused. "Not yet."

Giving the devil his due, Flanagan had no illusions about the extent of Sam's legal obligations under the best of circumstances. He did have to keep one eye on the various restrictions imposed by the courts. Many an open-and-shut case had fallen through the cracks because of a legal loophole or a policeman's procedural mistake. On that score Sam had lived a charmed life. When any quasi- or borderline-legal infringements had been attributed to the sheriff, he had always managed to deflect them. Which was precisely why he made such a juicy target for the newly antagonistic press.

"I'll find a way to get them back," Flanagan assured the sheriff. "Although I seriously doubt that anyone will be looking here in the immediate future."

"I don't like it," Sam said. It definitely was not like him.

"Growing a bit cautious in your old age?" Flanagan chided.

"Got some enemies on my flanks these days."

"You're the law," Flanagan said with an unmistakable air of challenge.

Flanagan watched Sam's face as it passed through some uncommon frozen moments of indecision. Then, as if to avoid the issue completely, Sam walked out of the bathroom. It was, Flanagan knew, an unmistakable signal and he quickly filled his pockets with the prescription drugs.

From below came the sounds of increasing activity. They started down the stairs and met the woman who had first greeted them, at its foot taking the coats of the first guests. She glanced at them curiously.

At that moment, Jessie Shanks came in the door followed by Kay Farnsworth and Amy. The women had lifted their black veils, revealing ashen skin and puffy red eyes. Flanagan studied their faces.

"Couldn't make the burial, Jessie," Sam drawled, offering his most endearing smile. "Came by to pay my respects." He looked at the women and shook his head. "And I'm really sorry, Kay and Amy. Lucy was quite a woman."

"Yes, she was," Kay said. She apparently had found the inner strength to control her grief, although her eyes revealed how much she had cried. Both women and Jessie Shanks barely noticed Flanagan, who felt somewhat guilty and awkward with his pockets stuffed with Lucy Farnsworth's drugs.

Tony Farnsworth suddenly appeared in the foyer. Seeing the sheriff, his reaction was one of agitation. Flanagan watched his discomfort and their eyes met briefly. Then Tony ran up the stairs.

Other guests began to crowd into the house while Kay and Amy went into the living room. A telephone rang. A moment later Flanagan saw Jessie answer it, talking in hushed, agitated tones.

"Didn't see you at the cemetery, Sheriff."

Flanagan's attention was drawn by the voice. It was Braker, the new newspaper owner, poised in an ominous predatory stance. Beside him, a scruffy Harry Ketchum smirked.

"Other things to do," Sam snapped.

"So I've heard."

"Coupla questions...," Harry Ketchum began.

"Not here," Sam said testily, turning his back.

"Later then," Braker intervened, a trifle unctuous.

"Maybe," Sam muttered, moving away. Flanagan followed.

"Better be careful with those birds," Flanagan said when he had caught up with the sheriff.

"Knew you'd say that. I'm not afraid of them."

"I know that. They're baiting you."

"I don't bait easily."

Easier to get flies with honey, Flanagan wanted to say. But he could see that Sam was in no mood to be lectured.

People began to mill about, most of them heading for the buffet. Flanagan saw Dr. Mowbray and Blatsford in the crowd, shaking hands and chatting. Both of them were appropriately solemn for the occasion. Eating standing up, most of the guests talked quietly among themselves. Kay and Amy formed a kind of seated receiving line in the living room. In turn, they greeted guests and chatted briefly with each, accepting condolences.

It was, Flanagan thought, a very civilized post-funeral event. In a way it wasn't much different than an Irish wake or a Jewish shiva. He had experienced each a number of times as grandparents, uncles, aunts and friends on each side were appropriately dispatched to their particular piece of heavenly turf. Flanagan felt a different kind of discomfort. He was not there out of respect but out of suspicion. Nevertheless, he observed the protocol of the ritual.

"If I had known how seriously ill she was," he told Kay, "I would not have bothered her about the dolls." He had waited his turn to speak with her.

"Don't be silly," Kay said graciously. "You were acting in good faith. You should not feel guilty about it. Not at all."

"I appreciate that. I was quite concerned." He paused for a moment. "She seemed to have failed so—well, so fast."

"It came as a terrible shock." There was a noticeable tremor in her voice. But Flanagan persisted, hating himself.

"An awful disease, diabetes." What he wanted was more information on her condition, more information about her last moments. "I shouldn't be talking like this. It must have been so traumatic. We all know how close you were." He felt overbearingly stupid. He was, after all, certainly a stranger compared to others in the room.

"Yes," Kay sighed. "We were very close."

"Like sisters. Just like sisters," he said hastily, still determined to keep the ball in the air. He started to say something more, but demurred. He looked directly into her eyes, which, despite the puffiness and bloodshot veins, looked clear and forceful. Observing her grief the other day, he admired the way she was bearing up.

"After awhile the memories will sustain you," Flanagan said with sincere feeling. "The grief will still be there, but it will be manageable. If it's any comfort, I adored my mother." She had been gone for five years by then, but her persona was still vivid in Flanagan's mind and her influence and values still the measured constant of his life.

"It just seems so odd that she declined so swiftly," Flanagan said cautiously. "She seemed so—so strong." He remembered the firmness of her handshake. "Just sort of faded away, I suppose."

"Yes. Like the air going out of a balloon. She just lost energy. Just like that. Her legs gave out. Even her eyes. Actually, it had been going on for a week or two," Kay said, as if to herself.

"When I was here...." Flanagan paused and cleared his throat. "That time when the doctor was here. He said she would be all right in a day or two." Flanagan wondered if he had properly disguised such an obviously impertinent question.

"Yes, he did say that," Kay nodded. "I had forgotten."

"Maybe she didn't follow doctor's orders," Flanagan said. Kay studied him with her Wedgwood blue eyes. He noted in them an air of apprehension.

"Mother was so good at that. Such a good soldier when it came to her taking her medicine." She shook her head in obvious response to some inner question. "No. That would not be mother." She turned away and he knew that she had dismissed any ominous ideas. Yet, he wondered if he had planted a seed of doubt.

"And what Tony did was beastly. He realizes that." The abrupt change of subject confused him. "He told me what you and he discussed about the dolls. Also about your unfortunate experience."

Flanagan wondered if Tony had told her about the rather sinister deal he had cooked up with Blatsford.

"I did have a long talk with him yesterday," Flanagan said in a last-ditch effort to keep the conversation going. From out of the corner of his eye he watched Sam talking to Amy Shanks, who was more his contemporary than Kay. Flanagan could see that there were others waiting to talk with her, but he was still not ready to give ground.

"And he's going to straighten himself out. He promised," Kay said.

"I'm sure he will."

He could not hold her up any longer. Others were pressing to get near her, pay their respects, and leave. Suddenly a hand tapped his shoulder. He turned and saw a well-groomed man with a dimpled smile.

"You're Josh Flanagan," the man said.

"I am."

"I'm Blandings. Just fitted your wife with contacts."

"Yes. Dr. Blandings. My wife speaks highly of you."

"Terrible about Mrs. Farnsworth," Dr. Blandings said, shaking his head. He looked toward Kay.

"Poor Kay, she's shattered."

Flanagan watched him. Blandings sighed, shook his head and looked toward Kay with obvious devotion.

"I guess poor Kay is on her own now. She and her mother were very close, you know."

Flanagan nodded and shrugged. Their glance met briefly, then the man turned back to observe Kay greeting more mourners.

Flanagan moved away toward Amy, shook her hands, found little to say but the usual amenities and joined Sam, who stood by the window looking out on the vast dormant orchard.

"So that will all be gone someday?" Sam sighed.

"The economics of land use," Flanagan said, looking up at Sam's profile. "Unless you can find a way to stop it."

"Nobody ever stopped the march of money," the sheriff said gloomily. "Obsolescence is setting in. Next step for us is to become decrepit strangers in an alien land. We're fading, Flanagan."

"It's a fade worse than death."

"I'm serious, Flanagan," Sam said grimly. "Amy reminded me of—well, my own mortality. Lucy and I were a sort of thing back in elementary school. Hadn't thought of it for years. She was a terrific athlete. Pretty as a picture." He shook his head. "Hard to believe."

"Not so hard," Flanagan said with perseverance. Sam was taking an unnecessary and dangerous detour, losing sight of their original objective. "She was helped along, Sam." Flanagan had lowered his voice, just as he spied Braker moving into the living room. A reflex, he thought. Braker's presence was now making them both nervous.

"Maybe," Sam muttered. He, too, had spotted Braker.

"It's not the time for maybes. Not now."

"She was sick and she died," Sam shrugged. "Amy said that in those last days she began dropping things. She was very miserable. Even stopped her favorite pastime, reading."

Stopped reading, Flanagan thought, remembering the pile of books beside her bed. It would be just one more idea to chew on. His first priority would be to get Sam off his philosophical kick.

"Maybe she's trying to throw you off the scent. Ever think of that?"

It was, of course, not without its own logic. After all, she was Jessie Shanks' wife.

"Amy? That scatterbrain?" Sam scoffed. Flanagan had no chance to respond, for Jessie himself had come up behind them.

"Understand you visited the construction site a while ago, Sam," Jessie said. Sam turned slowly to face him. Jessie, too, was a tall man but not as tall as the sheriff. In a quick glance, Flanagan saw Braker talking to Kay.

"Yes, I did," he responded. Flanagan was thankful for his use of the first person. He took a step away, just within earshot, and continued to look out of the window, hoping Jessie would ignore his presence.

"We violate any county ordinances?" Jessie asked pleasantly.

"None that I know of, Jessie."

"Got our people a little worried."

"I hadn't intended that."

"Just plain curiosity?"

There was a long pause. Flanagan held his breath. In his heart, he felt himself rooting for Sam. Go for it, he cried within himself.

"More than that, Jessie."

"I don't understand that implication, Sheriff."

Good, Flanagan thought, Jessie had unwittingly put it on an official basis.

"None of us thought you'd be able to gear up so fast. Matter of fact we thought the project had run out of money."

"It did."

"Now it's funded again."

"That's right. And, frankly, I don't see that it's any business of yours." Good again, Flanagan thought. If there was anything that got Sam's dander up it was a put-down, especially if it was tangy with belligerence and superiority.

"Protecting the citizens of this county from bodily harm is my business."

"What the hell are you talking about?"

He could hear Sam suck in a gulp of air.

"This is not an accusation, Jessie. There is reason to question. I said question. Not suspect. Question. That Lucy's death was something less than natural." Flanagan wanted to jump for joy. Sam was wonderful, although wild horses couldn't get him to ever say it publicly.

"Where in the name of God did you get that idea?" Jessie said, obviously panicked. Anything that might inhibit the disposition of the will was a matter of grave concern. It was obvious that Jessie had signed away Amy's inheritance as collateral for the bank to fund additional loans for the construction project. That, Flanagan knew, was a given.

"Wasn't Lucy's death rather sudden?" Sam asked.

"We hadn't expected it. No. But what you're talking about...."

Do it, Flanagan begged.

"Jessie, who is your principal financial partner in the ski deal?" Fighting any temptation to turn around, Flanagan heard what seemed like gurgling sounds. They seemed to inhibit Jessie Shanks' speech. Then he heard him cough and clear his throat. Peripherally, he saw Braker talking now with Amy, although it was clear that if he gave any attention to the agitated manner in which Sam and Jessie Shanks were conversing, Braker could not fail to be interested.

"That is the most presumptuous bit of crap that I have ever heard. In my mind, it disqualifies you from wearing that damned badge and I suggest that you leave this house immediately."

Jessie Shanks did not raise his voice. In fact, anger, thankfully, had modulated it. Besides, it was not the kind of information that Jessie wanted to be aired publicly. Nor did Sam. Indeed, neither of them could have failed to note Braker's proximity in the room.

"You can't do that, Jessie," Sam said.

"Can't I?"

"This is not your house."

Flanagan did not turn for a long moment, although he knew that Jessie had moved away. Still he did not want to make it appear as if he was Sam's alter ego, mostly because he did not want to be shut out from listening in. He wished he were a fly on the wall instead. But Sam's eyes met his and flickered and he followed him to the dining room. He could tell from the sheriff's deeper pink skin tones that the hook had bitten deeper into his craw.

Sam's conversation with Jessie had, of course, stirred things up. He could see Jessie Shanks in whispered intense conversation with Dr. Mowbray. The doctor's eyes flitted around the room and fixed ominously on Sam. Unfortunately, he was waylaid by Tony before he could observe what was to come next. Tony seemed considerably more relaxed since they had had their last conversation.

"You okay, Flanagan?" he asked pleasantly. He had changed his dark suit to a blazer with gold buttons and gray flannels. Although he was pale, his eyes seemed clear and at peace.

"Just a bit of a lump," Flanagan said, feeling behind his ear.

"I think they've gone," he whispered. "Why hassle me now? They know the money is coming."

"That must be a relief," Flanagan said. He chose not to tell him that Sam had locked up his tormentors.

"Thanks to Mother," Tony sighed. "She might have been right all along."

"About what?"

"Protecting us from ourselves."

"You really believe that?" Flanagan asked.

"I'm not sure," he admitted. "Kay and I had a long talk about that last night. About dependency. She made us dependent, you see. But we could have broken out at any time. So it was not entirely her fault."

"It's good to get those feelings resolved," Flanagan said, more to end the conversation and find Sam, who had disappeared from view. But Tony apparently had more to say.

"And we both agree about the dolls. Kay and I. Leaving it alone. This is beyond money, Flanagan. My debts will be covered by the will. And Kay doesn't need the aggravation. She's got enough to deal with. Who knows what it could stir up?"

It was a remark that could only refocus suspicion. Now that the initial shock of loss was over, none of the beneficiaries wanted to stir the pot. The cannibals did not want to get near the stew, he thought. If he had said it aloud, Emily would have thought he was presumptuous.

Another guest grabbed Tony's arm and led him away, offering a stream of condolences. More people had crowded into the house. Some he recognized and greeted. Others were only vaguely familiar. He saw Dr. Blandings now in deep conversation with Kay. Somehow, their conversation looked furtive, clandestine. He shook his head. Was he overreacting? The atmosphere was getting oppressive and Flanagan was more anxious than ever to get the drugs in his pockets analyzed.

He moved among the people looking for Sam, who was usually the first to be able to spot in a crowd. At one point he was jostled by a man who was vaguely familiar.

"Why, it's you, Flanagan." The man was broad shouldered and offered a warm smile of greeting. He put out his hand. "Alan Grant." Flanagan, recognizing the optometrist, experienced a sudden tug of guilt. Perhaps the feeling made him over-pump the outstretched hand.

"So good to see you again."

"How's Mrs. Flanagan?"

"Fine. Fine."

"Too bad about Lucy."

"Awful."

He looked up at Flanagan's eyes.

"Should have them checked. Haven't seen either of you for awhile."

It was true. He hadn't had his own reading glasses checked for a couple of years. Not that he was having much trouble. His vision was pretty good for a man his age. But he did need his reading glasses with accelerating frequency, although he resisted wearing them as much as he could.

"You're probably right."

"Just watching out for my patients."

"I understand."

Flanagan hurried away, not without another tug of guilt for Emily's defection. He saw Sam finally through the dining room window, deep in animated conversation with Dr. Mowbray. From a corner of his eye, he could see Jessie Shanks watching their confrontation from another window. Sidling through the crowds, he let himself out the front door. Others were saying their good-byes. In a moment the exodus would begin.

Mowbray was waving a finger in front of Sam's nose. He was livid with anger. Flanagan started toward them and stopped at that point where he could just make out some of the avalanche of angry words spewing from the doctor. Apparently, he had arrived at the tail end of the tongue lashing.

"So dig her up as far as I'm concerned. I did my job and my conscience is clear. But I tell you this—you'll be finished in this county after this—finished."

At that point, Mowbray turned and, like a disjointed tornado, stormed back to the house. Flanagan watched him disappear, but not before he saw two now-familiar faces watching them through a window, Herb Braker and Harry Ketchum. Apparently Sam hadn't seen them and Flanagan resolved not to draw attention to the surveillance.

"You sure take a lot of abuse in this type of work," Flanagan said pleasantly. But he could see that Sam wasn't buying any mollification. He followed him into the car and they drove back to Lakeside Falls without a word spoken between them. Yet, in an odd way, Flanagan was satisfied.

The dry grass had been fired and the wind was beginning to whip up the flames.

Chapter Thirteen

F lanagan upended the plastic container and spilled a few pills into the palms of Doc's hand. Doc studied them, moved them around with his fingers and pronounced judgment.

"Diabinese, probably," Doc said.

"That's just the point. No 'probablys.'"

"I've been pushing pills for more than fifty years...." Flanagan cut short the speech, which he had heard in varying forms for at least a couple of decades.

"I know you're infallible, Doc. But impartial juries, prosecutors and defense lawyers, the press, judges and most institutions of justice would expect some scientific backup in writing. It's like judging distance with your thumb."

"I say it's Diabinese. Insulin in pill form, for those with limited knowledge." He looked pointedly at his son-in-law, narrowing his eyes over his half-glasses. He put out the hand without the pills. "Let me see the container."

Flanagan hesitated and put the container behind his back.

"Only if you exercise the better part of valor."

"So now I'm an old busybody."

"I wouldn't say old."

Doc scratched his head.

"That important?"

"I'd say crucial," Flanagan muttered, handing him the container. Doc looked at the label, then shot Flanagan a look of deep concern.

"Always looking for trouble," Doc sighed, but his sense of intrigue was well honed and he relished his son-in-law's suspicious bent. Beyond a reminder about discretion, he did not need to be informed about the obvious. He put the plastic container down and opened a battered wooden card file cabinet. He had not yet fully succumbed to the world of computers, although they could not be ignored and he had no choice but to use them. But he could not give up his addiction to the cards and continued to use the old system, reversing the idea of backup. The old system was the computer backup. He took out an index card and looked again at the pills in his palm.

"I know it's Diabinese. She's been taking it for years." He waved his hand. "I know. I know. I'll have it analyzed."

He funneled the pills from his palm back into the container. Flanagan then handed him the other containers.

"Lucy had some complicated medical problems. She took oral insulin, digitalis to keep her blood vessels dilated, hydroDI-URIL, which is a diuretic, and a potassium supplement. The whole spectrum. Typical drug therapy for a diabetic with a heart condition. The diuretic caused her to pass more fluids out of her system and with them, essential electrolytes and minerals. Like potassium." He inspected a partial selection of the various pills.

"And you'll have them analyzed? All of them?"

"You think someone fiddled with them?"

"I don't know. Isn't there such a thing as look-alikes?"

"Yes, but the Big Pharmas go to great pains to color code and shape them all differently. And I am vigilant." He looked at his son-in-law and smiled.

"Do you think we are a house of pill repute?"

"Not bad, Dad," Flanagan laughed. "Where there's a pill, there's a way."

Doc nodded, then returned to serious mode. It was the wrong time for a punfest.

"Isn't this a matter for Sam?"

"He's resisting making it official."

Doc nodded. Like Emily, he understood his son-in-law's shorthand. Flanagan waited while Doc made a call to the lab for a pickup.

"Twenty-four hours all right?"

Flanagan nodded, but reluctantly. Doc packed the containers in an envelope, labeled it and put it aside.

"Cuppa?" he asked.

"Sounds great."

It meant, of course, that Flanagan had to go through Doc's pumping ritual. In halting spurts, he outlined his suspicions and the involvement of Sam Hazeltine.

"And if the lab confirms what I know, where are we then?"

"It's called the process of elimination. We'll have to get into some heavy what-ifs."

"I've got one for you," Doc said. Like Emily, he threw himself gamely into the spirit of Flanagan's compulsive crime solving. He wore a wry smile of friendly pride.

"With drugs, if you vary the program, eliminate one or the other therapy, you run into trouble. You don't necessarily have to substitute. You can overdose or underdose. Diabetes is essentially a problem in body chemistry."

"I'm aware of that."

"And these drugs, as far as I know, were self-administered by Lucy herself. I saw her myself only last week. She was alert and joked when she came in with Kay. Never thought she'd go this fast."

"Neither did Dr. Mowbray." He had saved the bit about Dr. Mowbray for last.

"Dr. Mowbray?"

"I was there when he said he had increased her dosages. More diuretic. He had said that specifically. Also her potassium."

"Doesn't sound ominous to me. I've known Mowbray for nearly as long as I know you. Frankly, Flanagan, I think you're barking up the wrong tree there. Not that he's not capable of some form of malpractice. Every doctor makes mistakes. Honest mistakes. But that's malpractice. Not murder."

"And tough as hell to prove the difference."

"I'd say almost impossible."

"Even if the benefit to the doctor was obvious and substantial."

Doc looked at him with growing awareness.

"So that's why you fished that out of me about Mowbray being the general partner with Jessie in that ski deal." He shook his head. "Stretching, Flanagan. Putting two and two together to make five."

"I'd hate to be on a jury considering the possibility."

"So would I."

Doc looked into his coffee cup, on which a film had already begun to form. Actually, Flanagan knew, it was only a prop.

"Hope I haven't got Sam in deep water," Flanagan said, giving voice to the thought that was beginning to bother him.

"Don't worry about him. He's too tall to drown."

"I just know I'm right, Doc."

His father-in-law shrugged.

"It's as wild a theory as most of the others. Got to admit, you've had a lot of base hits."

"And a few home runs, Doc."

Doc tapped him playfully on the arm.

Throughout Flanagan's career as an insurance investigator, there was always a moment when something hidden and inarticulate began to nag at him, as if his mind were groping in impenetrable mists for something that he knew was there but could not find. This was one of those moments. Actually it wasn't even measurable in time, more like a dull ache that simply appeared mysteriously. Patience, he had always cautioned himself. Don't force it. In due time it will surface.

Always, too, such a moment was accompanied by a wave of fatigue. He finished his coffee and stood up.

"I'll call you when I get the report. But don't expect any miracles."

He made a gesture of understanding and walked home, coming in the front door. He was surprised to find Emily and a young couple standing in front of a tall clock, the Hoogendyk. Flanagan felt a sudden rush of joyous excitement.

"Oh, there's my husband," Emily said, obviously relieved. "He knows more about these than anyone."

She cheerfully introduced him to a Mr. and Mrs. Parker, explaining that they were building a house on the lake. They were a tall couple who looked surprisingly alike, perhaps owing to Mrs. Parker's boyish haircut. Both wore glasses and seemed very serious and single-minded. Flanagan knew the type. They usually knew exactly what they were after, a fact underlined by Emily's various expressions and body signals.

"Sort of a modified Yankee barn with high rafters. We've been looking for the tallest clock we can find."

Manna from heaven, Flanagan thought. All fatigue melted away. A Yankee barn, the tallest clock. Like a girlie show hawker at a carnival, he stood before the Hoogendyk.

"This gorgeous baby was made by the great Dutch clock-maker, Steven Hoogendyk, in Rotterdam. Absolutely the finest in its class. Look at that marquetry. Cannot be duplicated." He pointed out the construction details, tracing the workmanship with his fingers. "A fabulous buy. I really stole it and can pass it along..." He wondered if his desperation was showing.

"How much is it?" Mrs. Parker asked. He looked at Emily. There was, he knew, at least $15,000 in it. Should he ask for twenty? Give him bargaining power. Go for it, a voice said. Emily's face loomed up at him, a faint goading smile on her lips.

Get rid of it. Her silent, silently hysterical pleading came through loud and clear.

"$20,000," he said. It came out like air from a punctured tire.

The Parkers looked at each other. There appeared to be no obvious protest. He wanted to dance with joy.

"It's a one-of-a-kind," he said.

"None like it in the world," Emily added.

"A masterwork."

"It will look exquisite in your Yankee barn," Flanagan pressed.

"It's lovely," Mrs. Parker agreed. "Should fit in perfectly."

Flanagan darted a glance at Emily. He felt his palms begin to sweat. Now? Emily sent him the go signal.

"It's even got an extra strike. Like one for good measure."

"It does?"

"The time's perfect. It's like a birthday cake. An extra candle for good luck."

"It's been lucky for us," Emily said.

Flanagan looked at his watch. Two minutes to five. He saw Mr. Parker reach into an inner pocket and take out a checkbook.

"Is that the way they made them?" Mrs. Parker asked.

"That's the way they made this one," Flanagan replied. "I suppose it was something like a signature."

"You just subtract one strike at the top of each hour. Simple. On the half hour it strikes just once, like the others."

The couple looked at each other for a long moment. Then the cacophony began. Flanagan's throat went dry as he watched their reaction. The other clocks stopped striking. Hoogendyk offered his signature. Suddenly a frown crossed Mrs. Parker's brow.

"Won't it be confusing?" she asked innocently.

"Not if you know what's happening," Flanagan said quickly. He was certain it was a question of living with the thing. Not morality. The value might be there in the future—maybe— despite the fact that no major dealer presently would touch it. Even in the antique business eccentricity was sometimes rewarded. He'd have to research some examples of that, he decided.

"But what about guests? We expect to entertain a great deal. Won't they be confused?"

"Not if you tell them in advance."

"But suppose they forget, or I forget to tell them."

The sale was fading and he knew it. Emily shrugged. He tried a last ditch gamble.

"I could let it go for less. If you really want it."

"Can it be fixed?" Mr. Parker asked. There was still a modicum of hope. He continued to hold the checkbook. Suddenly Lacey's image emerged in his mind. Moral hypocrite, he charged himself.

"I'm afraid not." It had the sound of defeat. He wished he had said: "Fix it? It's not broken. That's the way it was made." Which is exactly what Emily said suddenly, as if she had read his mind. He looked at her, but she turned her eyes away.

"We want a working clock," Mr. Parker murmured with some sarcasm and a not-too-kindly look at Emily.

"There are others here. Take this baby." He patted the George III by Lawson as if it were a used car.

"It's so short," Mr. Parker said.

"Short! It's one inch over eight feet tall."

"Not big enough," Mr. Parker said, glancing over the others with a sneer.

At that point, Mr. and Mrs. Parker exchanged glances familiar to Flanagan and his wife.

"Maybe we should think about it," Mr. Parker said. The couple smiled insincerely, turned away and moved out of the house.

"They'll bury us with it," Emily sighed. Flanagan looked at the clock, not without affection. "And I won't have us spend another nickel on it."

"You mean you'd let it go silent. Murder it."

"It's a clock, not a person. You've got murder on the brain, Flanagan."

Fatigue washed back over him.

"That I have," he sighed. She inspected him for a long moment and he sensed her careful assessment, which indicated she had something unsettling to say.

"And while we're on that subject, Audrey called. It seems Braker and his Herald cohorts have been all over Sam today. She's says they're driving him up the wall. He's very upset, chewing Maalox by the pound and blaming you."

"Par for the course," Flanagan muttered. It was one of the aberrations of their competition that Sam's complaints always came directly from Audrey through Emily.

"But you're not on the line. Sam is."

"I told him he ought to have done an autopsy before they put Lucy in the ground."

He sat down on one of a pair of Victorian grandfather chairs and crossed his legs. Emily sat on the other one, crossed her legs and observed him.

"All you need is a long curved pipe, Sherlock."

"Why couldn't she read at night? I saw books piled on her night table. She wore contact lenses. She could have read."

"I don't understand."

"I don't either."

It was no use. Soon, he knew, he would begin to rail against his own ignorance.

"It just may not ever be provable," Flanagan said wearily. He felt her eyes watching him as he mulled over his thoughts. Then he remembered what she had said that Audrey had told her about Sam.

"Why did you say Sam was going up the wall?"

"Audrey said."

"Of course, Audrey said." He resisted exasperation.

"Braker wanted to know what Dr. Mowbray was arguing with Sam about."

"Did Sam tell him?"

"Not according to Audrey."

"So he went to Mowbray."

"Probably."

"What will Mowbray do?"

"Do? He'll probably chew up every square inch of carpet he can get his hands on."

"That's a mixed metaphor."

"Only if you metaphor the first time."

"A good sign, Flanagan. The noggin is alive and kicking."

He ignored the compliment.

"And Braker's minions, according to Audrey, are now crawling all over the sheriff's office."

He felt genuine compassion for the sheriff, although he would never show it. The man's a big boy. He should be able to figure out how to get them off his back.

"Can't blame them. It's a damned good story. Rich local matron murdered by...." Suddenly Flanagan shook his head vigorously.

"Can't do that. No proof. No weapon. Only suspects."

"But that's not a real story."

"The story is in the stink."

"Leave it to Sam. He'll think of something," Emily said.

Mostly ways to skin me alive, Flanagan thought gloomily. He felt Emily watching him and sank deeper into his own thoughts. I am not wrong, he assured himself. Am I?

Chapter Fourteen

The telephone jangled Flanagan out of a dead sleep. Caesar jumped up and croaked a single bark, looked around him with his sleepy brown eyes, then put his snout on his paw and sank back into his canine dreams. Since the phone was on Emily's side, she had the receiver in her ear and was listening intently.

"You're kidding," she said after a long pause. He could hear the muffled sound coming through the phone. From its familiar cadence he knew it was Audrey. "I don't believe it."

"Believe what, for crying out loud?"

"You're not serious."

"What the hell is going on?"

Emily turned her head from the mouthpiece.

"She's reading from this morning's Herald." Then, turning back to the mouthpiece, she said: "Go on."

Outside, the first gray spears of daylight were seeping through the drawn blinds. Flanagan got out of bed, stepping on Caesar who squealed briefly, then dutifully followed his reluctant master down the stairs to the front where he quickly scooped up the paper. Barefoot, breathing vapor and chilled, he scanned the front page.

He saw it on the bottom right-hand corner, but the headline jumped out at him like a jack-in-the-box.

"Sheriff Hazeltine Investigating Downs Heiress Death."

Sweat seemed to break out on his goose bumps. It was the one thing Sam feared the most. Premature exposure. Braker and Ketchum had gotten a bonus for their trouble. In fact, a bonanza. Blinking to focus his eyes, Flanagan summoned the courage to read the story.

"The sudden tragic death of prominent heiress Lucy Farnsworth is apparently the focus of a quiet investigation by the sheriff's office.

"Mrs. Farnsworth, the oldest daughter of multimillionaire cherry king Edward Downs, died two days ago of cardiac arrest. Mrs. Farnsworth was a diabetic, but friends and relatives judged her death to be 'shockingly sudden.'"

Flanagan winced and shivered. The sweat over his goose bumps seemed to freeze.

"The heiress, who was known throughout Lakeside Falls as a philanthropist and patron of the arts, was buried today in the family plot after a funeral service before throngs at the Episcopal Church on Main Street. Sources close to The Herald have learned that the sheriff is exploring the possibility of foul play, but at this stage in the investigation, spokesmen for the sheriff's office were reluctant to comment.

"Adding fuel to the speculation was an unconfirmed report that two members of the Annunzio Mafia family of Chicago were picked up for questioning late yesterday in the vicinity of the Downs Orchards, where Mrs. Farnsworth resided with her daughter Kay. Sources in Chicago have confirmed that Anthony Farnsworth, the son of the deceased, has run up a mountain of gambling debts.

"A spokesman for the family, prominent local entrepreneur and developer Jessie Shanks, whose Cherry Ski Resort yesterday resumed construction, told The Herald that 'any allegations of foul play' in the death of his mother-in-law were 'scurrilous and absurd.'"

There followed a short history of Edward Downs, which jumped to an inner page and included old pictures of Downs with his wife and daughters in happier days. Flanagan flitted through the story again, noting the double byline by Harry Ketchum and Sue Livingston.

Caesar took the opportunity to perform his morning rituals among the front yard shrubs, sprinting up the porch steps just in time to miss getting his tail pinched in the slammed door. Flanagan stormed back up the stairs to the bedroom. He threw the paper on the bed. Emily was in the bathroom putting in her lenses.

"Sam is storming around the house asking for your head. Audrey won't let him call until he calms down," Emily said, coming out of the bathroom with moist eyes. She picked up the paper, read the story and groaned.

"A fishing expedition, is all," Flanagan grumped. "Like William Randolph Hearst, he wanted to start the Spanish-American War."

"Now poor Sam will have to do it in a fishbowl."

"As the culprit scurries for cover." Or culprits, Flanagan thought. He quickly jumped into his pants and shirt and shaved swiftly. Just like the Marines, he silently told his mirror image. Only the face was older, plumper, not the lean bony one that had griped back at him during the Vietnam War. As he shaved, he forced himself to put the story in a more favorable perspective. Braker had ordered his troops to set the mousetraps based purely on the image of Dr. Mowbray waving his finger at the sheriff.

Flanagan reconstructed the scenario. Ketchum and Livingston had questioned Dr. Mowbray, who would have snarled and flushed to the verge of apoplexy. Then Jessie Shanks would have been overly indignant, perhaps even threatening.

By then, Braker's dynamic duo would have been able to reconstruct a credible account of Lucy Farnsworth's last days and an assortment of comments about her swift and sudden demise. A call to the paper would have sent a reporter to the sheriff's office and the county jail. A snooping expedition.

In fact, Flanagan was certain that one of Sam's more lethargic staff people, sucking up to a reporter, would have spilled the beans about the two hoods. After that would come indignation on Sam's part, angry talk, unguarded revelations. Sam had probably never used the words "no comment" in his career, knowing that every utterance he would make would be suitably glorified by The Herald under its former owners.

The story, Flanagan knew, was the stuff of which circulation builders are made. The Lakeside Falls citizenry were no different than the rest of the country. They loved the sly and juicy sap of scandal and innuendo, and soaps were heady amusements in Lakeside Falls as elsewhere.

For Sam, though, the worst problem was that the good old boy network between the newspaper and the authorities had passed into oblivion with The Herald's sale. The Sanfords were six generations in Lakeside Falls. Nothing affecting the sheriff's office had ever gone into the paper without Carl Sanford's consultation with Sam. Them days are gone forever, Flanagan sighed. Braker was, as the saying goes, a bottom liner. Advertisers wanted exposure. The more readers, the more exposure. The harder the squeeze, the more juice. While the big-city newspapers swooned in the face of the digital onslaught, the local rags prospered, and the competition with the local computer entrepreneurs in the race for eyeballs was fierce. It was take-no-prisoners time in the news business.

The phone's ring exploded into his thoughts. He knew exactly who it was. Find the silver lining, he pleaded with himself. Emily looked at the phone and snickered.

"Be kind," she whispered.

He picked up the phone. Moisture on his palms made the instrument slippery.

"Thank you, Sam," Flanagan began the conversation before the other voice could speak.

"For what?" Sam said, surprised, but, Flanagan speculated, not disarmed.

"For ringing the phone and not my neck."

"I can assure you, Flanagan, the latter would have given me more pleasure."

"If I'm wrong, I'll set up an appointment and you can wring to an inch of my life. But if I'm right...."

"Right never worries me. Wrong is the problem. I keep my job because I am credible. Shall I spell it out for you?"

He was, of course, jousting at windmills. The story merely speeded up the time frame and put him on the line to deliver either way. The problem was that the allegation would be read as an accusation, which was impossible to deliver at the moment. Sam wasn't used to not holding all of the cards.

"Now I have to satisfy that SOB." He was not generally a cusser, which spoke eons for the state of his interior. "Already this morning I've had Jessie Shanks and Dr. Mowbray on my back. Also the mouthpiece for the Annunzio group in Chicago. Next thing we can expect is an editorial saying I was letting the Mafiosi into the county."

"Did you release them?"

"Of course I did. Unless you and Tony wanted to press charges. Which I doubted. If they continue harassing Tony, there's just nothing that I can do about it."

His anger was dissipating.

"I'll have a report on the drugs by tonight." It now seemed a redundant gesture to have given the drugs to Doc. Sam was quick to pick up the same implications.

"We don't want anything out of my control now," he mused. Flanagan waited for his next assertion. When it didn't come, he knew he was being goaded to press.

"Are you going to ask for an exhumation?"

"First let's see what the lab has to say."

Not bad, Flanagan thought, with strange pride. The man could, after all, rise to the occasion. But both knew the big if in the entire enterprise. What if the medical examiner found nothing of value, nothing to use as evidence of foul play? Nothing.

"So you still think there is a possibility?"

"I never said I did in the first place," the sheriff snapped. "I got carried away by your dramatics."

Not that, Flanagan thought. You sly fox. It was the challenge.

"In a way—" Flanagan hesitated, "—that story might have some good effects. Might force confrontations that would not ordinarily take place. Suspects are generally more vulnerable under pressure."

There was a long silence on the phone and Flanagan pictured Sam's face creased in rumination.

"It's not necessarily the who that worries me now. It's the how." He paused again. "I mean if there are any grounds to this at all."

Flanagan wasn't sure how to interpret that remark. Was the sheriff losing confidence in Flanagan's theory? Had the newspaper story been intimidating enough to weaken his resolve? Couldn't blame him, Flanagan thought. He was, after all, the man on the front line.

"You mean there's so much smoke you might not be able to see the fire?"

"Something like that," Sam sighed. "More like playing Russian roulette." There were times, Flanagan thought wryly, when their competition reduced itself to topping figures of speech. No contest there, Sheriff, Flanagan thought wryly. But his doubt had disappeared. Despite Sam's irritation, the hook had not been dislodged.

"Is there anything you would like me to do?" Flanagan said, with deliberate and, he hoped, credible humility.

"You've done enough for the moment, Flanagan," Sam said. "Let's just see how those lab results work out."

"I'll let you...." But the sheriff had already hung up. Emily, who had been watching Flanagan's face during the conversation, began to brush her hair in jerky movements.

"Sometimes I just hate your buttinsky ways," she said. "It's not that I think you're wrong. It's just that Sam is so vulnerable."

"He's a big boy. He could reject my theories."

"That's just the point. He hates them. But he trusts your judgment. Audrey says he broods over it constantly."

"I can't help that."

"And you never show him any...." She searched for the right word.

"Compassion," he volunteered.

"Yes. That's exactly what I mean."

"You think I just use him, manipulate him?"

"Sure you do."

She was, of course, reacting to Audrey's complaints, the main thrust of which was that Flanagan was always putting her husband in jeopardy.

"He doesn't have to listen to me."

He knew she wasn't really irritated at him, just frustrated. She really adored Audrey and Sam, and lived constantly with the threat that the strange masculine competition between him and Sam would somehow destroy her relationship with them, particularly Audrey. He tried not to think about it in those terms. Nor did he explore other psychological implications that lay just beneath the surface. Something about Flanagan somehow trying to make his old man proud or, the other side of that coin, besting him. He, too, had his own psychological ax to grind. But if you got into that, Flanagan knew, where would it end?

Lost in introspection, he felt Emily's cool, sweet kiss on his forehead.

"Where are you off to?" he asked.

"Promised Mr. Ingersoll I would stop by today."

"And the little girl?"

"Doctor says, the longer she hangs in, the better it is. Breaks your heart to see her little pale face on the pillow." She sighed. "Be back in a couple of hours."

He heard her heels on the stairs, sat for a few moments on the edge of the bed, then went out himself on his morning ritual. He whistled for Caesar, who oddly did not respond. It happened occasionally when a bitch in heat entered the nearby population and the mighty Caesar was pressed to conquer goals. There were various offspring sprinkled around Lakeside Falls, progeny of the mighty Caesar in all shapes and sizes. Under no circumstances would he ever have the mighty Caesar fixed. When his mighty sword was out of his scabbard, beware.

He took the long way around to the post office, mostly to clear his head in the crisp morning air, enjoying its bite on his skin. Mornings always gave a better forecast of weather to come. Winter was in the air now. Soon the snows would come and Lakeside Falls would be a winter postcard. Nothing like a Michigan winter. Memories of it had sustained him all the long years he was away.

It calmed him to think about it. Stopping by the post office, he picked up the mail and headed home. He was momentarily surprised to find the front door open, until he remembered that he had neglected to close it when he had come out that morning to pick up the paper. But once inside, the earlier explanation was superseded.

Nor was it merely instinctive. The sliding wooden doors that separated the dining room from the foyer were closed. He could not remember when they had last done that. Also, there was something else missing—Caesar, who by now would be slobbering all over him.

Then he heard the low whine. Dropping the mail on the floor, he slid open the dining room doors. In a corner under one of the Victorian tables, he saw Caesar, his brown eyes frightened. He was in pain and his low pitiful whine was heartbreaking. Flanagan kneeled and crawled beside the dog who rested his snout on his shoulder. Gently, he maneuvered the dog out from under the table. With effort, Caesar rose on three legs. A hind leg was obviously injured, but Flanagan's presence had given Caesar courage enough to gamely wag his tail.

"It'll be fine, old buddy," Flanagan said to the dog, lifting him off his legs in the cradle of his arms. For a moment, he staggered under the dog's weight and had to lean against the wall for support.

It was then that he saw them, tiny people, looking very much alive. They were seated in chairs around a child's table, an odd gathering of eccentrics waiting for dinner. It was eerier, an unexpected horror show, embellished by another bizarre sight. The doll sitting in the host's chair at the end of the table was headless.

Chapter Fifteen

Flanagan drove with one hand. With the other, he caressed Caesar's head and kept up a steady flow of reassuring patter and solemn prayers of everlasting fidelity.

"No more insults, buddy. No more snide remarks and put-downs. I was only joking anyhow. You must have known that. Just hang in there. The vet's not far."

He knew he was speeding, but promised himself that he would not stop for any reason. From time to time, Caesar licked his wrist gratefully.

"Slobber away, buddy. Caesar." He raised his eyes. "I promise to call him by his name. Always."

He sensed that he had been reduced to supplicant. Yet at the same time he felt slightly ashamed at his sense of personal guilt. The fact was, he knew now, that Caesar was an integral part of his life, a living, loving entity from another species, a devoted friend who was in trouble.

In fifteen minutes flat, he was at the vet's and carrying Caesar into the waiting room. The vet, Dr. Tommy Thompson, was a collector of animal weather vanes and Flanagan had sold him a stag, a steer, a horse and a really rare rooster, the latter displayed on a cupola on top of his house. The lower level was his office.

Normally, Caesar's professional visits were made in the company of Emily, who described him as a difficult patient. Tommy was a little man with a very bald head, thick horn-rims and small, white, gentle hands with which he probed at Caesar's wounds. To give him courage and allay his fears, Flanagan stood beside him, wincing at the needle the doctor stuck into Caesar's hindquarters. He watched as the dog slipped swiftly into unconsciousness.

"Just wait outside now, Flanagan," Dr. Thompson said. "Nervous Nellies just gum things up."

"I'm not a nervous Nelly," Flanagan protested, although he knew he hadn't the stomach to watch any surgical procedure on this spiritual brother from another planet.

He sat in the waiting room, surrounded by people with sick pets, including one with an exotic bird and another with two exactly matched kittens in two exactly matched little baskets. He picked up a magazine and pretended to read, while his mind calmed and began to concern itself more with the human species, many of whom showed a venality and ruthlessness that belied the biological fact that they were considered part of a higher order.

Mostly, he focused on Lacey, whose act of violence, he vowed, could not go unpunished. Reconstructing the scenario, he was certain that Tony had paid Lacey a visit and threatened the man or worse, and in some way thwarted Lacey from profiting from the dolls. Infuriated, he had stormed into the Flanagans' shop guarded by the mighty Caesar, who had apparently finished his husbandly chores and, satiated, returned to home base only to be confronted with a vicious human swine.

The big dog who had, as always, the good sense to bark and look ferocious at potential enemies, had received a near mortal blow from the furious Lacey who, seeing the place was empty, had proceeded to leave his brutal mark of frustration. Flanagan took his cell from his pocket and punched in Lacey's number, then aborted it. He was too livid to make the call.

"Bastard," Flanagan said aloud.

"What did you say?" the woman with the two kittens asked.

"Not them," Flanagan said, flustered. "I'm sure their parents were perfectly legal."

The woman gave him a sour look and turned away, concentrating on her sick kittens.

Since he was enormously down on the human species, he began to have regrets about his involvement in the entire Farnsworth mess. Generally speaking, perhaps with the exception of Kay, they were a greedy and confused lot. It wasn't that he was developing doubts about his instincts, only about his involvement, in which he could find no "up" side, except some obscure ego satisfaction or some deeply personal psychological vindication. Why this obsessive pursuit of—was it justice? The thrill of solution? Proof of superiority? A desire to prove one's importance? He was beginning to sink into a muddle of self-doubt. Luckily, Thompson intruded.

"I set the leg and casted it. A few weeks and he'll be good as new. But I suggest you leave him overnight for observation."

"I thought you had to shoot him if he breaks his leg."

"That's horses. You've been seeing too many bad movies."

"So he'll be as good as new?"

"And able to take his usual mighty thrusts. I was tempted to fix him under anesthetic."

"You didn't?"

"I'm not into personal risk." It was actually Emily who had warned him of swift vengeance.

Flanagan sucked in a deep sigh of relief.

"I'm looking for a grasshopper," Dr. Thompson said in an abrupt change of subject. "I saw one on top of Faneuil Hall in Boston. Made of copper, gilded. It even had green glass eyes."

"I'll do a search for you," Flanagan said. The vet patted him on the back and squeezed his upper arm.

"And don't worry about Caesar. I can see he really cares about you."

"How do you know that?"

"He barked it during the surgery."

"Very funny," Flanagan said, his mind searching for a comeback. Not finding any, he put out his hand.

In the car going home, he took a deep breath and called Lacey.

"How could you?" he rasped.

"You couldn't leave it alone," Lacey said. "I took twenty stitches in the scalp from that monster. And five in the leg from that shit you call a dog. You had to tell him. You just couldn't clam up. He demanded money. Ten grand on the barrelhead."

"Hail valiant Caesar," Flanagan whispered.

"What did you say?"

"You should have coughed up the moolah. Saved everyone pain, especially Caesar."

"Caesar?"

"And beheading that poor little lady. So, so Jihad."

"You're crazy, Flanagan. Now you deal with those fucking dolls. I never want to see them again as long as I live."

Lacey broke the connection.

The conversation brought him little comfort. Emily was right. He had an investigatory compulsive problem. The Farnsworth involvement had become a nightmare. How many others would be hurt by it? Even Lacey had a point. He regretted having told Tony about the true value of the dolls. Worse, he was actually worried about Sam, who he had dragged into what might turn out to be another fiasco.

The story in the newspaper had changed the ground rules. Not at all like when the Sanfords owned it. Now the paper had become an adversary, a watchdog, a big pain in the butt.

This new anger kept him from falling back into a state of depression. It made him contentious and combative, determined now to see the Farnsworth matter through to its conclusion—win, lose or draw. This new attitude steadied him.

When he got back to the house, Emily had not returned. He went into the dining room and inspected the broken doll. It was the Jumeau Bébé, the most valuable of the lot. Lacey had twisted off the head and placed it on the table in front of the seated torso. It could, of course, be repaired, but its value would be somewhat diminished unless it was so cleverly done that the dealer could fail to point it out to a potential customer. It was something he could never do.

As he fingered the head, he heard a tinkle of the overhead bell. Someone was coming in. He went into the hall and watched two people come inside. It was Tony and his sister Kay. Perhaps it was the proximity, but they resembled each other remarkably. It was something he had not noticed before.

"We have to talk," Tony said, putting out his hand. His ingratiating attitude telescoped the message he was there to convey. Not letting on, Flanagan took his hand and pumped it vigorously. He nodded to Kay and led them through the long hall. He was certain that he had moved them through with enough speed so they would not notice the dolls. Shepherding them into the den, be offered them coffee which they both refused.

He regarded them thoughtfully, hoping he was showing them a kindly, receptive exterior. He could tell they were ill at ease. They looked at each other with nervous, bird-like movements.

"We had no place else to turn," Tony said. Apparently they had agreed in advance who would be the opening spokesman. Kay held a handkerchief in her hands which she twisted and untwisted. Occasionally, her knuckles seemed to whiten with the tension. There was, Flanagan noted, a deliberate attempt to eschew all small talk, the basic protocols of politeness. Their attitude was obviously single-minded, without frills.

"We know that you and Sheriff Hazeltine are close friends," Tony continued, clearing his throat. Flanagan nodded, betraying no hint of the irony. Concentrating on Tony as he talked, Flanagan felt Kay's eyes fasten on his face. When he turned to confirm it, her eyes would move aside, sometimes downward to her twisted handkerchief. "And we do trust you. The way you handled the thing with the dolls. Let's face it, you could have been tempted to exploit it. Make a buck on it. Call it ethics or whatever. You didn't take advantage. And I promise I'll make up whatever you lost on the deal. That's a solemn vow."

With the dolls in the front room, Flanagan felt more foolish than self-righteous and he ignored any further comment on the subject. Luckily his two visitors had not seen the dolls.

"You did see the newspaper this morning?"

Flanagan nodded, grateful for the swift change of subject.

"The fact is that it's crazy, absolutely crazy. My mother was obviously a very sick woman. Why should there be any suspicion about her death? It's awful for me and my sister." He looked toward Kay, who reached out and touched his hand. "I mean, who but us could possibly know the truth?" His voice broke for a moment. "My mother died. Why can't they let her rest in peace?"

"They're talking of doing an autopsy, disturbing her corpse." Kay's eyes welled with tears, which she wiped with her handkerchief. "It's so—so ugly and demeaning."

"There is no logic to it. Nothing to support it. We were both there when Mother went downhill." Tony swallowed hard. "I don't understand it at all. Not at all. Neither of us do. She was a sick woman. Sure, she seemed to go faster than any of us would have liked. But that's not foul play. That's merely dying. Mother died. Why can't she just be left alone?"

He seemed to realize that he was rambling and he quickly gathered his thoughts again. In his eyes, Flanagan saw the full concentration of his intensity. "You've got to talk to your friend, Sheriff Hazeltine. We see no reason why Mother's peace must be disturbed."

"What makes you think I have so much influence over the sheriff?"

"It's well known in town that you've helped him in a number of cases. And, most important, by a curious set of circumstances, you were around when she—when she—was passing away. That's aside from the fact that both Kay and I, based on your own actions over the past few days and your reputation, trust you."

It was a long peroration on his history and virtues. A little embarrassing, he thought, in the light of his persistent suspicions.

"But what should I say to him?" Flanagan asked with somewhat labored ingenuousness.

"That it's wrong. A sacrilege to Mother's memory. Who knows what else? Maybe a scheme of some sort?"

It seemed obvious that Tony and Kay had some thoughts of their own.

"There's not an iota of doubt that your mother died in any way but of natural causes?" They exchanged bird-like looks.

"Not a shred of doubt," Tony said. Kay nodded. With the specter of doubt raised so conclusively, he wondered why his opposite view was so pervasive.

"It's true that I have discussed it with him," Flanagan said cautiously. Needing a gesture of uncertainty to convince them of his sincerity, he bit the side of his lip, shrugged and raised his eyebrows.

Tony exhibited a thin smile of vindication.

"We both assumed that."

"And there is a cause and effect consequence of your mother's death. For example, the start once again of the construction on the ski resort. Obviously, a bail-out based on your aunt's potential inheritance. And...." It was, of course, the pregnant pause. "Did you know that Dr. Mowbray was a heavy investor in the project with your Uncle Jessie?"

Although both did seem to register varying degrees of surprise, Flanagan felt that they both had a rudimentary knowledge of such a possibility.

"How heavy?" Tony asked.

"I'm not sure. But I believe that he could have borrowed up to his eyebrows to have made such an investment. I'm only speculating, of course."

"Has that been confirmed?" Tony asked.

"Why then would the sheriff's office be so interested?" he said evasively.

"But that's not strong enough to allege foul play?"

"What is, then?"

"That's the point. It's so obviously...." He groped for the right word.

"Circumstantial."

"Yeah. That's it."

"Like Blatsford," Flanagan said, his eyes leveled at Tony, who did not appear ruffled in the least.

"Kay knows about that," Tony muttered.

"And your deal with Blatsford?"

"That, too."

Kay nodded.

"We have no secrets from each other, Mr. Flanagan. Not now. Not after last night." She took a deep breath and once again reached out toward her brother. He took her hand and continued to hold it.

"She knows about my gambling debts, as well. In fact, about everything. We just opened up to each other." He looked toward his sister and smiled. "And about time, too. Confession time. We've both discovered that we've had a lot of the same problems."

"Like what?" Flanagan asked. It was, he knew, a step over the line, but he took it anyhow.

"Let's face it. It doesn't exactly build character to be a dependent all your life. It ruins all incentive. You take the easy way out. And sometimes you become self-destructive because you have such a lousy sense of self-worth." He seemed a little too glib on the subject, as if he had spent a great deal of time in creating an explanation. "A mistake on Grampa's part, as well. Giving Mother all that responsibility. It wasn't fair to her, either. Not even to Aunt Amy. "

"Your grandfather obviously wanted to preserve his fortune."

"I don't fault him for that," Tony said hastily. "He should have set it up impersonally. Not given it all to Mother to administer. Her financial decisions were based too much on emotion. Even when it came to me. I wheedled thousands out of her." He looked at his sister. "I am very much ashamed of myself. And finally, she reacted by cutting me off. What I'm saying is that it would have been better for Grampa to have put it all in the hands of a third party, a lawyer who would be administrating some unbreakable covenant. Fact is, I loved my mother, deeply. I also respected her. And she loved me, but didn't respect me. I abused her. I admit that. Maybe the sheriff's office suspects me as well."

It was a fishing expedition, but Flanagan refused to bite.

"And me," Kay added. "Look what my life has been." Her eyes narrowed, perhaps to hide a wince of pain. "My mother was my companion, my confidante and friend, my financial supporter." Now her eyes widened. She grew introspective. "But I've had absolutely no life without her. No beaus. Oh, I did have them when I was younger, but then they stopped coming."

"Surely she didn't prevent you from having a social life? Male friendships."

"You mean sweethearts?"

"Of course, what's wrong with that?"

"You just don't understand dependency, Mr. Flanagan." For a brief moment, he could see the anguish. Oddly, the image of Dr. surfaced in his mind. "I depended on her and she depended on me. As her health declined, my sense of responsibility toward her grew. We were, in fact, a couple. Mother and daughter." She sighed. "I miss her desperately. I miss taking care of her...." She dislodged her hand from her brother's and dabbed her eyes with the handkerchief. "Time passed and we grew closer and closer, inseparable." Suddenly, she sat upright and straightened her shoulders. "But one thing is certain. We will not suffer the humiliation of her being made a spectacle now, after her death. She was not a spectacle in life." She seemed stronger, more assertive than he had imagined. "The implication of the story in the paper is that Mother was murdered. And you're broadly hinting that the sheriff believes that Uncle Jessie and Dr. Mowbray contrived a way to kill her with poison or whatever to save themselves from financial ruin. Right?"

"I would say that could be one of his assumptions."

"Or even that Mr. Blatsford found a way to eliminate her," Tony said. "Also for money."

"I'm sure a case could be made for his being benefited."

"For me as well," Tony said calmly, looking at his sister.

"Well then, you can't blame the sheriff for taking a closer look. That's his job."

"It's just so beyond logic," Kay said.

"Not really," Flanagan said gently.

"And would it resolve the question once and for all?"

"You mean if they found nothing amiss in an autopsy?"

"No poisons or such things."

"It would certainly clear the air."

"I still believe it's wrong," Kay sighed.

"Nor do we want to oppose it legally. Just the time and effort would be ridiculous."

Flanagan turned pointedly to Tony.

"You mean by time... holding up the will?"

"Frankly, yes. Who knows what all this legal maneuvering would do to a reasonable time frame for getting our rightful inheritance? Let's face it..." He turned to his sister. "My situation is desperate. Not quite like my sister's, here." Flanagan was surprised at that remark.

"What he means is that there is the house, and I do have a small savings account. Not much. But enough to scrape by for a year or so if I live modestly. Just money set aside from my allowance and small sums that Mother provided from time to time. You'd be surprised how dependence makes for frugality." She paused, twisting the handkerchief. "But I want you to know... for me, the issue is not money. It's Mother. I can't bear the thought of taking her out of her grave, cutting her up—" She choked up, holding back more tears.

"He really doesn't have to go ahead with this madness, does he?" Tony asked, pleading.

"Not unless he really believes it's essential to his investigation."

"Is it possible that the newspapers are exaggerating things?" Tony asked hopefully. "Merely speculating?"

"Anything is possible when it comes to the press," Flanagan said.

"But do you think he would be open to dropping everything? I mean, how far is he committed?"

Flanagan shrugged, hoping that uncertainty was, indeed, an honest assertion.

"Then all we can ask is that you talk to him," Kay said.

"That I promise," Flanagan said.

They stood up and Flanagan shook hands.

"At least there's someone around here we can trust," Tony said as they followed him out through the hall. But as they moved through, Kay stopped suddenly.

"What lovely objects you have, Mr. Flanagan." She put her fingers caressingly on a table inlaid with a checkerboard. "I'm afraid that whatever objects of value Mother had were sold long ago. She had more trust in cash and stocks than things."

"Yes, I know."

With his heart in his throat, Flanagan watched as she browsed, from room to room. Tony followed her, but it was easy to see that his mind was elsewhere.

"And in there?" Kay asked.

"Nothing spectacular, I'm afraid."

"You're much too modest, Mr. Flanagan," Kay said, moving into the room. Flanagan cursed his stupidity in not closing the doors. Following fast on her heels, Tony suddenly shed his vague look. He saw the dolls and glared at Flanagan. Kay saw them as well.

"I think the dolls on chairs is a very droll idea—" She turned to face Flanagan.

"They're Mother's. The ones I sold to Lacey," Tony said, lowering his eyes. "I guess the bastard turned them over to you."

"They're not mine, Tony. They're now yours and your sister's."

"You can have them," Tony said. "They've caused enough trouble." He turned to Kay. "Okay with you, sis?"

"Maybe they can do some good for you, Mr. Flanagan," Kay said. "And for that little girl."

"It's not a bribe," Tony said.

"One of them lost its head," Flanagan said.

"She's not the only one," Tony sighed.

"Just talk to your friend," Kay said as they left the store.

Chapter Sixteen

Flanagan broke the news about Caesar to Emily starting backwards, revealing first the good result that Dr. Thompson predicted. Then he proceeded to illustrate Lacey's venality by showing her the dolls placed around Emily's grandmother's Victorian dining room suite. He was particularly dramatic in exhibiting the doll with the broken head, dangling the head and trunk in each hand as if it were the remains of Anne Boleyn.

"The man's an animal," Emily said, visibly shaken.

"Worse, he's human."

Shuddering visibly, she had her own bad news to impart about little Charlotte, who had been rushed back to surgery.

"She was just not responding," Emily sighed, prompting Flanagan to put down the broken doll with a sense of shame.

They went into the kitchen. Emily made fresh-brewed coffee and they sat at the table in silence for a long time, each lost in his own thoughts. To break the growing gloom, Flanagan told her about the visit from Kay and Tony Farnsworth.

"They think I have influence with Sam," Flanagan said, "and denied giving us the dolls was a bribe."

"You do and it was," Emily said. "You have influence with me and I have influence with Audrey and Audrey has influence with Sam. As for the dolls, it could be construed as a bribe."

"Always a bridesmaid and never a bribe."

"Here is the solution to the moral dilemma," Emily said, kissing Flanagan on his still-sore nose. "I will not try to influence Audrey who will not try to influence Sam. The bribe then becomes a gift. We have already gifted one to little Charlotte. I say we repair the headless one and try to get back our five thousand dollar investment, then donate the rest to the hospital to be given to any little girl who is gravely ill. Makes us dead even."

"Illogic triumphs. Your solutions, unlike some, are far from poisonous."

"You just can't let go."

"That's me," he said, pointing to the tumble polisher. It hummed along relentlessly, so much a part of their audio environment that he no longer noticed it.

"Never stops until the job is done."

"Not at all," Flanagan agreed. He knew she was not being judgmental and her concentration on the little machine was simply the way in which she coped with stress. She refocused her concentration.

"Unless they had something to hide," Emily said vaguely.

"Which is the purpose of the exhumation."

"But they do have a point. I wouldn't want anyone I loved to be exhumed." He watched her body dissolve in a wrenching shiver. "Even the word is so yucky."

"That's what makes this whole thing so frustrating. On the surface everything makes sense. It all seems so natural."

"Natural?" Emily mused. "What's natural?" Her eyes suddenly filled with tears. "A man kicking a dog?"

"Now that's definitely not natural. But I want you to know, Emily, I gave him all the puppy love I could muster," he said with reassurance. "And I apologized profusely for all the insults."

"I'm sure he understands," Emily said, reaching out and

touching Flanagan's cheek. "Do you think that Lacey has broken some law? Something about cruelty to animals?"

"Must be," Flanagan mused. "But I just don't think it's the appropriate time to get Sam or any of his staff involved. Not just yet. He's got enough on his plate at the moment."

She came closer to him and he took her in his arms. For both of them there was always succor in an embrace. They held each other tightly and he breathed in the familiar scent of her hair and skin. The act did not need words. It soothed, chased insecurity, pushed back the hurts and psychic injuries.

"Perhaps I should have left it alone," he whispered. "It's all hypothesis."

"Cut it, Flanagan," Emily said firmly. "No self-doubt. The chips must fall where they may."

When they disengaged, he felt better.

"To thine own self be true," he said.

"That's my boy."

"When rain falls, it gets up again in dew time."

"Recovery complete."

"For you, too?"

She nodded and smiled.

He spent the afternoon gathering up the dolls and wrapping them properly. He also called people who specialized in their repair, packed both parts of the Jumeau Bébé carefully in a box filled with plastic chips to prevent jarring, and mailed it off parcel post. Then he called Doc to see if the lab report was ready.

"Not yet," Doc said.

With some trepidation, he decided to walk over to Sam's office, if only to be with him when the report came in. Peggy Bilton greeted him with a deep scowl. He was surprised to find Harry Ketchum camped in the sheriff's waiting room. With him was the dark-haired girl he had noticed at the funeral. He assumed that she was the Livingston of the double byline.

"See you have company," Flanagan whispered to the scowling Peggy Bilton. She mimed a curse in the direction of the reporters.

"What have you got to do with all this?" Harry Ketchum called from across the room where he was sitting, thumbing through an old issue of Time. His curiosity on that point seemed only lukewarm. In an odd way, Flanagan resented his disinterest, but was thankful for it. The common understanding was that Flanagan and Sam Hazeltine were close friends. Which, Flanagan thought at that moment, testified to the unreliability of unscientific perception.

"I'm in antiques," Flanagan mumbled. It had become a standard answer when the overcurious singled him out.

"Collecting old sheriff's badges?" Ketchum chided, showing a mouthful of bad teeth.

"I also collect clippings. The inaccurate kind."

Ketchum chortled.

"Hope for you yet," Peggy Bilton said with the faintest hint of a smile.

Sam came out of his office, looked at the two reporters, shook his head ominously and waved Flanagan inside. His crinkles were more like worry lines and his shoulders seemed to sag with fatigue.

"Like a snowball going down a high mountain."

"That bad?"

"You saw them out there. Braker's got his teeth in my butt."

Flanagan nodded in sympathy.

"That's only part of it. First thing in my office, I get a call from the Detroit bank putting up the money for the ski resort. Chairman of the board himself. Scared to death. They've already got five million in it and they've just put up another five." Flanagan whistled, if only to emphasize his attentiveness. "Like a dummy, I took the call. I gave him the usual deadpan comments, which I'm sure only panicked him further. Then came a call from good old Jessie. Fit to be tied. Threatened to run me out of the county. Called me names I wouldn't even use in the privacy of my own thoughts. And then some. After that came another call from the good doctor Mowbray. You can imagine his reaction. Then came... I kid you not... a call from Chicago."

"Annunzio?"

"Never said. But the hints were broad."

"Cement shoes?"

"Not at all. Butter would melt in the man's mouth. He said his people would never ever stoop so low as to harm a sick lady. He also made it clear that if his associates did not get satisfaction —that was the term he used—he would extend operations into this county." The sheriff paused. His eyes grew vague and he brushed a palm across his forehead. "Tony did not get high marks. And still, that's not all."

"Listen, all you got was phone calls. I got a visit from Tony and Kay."

"At least they left. Those sweaty palms outside have crawled all over the place. And there's nothing I can do about it. Something about freedom of the press and the right to know. You'd think I was one of those Southern sheriffs favored out in movie land, the kind that chew tobacco and wear those pilot sunglasses."

"But what do they know?"

"Since when does that matter?"

"The stuff of circulation builders."

"Tomorrow it's going to look like we're involved in a giant cover-up. I can't believe it." He looked the soul of outraged innocence. Which, in fact, he was. What have I wrought?, Flanagan asked himself.

"You want to know the funny part, the real funny part?"

Flanagan studied Sam's face. It had never really been impenetrable, but it was now. Flanagan was not sure whether the question was rhetorical or required a response. It was, he decided, more politic to remain silent.

"I believe it. As much as I would like to ignore it, sweep it away. I believe it. It smells and I hate to admit it, your dumb nose picked up the stink."

For Sam, it constituted an important admission. Publicly, as least as far as Flanagan was concerned, his posture was to maintain doubts, keeping his true feelings secret until the last possible moment. Flanagan, however, would not press him to be more specific on the matter of the suspected perpetrator. Neither of them would ever commit to that until they were dead certain. After all, therein lay the prize and for the other, the humiliation. So, for the moment, Flanagan realized, they were to be staunch allies, like Churchill and Stalin. Besides that, Flanagan thought wryly, the big galoot needs me.

"And the stench gets more gamey by the minute," Flanagan said without arrogance.

"Instinct and feel. Nothing at all to do with logic."

"Exactly."

"The only thing missing is the murder weapon," Sam said gloomily.

At that point the telephone rang.

"It's Doc for Flanagan," Peggy whispered through the intercom. Sam flicked a switch and turned on the squawk box.

"Sam is here beside me, Doc."

"Well, I got the report," Doc said. His voice coming from the loudspeaker seemed hoarse.

"And?" Flanagan prompted.

"Sorry, fellas. Nothing amiss. All the medicines are exactly as prescribed."

"So that rules that out."

"Which is not to say that she couldn't have over-medicated herself. Something like that. People misuse drugs all the time."

"Can't prosecute a person who takes his own life," Sam said.

"And if she was poisoned," Doc said, "nobody would be dumb enough to leave the poison standing around for anyone to see."

"That's another matter," Sam said, looking at Flanagan. What went unsaid was the matter of exhumation, which was, as they all knew, the next option. Or the first, as Flanagan had suggested.

"There was one thing...." It was Doc's querulous voice, almost a whisper. "It happens."

"What are you talking about, Doc?" Sam asked.

"Just a note on the lab report."

"A note?"

"The technician noted that one of the diuretic pills was in the bottle of potassium supplements. Probably got mixed up when we inspected them. Or Lucy might have dropped one in by accident. No big deal, though. Just one pill."

A tiny light went on in the corner of Flanagan's mind.

"Why are potassium supplements prescribed, Doc?" Flanagan asked.

"When you take a diuretic for the kidneys, you lose electrolytes. Potassium supplements counteract the loss of electrolytes. It's a standard procedure for heart cases. The diuretic is called hydroDIURIL. Very common stuff."

"And the other pills?" Flanagan asked.

"Diabinese." He said it with what Flanagan detected was an air of victory. Doc cleared his throat with exaggerated pomposity. "As I told you earlier."

"So if she took everything as prescribed, she would have sailed along, chemically controlled?" Flanagan asked rhetorically. Sam nodded, as if in approval. This was, after all, his office, his job.

"No guarantees in that. She wasn't exactly normal."

"But she was being monitored by a doctor," Flanagan pressed.

"Doctors," Doc harrumphed.

"What was the official cause of death?" Flanagan asked Sam, who pushed over a copy of the death certificate.

"Cardiac arrest," Flanagan read aloud.

"Means the heart stopped beating," Doc joked. "Only an autopsy tells the truth. Or as near the truth as possible."

Flanagan looked at Sam, but resisted a smile.

"Unless it proves conclusively that the woman was poisoned," Sam began with an air of futility, sucking in a deep breath of resignation, "—there is no case to be made. It is very difficult to prove overmedication as a murder weapon, except in hospital cases where the monitoring is carefully documented. I've checked that out."

A tug of failure started to nip at the edges of Flanagan's theory, but he quickly shrugged it off. Why was he being nagged by this instinctive compulsion to declare Lucy Farnsworth's death murder? After an inordinate length of silence, Doc croaked into the loudspeaker.

"You guys still there?" he asked.

"We're here, Doc," Sam answered, revealing suddenly that he had used the pause profitably. "But I have this question."

"Shoot," Doc said. Flanagan sensed his relish at the attention.

"How exactly would she fatally overmedicate?"

"Or undermedicate," Doc added wryly.

"Go on."

"If she didn't take her insulin she'd go into diabetic coma. If she didn't take her diuretic, she'd fill up with fluids which could have killed her. If she didn't take her potassium she would have picked up hypokalemia, another killer."

"So you didn't really have to substitute different drugs. All you had to do would be vary the mix."

"Look," Doc said patiently. "A sick person like Lucy Farnsworth needed these drugs to live. She knew it. It was part of her daily habit to administer them to herself. Fiddle with any combination of these drugs, of most drugs, and you have a form of suicide. What you guys are looking for is murder. We can sit here all night and speculate. She couldn't live without insulin. These are not placebos. Couldn't live without the diuretic. No placebos there. Couldn't live without potassium. No placebo there. I don't know a damned thing about murder. Sure, she could have been induced to take lethal doses. You may or may not find that out in an autopsy. As Sam says, the case can be made for poison as a specific killer. The rest is pure speculation."

"Suppose," Flanagan said, after a long pause, "only speculation, mind you, but what type of misuse would be the most difficult to detect by a doctor?"

There was a long silence at the other end of the phone.

"I'm no doctor, but...." Sam's head cocked forward as if to capture every subtle nuance. "I'd bet on the potassium."

"You mean not taking it?"

"In terms of your question, I think the symptoms of over- or underdosing on the diuretic and insulin would be very quickly identifiable. Potassium, I think, would be trickier." Doc laughed. "But don't hold my feet to the fire."

"Could you find it—or lack of it—in an autopsy?"

"I'm a pharmacist, not a pathologist."

He was loving it, Flanagan thought. A glance at Sam showed that the sheriff's face had grown a shade paler.

"Thanks, Doc," Sam said.

"I tried. Hope I helped."

They heard the click and looked at each other with raised eyebrows and unmistakable resignation. Sam frowned and shook his head.

"It's poison we need to find."

But Flanagan's head was spinning with new possibilities.

"He said they found a diuretic pill mixed in with the potassium supplements."

"Happens all the time."

Sam glanced at Flanagan, shrugged, then reached for the phone. Then he switched on the loudspeaker again. Conditioned reflex, Flanagan observed. The hook is so deep he's thrashing. Doc's voice crackled in the air.

"How different-looking are the pills?" Sam asked. For a moment the color came back into his cheeks. "The diuretic and the potassium."

"They're capsules, actually. Different in color and size. Easy to tell the difference. And, of course, they're supposed to be in different containers."

"Except one pill," Flanagan interjected.

"One is still one," Doc shot back. "There was plenty of potassium in the container."

"Thanks, Doc," Sam said, hanging up. He shook his head. "So

someone might have made the substitution. So what? Without poison we're still on square one." He looked at Flanagan, offering a wry smile. "And if we don't find poison, we've nothing on our plate."

"But we could find the other. Evidence of misuse of the drugs."

"Which proves what? That the woman made a mistake. And I look like a bumbling bull."

"Listen, Sam," Flanagan said with a rare degree of intimacy. "Like in Spain. I enjoy the fight, but I'm not interested in killing the bull."

"Who is both brave and stupid," Sam said.

"No aficionado of the bullfight ever calls the bull stupid. He is a creature of courage who commands great respect."

"We're not in Portugal," Sam muttered.

"Not in Spain or Mexico, either."

Flanagan was happy to see that the subtlety was not lost on the sheriff. His mind could have continued the image. Instead, he spoke to himself silently. "And I am being gored on the horns of a dilemma."

Chapter Seventeen

Flanagan awoke long before dawn and it was soon apparent that he would not be able to get back to sleep. He tried to keep his mind from aggravating his physical restlessness, but he soon knew that that was impossible as well.

"You up?" he whispered. It was not that they disregarded the other's necessity of sleep. It was, after all, a whisper. But they were so tuned in to each other after so many years sleeping side by side that it simply was not possible, Flanagan believed implicitly, to escape the subconscious rhythm of proximity.

"I am now."

It was the inevitable response. Him to her. Her to him. Indeed, some of their most perceptive and insightful conversations were carried out at such times.

"Sam's between a rock and a hard place."

"Tell me something I don't know," Emily said, turning over.

"He has ordered the exhumation and autopsy."

"I thought that's what you wanted."

"They won't find any trace of poison. Not a traditional poison. It might show biochemical deficiencies, evidence perhaps of a medicine overdose, but not enough to say for sure that Lucy Farnsworth was murdered."

"Which leaves Sam?"

"Looking foolish. The paper will dump on him. And all those years of careful image nurturing will go down the tube."

She was silent for a long time.

"Things always look worse at night."

"In a few hours the sun will come up and things will look just as bad for Sam."

"Audrey thinks it's all your fault."

"In a way she's right."

"Not completely. It was Yours Truly who called Lucy Farnsworth in the first place. If I hadn't called her, no one would be the wiser."

"That's the terrible irony. Of all people, I had to arrive on the scene."

"A man with a hyperactive suspicious nature."

"Exactly."

"But Sam could have backed away."

"He always tries to at the beginning. Then he gets cold feet. Then he begins to think that maybe I've got a point. Finally, he gets to think it's his idea and he believes in it completely. Which gives me an awesome responsibility."

"To prove you're right so that he can be right."

"Something like that."

"So what's holding you back?"

"Well, now. It's 'one for the Gipper' time."

"Isn't that why you woke me?"

"The least you could do is air your doubts."

He lifted himself on one elbow and looked at her shadowed features.

"I have no doubts about the possibility," Emily said, blinking up at him. "Most drugs can be lethal if abused. From the lowly aspirin to the most sophisticated steroid. I'm, after all, a pharmacist's daughter."

"And all the horsemen knew 'er."

"Doctors have the weapons of destruction, too," she said with a mild harrumph, pointedly ignoring the pun. "Many have prescribed lethal doses. Some inadvertently. Some deliberately or out of ignorance." She looked up at him. "I'm only saying what you know already."

"So we're discussing here malpractice and carelessness."

"But you and Sam are looking for murder."

"A murderer. Singular or plural."

"Shanks and Mowbray?"

"They had the motive. And Mowbray had the means. They were going down the skids financially. Lucy's death was a bail-out. Why not?"

"It takes a lot of desperation to kill another human being."

"Done every day. Especially in families."

"Does the moving finger of accusation also point to Tony Farnsworth?"

"He has, as some say, an airtight motive. He could have also been a surrogate for Blatsford, whose gain because of Lucy's death is supposed to be rather extensive. And, we know, of course, that he is being pursued by Mafioso goons." He rubbed the knob behind his ear, which still pained him under pressure. "I can testify to that firsthand." Now it was his turn to sink into silence. He was heading into an area of complex psychological implications. "He told me he loved his mother deeply."

"And you believed him?"

"Yes I did. I can relate to that. Matricide strikes me as the most vicious of all crimes. To kill someone who has nurtured you. Even more than patricide and fratricide." He felt a shudder run through him. "A son especially. But I see a son more as a father killer, for some reason."

"More like daughter's work?"

"I can't relate to that, either. But the competition is usually with parents of the same gender."

"So you remember your Freud?"

"Sex is not for him that is a Freud."

"We were discussing gender, not sex."

187

He bent lower and kissed her ear.

"It's a subject in which I graduated magna cum lewder."

She brought up her hand and gently lifted his face.

"Does that mean that poor Kay is also suspect? And Amy Shanks?"

"Since we are essentially hypothetical, who can be ruled out?

"Why do you answer a question with a question?"

"Because I'm half Jewish."

She shook her head and he could see the broad smile form on her face. He traced it with his fingertips, and she opened her teeth slightly and bit one finger gently.

"Ouch," he screeched, feigning pain. "You see, women love to inflict pain."

"What would have been their motive?" Emily said, suddenly reflective. He had, he realized, touched the magic button of the biological kinship, the alliance of sisterhood.

"Amy Shanks would be manipulated to do it for her husband."

"Greed?"

"She would benefit considerably. A wife always benefits from her husband's prosperity. They are, after all, lifers like us." He paused for a moment. "Unless you've caught a whiff of scandal about the Shanks."

"What makes you think that it would have gone over your head?"

"Women often have secrets between themselves."

"That they do, but men are far worse gossips. No. I've never heard anything at all to question the faithfulness of either Shanks. And in this glass bowl of a town, the absence of that kind of gossip is gospel."

"What about jealousy?"

Still watching her face in the quickening light, he could see her growing thoughtful, as if she, too, recognized the full weight of the question. Suddenly, he had the urge to kiss her fluttering eyelids, which he did. They tickled his lips.

"Of course, they would be jealous. It is the natural condition of sisters in varying degrees. Amy had good reason to be jealous. Her father left her finances in the hands of her older sister. Oh, I know that he might have felt that she was protected by Jessie and Lucy was, after all, a widow. But still, when a parent favors one sibling over another, there is bound to be some form of conflict." She shrugged. "Perhaps resentment, a troubling inner questioning of one's self-worth."

It was a caveat of their parenthood to never, under any circumstances, create unnecessary competition for their own children by showing favoritism. He suddenly saw the flighty Amy Shanks in a new light.

"Enough resentment or jealousy to kill her sister?"

Emily brought her hand up to her mouth and began to tap thoughtfully on her teeth.

"Women have an enormous capacity for hate. Much more than men, I believe. But a lot less capacity for violence."

He knew, of course, that statistics backed that up. Most of the murders ever documented were committed by men. He appreciated, as always, Emily's insights, especially about women. In fact, he trusted it more than his own analysis, believing that a mysterious abyss separated the sexes, one that could rarely be bridged except by the most fragile of constructions.

"What about Kay?"

She was a long time in answering and he took advantage of the pause to gently touch her eyelids with his lips, exploring further down her cheek to her ear, then her neck. With one hand, he caressed her form through the smooth silk of her nightgown.

"Of course, it's possible. But where is the motive?"

"I've wracked my brains on that score. And I've come up with only one."

He saw her eyes open with expectation, noting that their whites had caught the glint of false dawn. It struck him that the shadows on her features seemed to erase all signs of age. She appeared now as the young girl who had fired his heart and body nearly thirty years before. He felt the strength and warmth of the feeling wash over him. Bending over her, he brought his lips to hers in a deep kiss which she returned.

"You can't leave me in suspense," she said girlishly, enhancing the image that had jumped into his brain.

"Independence," he said. "The stuff of which revolutions are made. What is the saying? You can't make an omelet without breaking eggs."

From the way her forehead creased, he knew she was disappointed in his explanation.

"You don't think that's reaching?" she asked.

"I admit it, but I can't come up with another thing. Ideas, yes."

"Like what?"

"A man, for example."

"Is that the most accepted explanation as to why women kill?"

"You don't think so?"

"I'll tell you what I do think."

"What?"

"Killing for a man is a man's idea. Macho macho."

"See what I mean about a gender gap?"

"I'm so glad you woke me for this little chat," she said. Her hand pressed his head down so that his lips could meet hers.

"And that's not all," he said breathlessly when their lips parted again.

"Hardly," she whispered as their arms twined about each other.

* * *

HE AWOKE REFRESHED as if from a catnap. The space beside him was still warm. Opening his eyes, he saw her in the bathroom, squirting drops in her eyes. Sensing that she was being watched, she looked toward the bed, blinked and smiled.

"Shall we meet again tomorrow at four a.m.?"

"And every morning thereafter."

She looked at him and smiled.

"I am absolutely amazed at the marvelous endurance of the human body."

"Not any human body. Mine is not representative. I am outside the Viagra profile."

"Braggart. On the other hand, inspiration is required to raise the stakes."

She moved her hips in imitation of a hula dance, sans grass skirt.

"Now there's a twist," he said, showing his reaction as he rolled out of bed and approached her.

She saw him in the mirror, observed him and waited.

"I see what you're angling for," she said expectantly.

"Assume it then."

It was quick. For both of them.

"The secret is in the fit," she sighed.

"My fit is your fiddle."

"You have a dirty mind," she laughed, moving away. "Now go and strum your fiddle yourself."

"My sturm is dranged."

"Whose wouldn't?" she laughed then ran off to the shower.

He jumped into the shower after her. She was out quickly. Toweling off, he could hear her steps on the stairs. He knew she was headed for the newspaper. Her screech sent him bounding down the stairs dripping in his bare feet as he put on his robe. She was standing in the long hall, muttering under her breath as she read the paper.

"It's headline stuff now."

"Sheriff orders autopsy on Lucy Farnsworth's body," he read aloud. It was all there, as Sam himself had predicted. The not-so-subtle accusations, according to the story, were based "on supposition, poor theory, psychological intimations and mere circumstantial evidence."

Ketchum and Livingston were bylined, but three additional

ones were cited below the story. The thrust was that the sheriff was acting on the basis of "either undisclosed information or a personal vendetta," as if he had cards up his sleeve. Appropriate outrage was lavishly reported, complete with pictures of Jessie and Amy Shanks, Dr. Mowbray, Tony and Kay Farnsworth and, surprisingly, Sam Blatsford. There was also a picture of two men walking out of city hall with hats covering their faces, and a larger photograph of the Detroit godfather Annunzio under the headline: "Head of the Largest Midwest Mafia Family."

"This is disgusting," Emily said.

"A setup," Flanagan said angrily. "It's the way they work. Build up to tear down. But it's the stuff of which newspapers are made. Got to hand the bum that.

"Innuendo and speculation. Reputations smashed. Hints of horrors. Even the outrage appears as hysteria. All the dirty linen is thrown in together. It's as if they've all been declared guilty."

Nothing had been left out. But the worst of it was the buildup of the autopsy, which would make lascivious reading the next morning, like a TV miniseries. At the sound of the phone's ring, Flanagan's stomach twisted in knots. Emily rushed to the kitchen to answer it.

"It's awful, Audrey," Emily said with a catch in her throat. It was obvious to Flanagan that Audrey was crying at the other end. Then tears began to stream down Emily's cheeks and she handed the phone to Flanagan. He heard it drop at the other end. In a moment, it was picked up and he heard Sam's voice. Contrary to expectations, it was firm and confident.

"Flanagan at this end."

"If ever a new idea is needed, it is now," Sam said.

"I'm working on it," Flanagan said. Ideas were germinating in the subconscious. He was sure of that. But at this point, it would be fatal to offer an idea that could be Sam's ticket to oblivion.

"We did outfox them on something," Sam said.

Flanagan's long pause was his answer.

"We exhumed in the middle of the night. Which prevented

them from taking a sick, ghoulish graveside photo." From his voice, Flanagan detected his pride. "Then I had the grave covered as if nothing had happened. Just to throw them off—even though they know I got the exhumation orders."

"And the results of the autopsy?"

Flanagan felt his heartbeat accelerate.

"Not yet." Sam's voice grew lower, as if someone might be listening. "I flew the body down to the medical examiner in Detroit. Worked it out on the buddy system. Should at least have that behind us in a few hours."

"And then?"

"We'll take it a step at a time."

Flanagan was already making assumptions but he kept them to himself. He looked over at Emily, who was dabbing her tears with a napkin. Suddenly, the embryo of an idea began to take hold somewhere deep inside his mind. He felt himself reaching out, groping.

"Audrey okay?" Flanagan asked. It was, they both knew, an oblique inquiry as to the state of Sam's mental health.

"Takes a while for an old dog to learn new tricks," Sam said. He was suspiciously ebullient. Flanagan waited for the explanation he knew would come. "Reason they were able to juice up the story was that everybody talked too much, including me. Especially me. Used to be you could trust people, give them access. That's over. We're going to show those buzzards what us hicks can do."

Flanagan detected the bravado. Was it the sound of a frightened boy whistling in the cemetery? Or a man learning his first hard lesson on how to live with an inquisitively ruthless press?

Chapter Eighteen

Since the dog couldn't rear up on his hind legs to greet his masters, Flanagan had to bend down. He rubbed Caesar's neck. The dog's tail waved happily.

"He'll be fine in a few weeks," the vet said, handing Flanagan an envelope. "If he seems to be in pain, pop him one of these."

Flanagan noted that the vet was looking at him with an odd expression.

"Forgot to ask you how it happened."

"A long story," Flanagan said, somewhat annoyed at the vet's obvious skepticism. "He's like my brother, for crying out loud."

"You got me wrong," the vet protested. "It's just that it looks like a glancing blow did it. A toe of a shoe...."

"Sure he'll be okay?" Flanagan asked.

The vet rubbed Caesar's head.

"He's in good shape. He'll pull through with flying colors."

Flanagan led Caesar to the SUV. He walked on only three legs, as the fourth was cast in a slightly bent position, just off the ground. He lifted Caesar in beside him and while Flanagan checked to see if the dolls, all securely wrapped, were still in the back, Caesar slobbered a wet kiss on his cheek. Flanagan embraced and patted him.

"Couple of things we have to do before we take you home to Mama," Flanagan said aloud. He felt exhilarated by his sense of mission.

He eased the car out of the vet's parking lot and turned into the highway heading for Tucker. As he drove, he periodically dipped into his pocket and pulled out a dog biscuit which Caesar took gratefully.

"Gotta count your blessings, kiddo," Flanagan said.

He accelerated the SUV, noting that a deep growl was already bubbling up in Caesar's throat long before they reached the turnoff for Tucker. By the time they reached Lacey's Antique Shop, Caesar was straining at the leash with bared fangs. Flanagan reached out and embraced him around the neck, whispering in his ear.

"Don't get mad. Get even."

He attached the leash to Caesar's neck chain, held on, and felt the heavy dog, three legs notwithstanding, barrel ahead into the store. Straining and growling menacingly, he saw Lacey's fat, frightened face turn white at the sight. A bandage partially covered his head. A number of customers were browsing in the store.

Caesar's nose fastened onto his quarry and Flanagan let the dog drag him to within a few feet of Lacey, who seemed paralyzed, rooted to the spot. In his haste, Caesar had knocked over a clutch of glass taper sticks that were placed on a Sheraton inlaid mahogany urn stand. All went down in a crunch of broken glass. The fearful customers, Flanagan noted, suddenly vanished.

"He just wanted to stop by and say thanks," Flanagan said. It was taking all his strength to keep Caesar from moving toward Lacey.

"You can't do this. I'll call the cops."

"Go ahead."

The big man finally found his sense of mobility, limping cautiously toward the back of the store. Unfortunately, he hesitated briefly before a locked breakfront filled top to bottom with

Royal Worcester figures. He had often bragged about it as being the pride of his collection. Caesar reared on one leg, supported, of course, by Flanagan's pulling back on the leash. Down went the breakfront in an explosion of shattered china.

"You can't do this," Lacey screeched, his face beet red, his voice trembling with hysteria.

"All he wants to do is lick the boot that broke his leg."

"You're crazy. You can't do this," Lacey screamed. He started to move again, then stopped abruptly in front of a Meissen collection. Flanagan noted that Lacey's most valuable pieces were exhibited close to his desk on which stood the phone. Caesar strained at the leash. It wouldn't have taken much give to get him to rear up on one leg again and destroy most of the collection. By then Lacey had gotten the message. His body took on the frigidity of porcelain, except for the sweat and tears running down his face. Caesar continued to snarl and offer an occasional mean-sounding bark. Flanagan bent over and patted his head.

"He'll probably settle for an apology," Flanagan said.

"Please," Lacey begged, barely moving a facial muscle, although he could not fail to control the tremble in the puddle of fat that hung from the lower part of his face.

"Not to me, Lacey." He pointed to Caesar. "To him."

"I'm sorry. What can I say? I'm sorry."

"Sorry, who?" Flanagan smiled. "The pooch's name is Caesar."

"Sorry, Caesar," Lacey whined. But then he made the mistake of moving once again toward his phone. Caesar reared, but Flanagan held back slightly and only a few plates of Meissen were destroyed. At that point, Lacey dropped to his knees and surrendered to a paroxysm of shoulder-shaking hysteria.

"Actually, he likes antiques," Flanagan said, pulling sharply on the leash. Caesar obeyed, following him more cautiously toward the entrance of the store. Halting briefly, Flanagan turned. "I wouldn't discuss this with the police, Lacey. It just wouldn't be politic."

Before the dog and man could leave the store, Caesar paused briefly before what looked to Flanagan like a Neapolitan mandolin. Against this instrument, albeit awkwardly, Caesar left his mark.

"He's quite musical, you see," Flanagan said, tendering Caesar a dog biscuit and letting him lead him back into the SUV. "It will enhance the meaning of that lyric: Urine the money."

* * *

THE DRIVE to the Farnsworth place was more leisurely. Flanagan needed time to think. Caesar, obviously exhausted by his sweet vengeance, curled up in the seat beside him and snored away peacefully. Flanagan had a specific goal in mind. He needed to have another go at Lucy Farnsworth's medicine chest. All morning, he had been trying to picture it again in his mind. There were the four containers he had brought to Doc, those with prescription labels on them. But something was missing. He couldn't tell exactly what it was. Only that he would know it if he saw it.

It troubled him not to have perfect recall. Had he ever had that? He doubted it.

He pulled up to the Farnsworth house and hit the knocker. He had to hit it repeatedly and loudly to summon up a response. It turned out to be Tony himself, unshaven and hollow-eyed.

"Haven't we seen just about enough of you?" he said, with a snarl that reminded him of Caesar. He was a lot less congenial than he appeared yesterday.

"Newspapers exaggerate," Flanagan said.

"You were going to help, talk to your buddy Haseltine."

Flanagan was confused for the moment. Tony went on.

"They did it in secret. Exhumed Mother's body and shipped it off to Detroit. And where did I get that information?"

Such inside knowledge surprised Flanagan.

"There are no secrets from that crud. I thought you were going to help."

"I never said I would or could. The sheriff runs his own show."

Tony's eyes became menacing.

"Ever since you came on the scene, everything has gone downhill. Now my whole family is among the suspects of murdering my mother. How do you think we feel? And all this talk will surely hold up the disposition of the inheritance." He shook his head. "My poor mother died of natural causes. Where did all this doubt come from?"

Unfortunately Flanagan had no illusions of where such doubts had come from.

"You have to admit, Tony, that the prospect of inheritance has certainly had its impact."

"Yeah," Tony mused. "It sure helped with that shitty ski deal. I called that bank to help bail me out. Said I'd sign anything to make them whole. When the money passes I'll get more than enough to pay them off. Greedy bastards."

"Then try another bank."

"You really think so?" Tony rubbed his two days' growth of beard and it suddenly occurred to Flanagan that his being unshaven was not merely the act of neglect. He was deliberately cultivating a beard.

"Happens every day," Flanagan replied, plumbing some vague memories from his insurance days. Collateral was the bottom line for banks. Flanagan presumed that a will could be collateral, although he wasn't sure.

"How fast do these things usually happen?" There was something in the way he said it that suggested that speed was Tony's primary interest.

"I think a local bank, one that your mother dealt with, might move pretty fast." Flanagan felt himself growing impatient.

"The whole thing, you think? Or just a portion of it?"

"I'd say at least fifty percent. Maybe more."

"Not a hundred?"

"Listen, I'm not a banker. The name of the game is risk. The estate, after all, has to be distributed sooner or later, regardless of the complications."

"But all this crap could hold it up?"

"I'm also not a lawyer," Flanagan muttered.

"They'll probably eat me up with interest," Tony said bitterly. It struck Flanagan as absolutely the least of the man's problems.

"But it will get them off your back."

"I suppose—."

"Unless you're figuring out ways to get out of the debt."

Flanagan had expected a feisty reaction. Its mildness surprised him.

"I wish I could," he muttered. "Not with those people. They never give up."

"One good thing," Flanagan said brightly. "The sheriff sure shooed them out of town. At least they're not breathing down your neck."

"He did that to protect his reputation. Not me. And what he's doing with my mother's death is the worst. We're not perfect. Lord knows that. But to think that any one of us would want to take Mother's life. That's bastardly." His anger rose. "We'll get that rat someday. That I promise."

"Maybe it's more the fault of the newspaper," Flanagan said cautiously. He could see that Tony's thoughts were drifting.

"We all talked too damned much," Tony said vaguely, as if he were addressing no one in particular. "We should have all shut up about it. Who the hell would want to poison Mother? She was a good and gentle soul. Never hurt a fly. All she did was what Grampa wanted her to do and that was keep the family coffers intact. She did that pretty well." His eyes moistened and Flanagan was afraid that he would soon get maudlin.

"And you have absolutely no doubts?"

"Look, all us of have our faults. I don't really like my Uncle Jessie. Aunt Amy is a flake. Dr. Mowbray may like the good life a little too much. But he's treated the family for years. It's inconceivable."

"And Kay feels the same way?"

"Even more so. She couldn't even bear to read the paper this morning. It was so upsetting to her, she just couldn't even stay in the house."

Flanagan looked for an opening and it came when Tony seemed to fall into a deep funk. He shook his head and stared down at his hands.

"I have to go the washroom," Flanagan said foolishly, getting up. He left Tony slumped in his chair, walked into the hallway and bounded up the stairs.

He quickly found Lucy Farnsworth's room, padded on tip toes into the bathroom and opened the medicine chest. It was, as he had feared, empty. Again he tried to jog his memory as to the items that were in it when last he looked. Without striking a chord, he went out of the bathroom and looked in the drawers and closets. Lucy Farnsworth's clothes were still there. He wondered what to make of that. He tried to remember what they had done when his mother had died, how long it had taken to remove her effects.

Closing the door silently behind him, he started toward the stairs, stopped, turned and moved toward other doors that opened on the corridors. The first one he opened was Kay's, a bright, cheerful room done in floral prints with yellow backgrounds. He took a quick look around, trying to observe what it might tell him about Kay's character. The overall impression was that the room seemed to be that of a younger person, a girl really. Not that there were posters of rock stars on the walls or the usual teenage clutter. He had gone through that stage with his own daughter. It just did not strike him as the room of a woman over forty.

He moved into her bathroom and looked in the medicine chest, studying the contents. No prescription drugs. The usual women's night creams, aspirins, mouthwash. Nothing out of the ordinary. Suddenly he felt intrusive, uncomfortable.

He let himself out of her room and moved to another, which

looked as if it had not been used for quite awhile. Then he moved to another and opened the door. Unmistakably Tony's room. He recognized the suit Tony wore at the funeral, badly creased and thrown carelessly over a chair. He noted, too, that a suitcase on the bed seemed fully packed. It did not come as a surprise. He went into the bathroom and inspected the medicine chest. Except for some half-filled bottles of aftershave, it was empty. Apparently, he had even packed his shaving things. So Tony is getting ready for a quick getaway.

In the distance he caught the faint sound of someone stirring below. Quickly, he came out of Tony's room and ducked into the hall bathroom. Apparently, when the house had been refurbished, all bedrooms on the floor were fitted with their own bathrooms. The hall bathroom was, therefore, an auxiliary one for guests. As he expected, except for a deodorant spray, the medicine chest was empty.

He flushed the toilet and moved quickly down the stairs. Tony was standing in the foyer.

"When you gotta go, you gotta go," Flanagan said cheerfully, noting only the briefest spark of suspicion in Tony's eyes.

"So you think I should go to a local bank?"

"Nothing to lose."

"That's the way I look at it," Tony said. He put out his hand. Flanagan gripped it. It was warm and mushy. When he got outside, Flanagan rubbed it against the flank of his corduroys.

<h1 style="text-align:center">Chapter Nineteen</h1>

"A great day for the innocent," Emily said sweetly, embracing the limping Caesar as he bounded three-legged and tail wagging through the door. She kissed his snout and Caesar returned the gesture of affection with moist intensity. Flanagan enjoyed the spectacle. Emily looked up at him. "And Charley is showing signs of improvement. How about that?"

"Great," Flanagan said. Emily stood up and pecked him on the cheek. For the guilty, maybe not so good, Flanagan thought. But it was too early to tell.

"Sam called twice," Emily said. A tiny frown crossed her brow. He picked up the phone and dialed the sheriff's office. Peggy put him through immediately without her usual caustic comment.

"Meet me at Doc's in half an hour," Sam said.

Flanagan grunted acknowledgment and looked up at Emily, who had been watching him expectantly, waiting for an explanation.

"If I talk it, I might shake the hook loose," he said. She caught his meaning, offering a smile and a reassuring pat on his arm. What was coming together in his mind still needed cohesion. Large and important pieces of the puzzle were still missing.

Instead of going directly to Doc's, he walked around town for a while trying to keep the trail fresh in his mind, rewalking the ground, head down, seeking things he had missed. It was, he knew, typical of the agony of detection which he had experienced many times before.

When he arrived at the drug store, Doc and Sam were already crowded into Doc's little office behind the pharmacy. There was barely room for Flanagan to sit down. Doc kicked the door shut with his foot.

Sam's face was stern, but not gloomy. Flanagan noted that Doc held some official-looking papers in his hand.

"As expected, no poison," Sam said.

"So why all the hocus-pocus?" Flanagan said.

"Hypokalemia," Doc whispered, looking over the paper again. "Severe loss of potassium. Deductively interesting. We should all get a medal for it." He looked at Sam. "Sam here told his buddy in Detroit what to look for. So he found it in the eye tissue. Our county man would have looked in the blood, which breaks down too quickly and is unreliable." He looked again at the paper in his hand. "The woman died of heart failure. Pretty typical. You can't fault Mowbray on cause of death. It's the hypokalemia that is spooky."

"We were right about something," Sam drawled. "Now we have to keep it away from our friends at The Herald. Can't even work in my own office these days. Don't know who to trust anymore." It was meant, Flanagan knew, to be a backhanded compliment. He looked at his father-in-law and nodded slightly, which was about the only way to accept it.

"But I distinctly heard Mowbray say that he had increased her dosage of diuretics and her potassium," Flanagan said. "I remember that clearly."

"Obviously she didn't follow instructions," Sam said.

"But why wouldn't she?" Doc asked. "She knew how important it was."

"Two possibilities. Either she made a mistake or someone

substituted her drugs. Doc, was the single diuretic capsule found in the potassium container analyzed?"

"Yes it was. Checked out, too."

"But even if one drug was substituted for another, how could she not know it? She's been taking this medication for years," Sam said.

The room was warming up. Flanagan felt his pores open.

"Doc—bring us Lucy's medication," Flanagan said to his father-in-law.

Doc rose from his chair and went to his workspace behind the counter. When he returned, he had with him the four original containers of Lucy Farnsworth's drugs.

Flanagan took them, removed their caps and upended the containers on the table. Then he pointed to each drug in turn, noting how they differed in appearance from each other.

"They just don't look alike," Sam said.

"Look at the diuretic and the potassium. Different, to be sure. We see it instantly. But now close your eyes and feel them."

Sam and Doc followed directions to the letter.

"A little tougher to distinguish," Doc admitted.

"Except for size. One capsule feels the same as the other," Sam said. He nodded slowly. "Are you suggesting a substitution could have been made?"

"That's the only logical explanation," Doc said with a shrug.

"But the woman would have to be blind not to see the difference," Sam said.

"That's where I come to the end of the line, gentlemen," Flanagan said.

"I'm not at the end yet," Doc muttered.

"Well, almost to the end of the line," Flanagan interjected.

"I'm all ears," Sam said.

"I suppose I could check the remaining numbers against the numbers prescribed," Doc said. "Might tell us something." He went out of the room and they could see him looking through his file of prescriptions and making calculations on his old-fashioned adding machine.

"Of course, someone could have been administering her drugs," Sam mused. "Doling them out. Deliberately giving her the wrong pills."

"I saw her taking them herself," Flanagan said, as if the statement was not meant to be spoken aloud. "It was actually the day before she died. Yes. I remember that. She was lying on the living room couch. Beside her on the table were these containers and a carafe of water." And something else, he thought.

Doc came back into the room. He squinted at a paper tape from the adding machine.

"Generally speaking, it's in balance," he said. "Not perfect. But not enough potassium tablets left to indicate that she was shortchanging her body. The fact is she would have had to take none of them at all to come up with hypokalemia. No, I'm afraid that the drugs are essentially in balance."

"Are you at the end of the line now, Doc?" Flanagan asked. But Doc shook his head in the negative.

"Chances are that she took these medications by rote," Doc said. "It was part of her daily ritual. Although...."

"Although what, for crying out loud," Sam muttered impatiently.

"You may call me Doc, but you know I'm not a real doctor." He said it mischievously, as if deliberately encouraging their exasperation. Flanagan, of course, and most of the old-time residents of Lakeside Falls, had heard that statement ad infinitum. Not that Doc's diagnoses were infallible, but he was right most of the time. Unfortunately, the preface to his considered and probably illegal medical opinion had to be endured. "Chances were that the hypokalemia was making her lethargic, weak, drowsy, restless, fatigued, nauseous and, owing to the toxic effects of digitalis, very irritable. Maybe even unable—as she declined—to take her own medication."

"So you are suggesting that someone else was administering them?" Sam asked.

"Only at the end."

"Like who?" Sam asked, quickly answering his own question. "Kay? Tony?"

"Her sister Amy," Flanagan interjected, remembering that Amy had come in as he had left on that last day.

"Won't necessarily wash," Doc said, once again exhibiting his air of mischief. "She died too fast. The process had to have been begun earlier. Hypokalemia is something that wouldn't happen abruptly. She would have had to administer to herself first. Then as she gradually declined, others might have had to do it for her. They would simply have opened the containers and put the pills in her hand, following the directions on the labels."

"So we're back to square one," Sam said, shaking his head. He turned toward Flanagan, who noted the pained look of frustration in his eyes.

"We never really left it," Flanagan said. The sound of his voice suggested an intonation. "It's quite obvious that the lady died of a deprivation of potassium. To put it another way, she probably OD'd on hydroDIURIL."

"That's not murder," Sam snapped. "Provable murder."

"In the absence of poison, a perfect crime," Doc said, unable to hide his enthusiasm for the idea.

"And I'm the town clown," Sam said, glaring at Flanagan. "The hick sheriff, bumbling and fumbling. Now that I've been painted into the corner, what would you suggest—." He stopped abruptly, while Flanagan filled in the gap. Murder maven, he thought, with a dollop of sarcasm. He was conscious suddenly of smiling, a gesture that was definitely not soothing to the harassed sheriff, who stood up abruptly. The table trembled and the little mounds of pills lost their definition. More fell on the floor.

"It's largely a question of commitment," Flanagan said, remaining seated, which effectively blocked Sam's way.

"What the devil is that supposed to mean?"

Doc glanced at both of them alternately, as if he were watching an intense tennis match.

"The basic question remains, Sam. Do you believe this woman was murdered?"

Sam rubbed his chin. His eyes flitted around the room, deliberately avoiding Flanagan's.

"That's irrelevant. Murderers are caught by evidence, not instinct."

"So you still believe in the possibility?"

"Would I have been in this spot if I didn't?"

Always questions with questions, Flanagan thought, girding himself for the new proposal he was about to advance.

"I have an idea," Flanagan said, conscious of using the full range of his humility.

"Speaking of instinct," Sam said, "mine is to cover my ears."

He didn't, sitting down instead.

"It's time you began to lead the press by the nose, instead of them leading you."

Flanagan could see that he had struck a chord. The sheriff briefly crinkled and indicated his approval by a delayed flutter of his eyelids.

"If our instincts are right," Flanagan said with dramatic inflection, "then a certain person—or persons—is or are very, very nervous. And will continue to be as long as they think an investigation is in progress. That's a given, right?"

"We're not dealing in geometry," Sam said irritably.

"So why not add fuel to the media fire and keep the pot boiling?"

"And the killer or killers will get more and more nervous," Doc interjected, an excited flush rising on his cheeks.

"People who have the nerves to deliberately kill, usually have the acting ability to hide their anxieties," Sam said. "Barring a sudden attack of conscience. Which continues to leave me boiling in the pot."

"It's a suggestion that needs a devil's advocate," Flanagan said.

Especially, he thought, since it was barely worked out in his own mind.

"My inclination is to get it behind me," Sam said.

"And abet a perfect crime?" Flanagan said, holding his breath. Sam paled.

"Is this an appeal to my conscience, Flanagan?"

"Just pulling out the stops, Sheriff. Look, you've already got them snapping at your heels. Mowbray, Shanks, Tony, Kay and Blatsford. You're gumming up the works, even for the innocent, whoever they may be. The objective here for most of our principals is now money. The inheritance. Big things are riding on that. That's probably in legal limbo for the moment. Pending the completion of your investigation. All I'm saying is that you keep it in limbo for a day or two. In other words, tickle their feet."

"What?"

"It drives the baby buggy."

Sam shook his head and tried a sneer, but could only work out a thin smile.

"I know. Put me in the punny farm." Flanagan shrugged.

"Be kind of fun throwing Herb Braker some red herrings."

"He's pretty fishy to begin with."

Problem is, Flanagan thought, a fish stink has a tendency to rub off on anyone within smelling distance.

"So what do you suggest?" Sam asked.

Flanagan told him. It was an idea not without the possibilities of improvisation.

Chapter Twenty

Overnight it had turned freezing and by the time Flanagan had picked up the morning paper and come upstairs again, his feet felt like icicles. He crawled back into bed, turned up the electric blanket and put his iced feet on Emily's exposed haunches.

"Yipes," she screamed, kicking him away.

"Just trying to catch your attention."

Swinging one leg over the side, he nestled it under Caesar's warm coat.

"Next best thing," he said, putting on his reading glasses. He did not want to miss a single word. He began to read silently.

"Not just to yourself."

She hadn't yet put in her contacts. He began to read aloud.

"The headline reads: Farnsworth Investigation Continues."

"You Machiavelli." She pinched his arm. He had filled her in on the ploy that he and Sam had planned.

"I know a very good tailor who can Machiavelli good suit for fifty bucks."

"Not before breakfast."

He ignored her and continued.

"There is a picture of Sam and another showing Lucy's grave.

There are two bylines—one is Harry Ketchum, the other Sue Livingston."

"Never expected it of Carrie Livingston's daughter. Carrie was always such a goody-goody in high school. Would you call the girl a muckraker?"

"There's lots of muck to rake. Unfortunately, Sam's muck is the least rakable."

"You're losing me. Read on, MacFlanagan."

Flanagan cleared his throat for dramatic emphasis.

"Sheriff Sam Hazeltine, in an exclusive interview with The Herald, has revealed that foul play in the death of Lucy Farnsworth remains a possibility. An autopsy report prepared by the medical examiner's office in Detroit is already in his hands, but the sheriff has indicated that it is too early to comment on the findings.

"The sheriff justified the secrecy surrounding the exhumation and shipment of the body to Detroit as necessary in the light of intense media attention.

"'It is impossible to investigate a murder in the glare of publicity,' the sheriff pointed out, 'although I have absolutely no objection to keeping the public informed when conclusions are reached. A murder investigation requires extreme secrecy so as not to forewarn the culprits.'" Not bad, Flanagan thought.

"As for possible suspects, the sheriff reiterated the point that his department was still in the 'gathering evidence' phase.

"When pressed to reveal what first gave him the idea that Mrs. Farnsworth might not have died a natural death, the sheriff refused all comment. The autopsy should reveal whether or not Mrs. Farnsworth died because of the ingestion of foreign substances. Indeed, it is apparent that family and friends, including Mrs. Farnsworth's doctor, Dr. Mowbray, prefer to remain silent at this moment, but there was speculation that some family members have had preliminary interviews with counsel.'" Flanagan paused. Good touch, he thought. Sam was learning fast. 'Mrs. Farnsworth was ailing with a variety of diseases....'"

The telephone rang. Emily picked it up. It was Sam Hazeltine.

"He was just reading it to me," Emily said. They exchanged pleasantries. Then Emily handed Flanagan the phone and went to the bathroom. As he listened to Sam, he read to the bottom of the story. The reporters had gone into elaborate detail about Lucy's illnesses, with an explicit explanation of the drug therapy that had been prescribed.

Part of their plan was to allow Doc to provide the reporters with "background" material without attribution.

"They print anything," Sam said.

"They love to believe."

"Pure innuendo. That's all it is," Sam said. Flanagan detected a note of shame in his voice. "Doesn't seem honest. All this about drug therapy, when they were really asking about poison."

"The wielder of the weapon will get the message."

"If there was a wielder."

"Are you starting to hedge, Sam?"

It was a direct challenge.

"Not really. Just concerned about what happens if nothing happens."

As Flanagan listened, he watched Emily put in her contact lenses. She seemed to be getting quicker, defter with her fingers. Then she picked up the eye drop container and squeezed a few drops in her eyes with equal efficiency. It was then that he realized what his mind had been groping for.

"Of course," he said aloud.

"What?"

"Give me a couple of hours."

"For what?"

"When nothing happens it's still something happening."

He dressed quickly, rushing through a shave while Emily continued to use the bathroom mirror to comb her hair.

"Where are you going in such a stew?" Emily asked.

"Got to see an optometrist."

"Well, it's about time. I wouldn't have it any other way, now that I've got these. You don't have to worry about those horrible glasses. You'll see, Flanagan. And Dr. Blandings is marvelous."

"I'm not going to him. I'm going to Dr. Grant. I'm no traitor."

"I've provided you with living evidence of his competence." She batted her eyelids, then opened her eyes wide. He saw the faint outlines of the lenses.

"My eye," he said.

She gave him an indignant look, which he ignored. He pecked her on the forehead and was down the stairs and outside fumbling with his SUV keys before he realized that he had not brushed his teeth. He knew what that meant. The magnet of discovery was pulling him compulsively forward without regard to anything, including old habits. It's out of my hands, he assured himself.

Until he arrived at Dr. Grant's office on Second Street, he had not realized that it was much too early for him to open for patients. He had seen him at the funeral and briefly at the Farnsworth house. Pulling the SUV up to the front of Grant's office, he got out with the intention of calling the optometrist's residence. But the office was at street level and he first peered through the glass door. He saw the glow of reflected light in the rear and proceeded to rap on the door with his knuckles.

Dr. Grant emerged from the rear. Recognizing Flanagan, he waved and proceeded to open the door. Solidly built, with broad shoulders and blond hair going to gray, he gave Flanagan a broad smile and a look of acute curiosity.

"Better early than never," Dr. Grant said.

He had opened his office directly after graduation from optometry school more than twenty-five years ago. His practice was an instant success, with patients recommended by his father, who owned a small supermarket on Main Street. It wasn't that Dr. Grant was old. But because he had been around for more than a quarter of a century, the perception existed that he was not keeping up with the times. Perhaps that was the reason, Flanagan noted, that his office was recently redecorated with portraits of beautiful men and women in designer spectacles, thick carpets and displays of glasses on floor-to-ceiling mirrored shelves.

"Real nice, Alan," Flanagan said. The last time he had visited his office it was musty and dusty with pictures on the walls from the fifties.

"Nothing like competition to put a poker up one's you-know-what."

"They'll all be back." He had the sudden urge to apologize for Emily's defection.

"Blandings is competent. I can't deny him that." Nevertheless there was an air of begrudging that was understandable.

"Bumped into him briefly," Flanagan acknowledged.

"He's a loner. Sticks to himself." He paused. "Frankly, I was surprised to see him at Lucy's funeral."

"He did fit her for contact lenses."

"I guess his relationship was more than professional."

Flanagan filed away the comment, which had seemed rather curious.

Dr. Grant proceeded behind the reception counter to an examining room. He motioned to the patient's chair. Flanagan obeyed the command.

"I'm not here for that," he said, but with not enough conviction to inhibit the examination. Dr. Grant had already taken out an instrument and was shining a light into his right eye.

"Call it a might-as-well. You're here. Eyes need constant monitoring after a certain age."

Actually, Flanagan decided, it did seem like a good idea and since it did not stop him from asking questions, he let the examination proceed.

"I'm going to spin out a scenario while you play with my eyes —okay?"

"As long as you pause long enough to read the chart." He pressed a switch and the familiar letter chart lit up across the room. He read as far as he could. Dr. Grant wrote something on a card.

"Now?"

"Now."

"Scenario. This woman suffers from diabetes and heart failure."

"Lucy Farnsworth."

"There are no secrets in this town," Flanagan sighed.

"Not many."

"She takes various drugs."

"Digitalis, Diabinese, HydroDIURIL, potassium supplements."

Flanagan turned toward his face. "I was her optometrist, remember. She was approximately four diopters farsighted. She wore bifocals to correct very blurred vision."

"What kind of lenses would Blandings have fitted her with?"

"Probably a monovision system in soft lenses. One for distance, one for reading. Corrects up to twenty/thirty in her dominant eye...."

Flanagan lifted one hand, palm up.

"Now don't get ahead of me."

"Sorry. It's my business."

"She'd need drops?"

"Especially her. Because of the diuretic, her corneal tissues would dehydrate excessively. I'd say she'd need to give herself a dab of artificial tears about three or four times a day to supplement her inadequate tear flow and...."

"Easy. Let me you walk you through it."

"Heavy stuff?"

"Extremely." Flanagan concentrated his thoughts. "Now, let me try to understand how it would work." Dr. Grant started to speak. Flanagan lifted his hand. "No, let me. You correct me." He paused, then continued. "She would take out her lenses before she went to bed. Probably in the bathroom. Put the lenses into a case filled with some fluid. Then get into bed."

"Probably. Although people are different and...."

"Then if she wanted to read in bed?"

"If she took the lenses out in the bathroom, she'd probably use her old bifocals. Distance-wise, reading a book would not present much of a problem."

"Would the old bifocals be adequate?"

"Might have to hold the book closer, but under normal circumstances probably adequate."

"Then why was she complaining about her eyes?" Flanagan asked. It was almost rhetorical.

"Hard to say about a diabetic. Lots of things happen."

"Like what?"

Dr. Grant grew thoughtful. Flanagan wondered if he was coming to the outer limits of his knowledge.

"Sometimes in older patients," Dr. Grant said with some hesitation, "they get what they call diabetic neuropathy."

"What's that?"

"They lose some tactile sensation in their fingertips. Makes it harder to get their contacts in."

"What about the eyes?"

"Well, if she was having trouble reading, she probably didn't have good focus control. Like the pupils were dilated too much."

"From drugs? From any of the drugs she was taking?"

"I don't think so."

"Then what?"

Dr. Grant shrugged, rubbing his chin and scratching his head. For the first time, his self-assurance seemed assaulted.

"She was no longer my patient." He sighed with unmistakable regret. "I'm sort of flying blind."

"Hope that's not a pun."

"Not for someone in my business." His response seemed vague. Obviously, he was chasing down possibilities in his mind. "I think you're suggesting something, Flanagan."

"I am," Flanagan admitted.

"Like someone tampering with the medication?"

"I'm listening."

"Dilation. I said it myself. Someone might have tampered with the drops. I mean, I don't quite understand...."

"Explain the tampering."

"Well, in that case," Dr. Grant shook his head. "A little dab of atropine sulfate in the solution would dilate the pupil from three to five millimeters." Dr. Grant paused, smiling broadly again. "It wouldn't show cosmetically. Lucy had brown eyes. Also, it would paralyze the ciliary muscle within the eye, which is responsible for changing the shape of the crystalline lens inside the eye." This time Flanagan let him go on without interruption. It was becoming quite clear, opening up inside of him. "This would eliminate whatever residual ability she may have had to refocus her vision from distance to near."

"What about the bifocals?"

"While she was wearing the contact lenses, other than some peripheral shadows around objects she would be viewing, she would still see very well, but when she removed the lenses at night and reverted to her old prescription eyeglasses, her close vision would have been worsened so that she could see, at normal distances, nothing smaller than large newspaper headlines."

"So she would have trouble reading? Trouble also recognizing close objects?"

Dr. Grant nodded. He had completely forgotten about the examination.

"And because she had lost some tactile feeling in her fingertips she would not be able to discriminate very accurately by touch...." At that point, Flanagan stopped abruptly. "I think we should continue with this examination."

"Have I been helpful?" Dr. Grant asked.

"I want to see things a lot more clearly," Flanagan said.

"Which is precisely why you are here," Dr. Grant said, shining the flashlight beam in his left eye.

Chapter Twenty-One

It had to be done with extreme delicacy. The last thing he wanted was for Sam to feel that Flanagan had one-upped him. Not quite yet. In fact, his report of his meeting with Dr. Grant was deliberately halting and tentative. It was important for the sheriff to come to this delicate point of acceptance himself, to deduce that Lucy Farnsworth was, for some still unexplained reason, not distinguishing the difference between her diuretic and potassium capsule. Of course, Flanagan had to prod things along in subtle ways.

Sam ruminated as he listened to Flanagan's account of Dr. Grant's information, lifting his long legs to the leather hassock and looking out into the cold, gloomy morning. Flanagan had rushed to the sheriff's office after his meeting with Dr. Grant. Once again, he had to pass through the gauntlet of The Herald's two snoopy reporters. Peggy ushered him directly into Sam's inner sanctum.

"Has some logic," Sam said, still noncommittal as to his acceptance.

"But is it compelling enough?" Flanagan asked hesitantly.

"It probably is worth going with," Sam said, obviously hiding his own excitement. He removed his legs from the hassock and sat upright, a sure sign of his commitment. "It certainly explains a lot. She probably couldn't tell the difference. Not by sight. Not by feel."

"I'm inclined to think you're right," Flanagan said cautiously.

"All one had to do was substitute the diuretic for the potassium. And if Mowbray had upped the dosage...." He clicked his tongue. "...my God."

"Voila, hypokalemia," Flanagan said, as if the idea had suddenly burst into his head.

The sheriff's face crinkled into a broad smile. He slapped his desk. It was his turn now for a little magnanimity.

"I sensed you had suddenly gotten something when we talked this morning on the phone," Sam said, as if to validate his acute perception.

"I saw Emily putting those artificial tear drops in her eyes."

"And you remembered that the drops were missing when we looked into Lucy's medicine chest?"

He was giving no quarter now, implying that he had remembered the missing drops all along. Which well he might have. Sam, too, was not above holding back information from Flanagan. Gave their competition its edge, Flanagan thought. Wouldn't be much fun without a worthy opponent, he assured himself.

"And you rushed over to Dr. Grant?"

"Who else to trust but the old natives?"

"You're right there," Sam said. Slowly, reality arrived and the color drained from his cheeks. "Unfortunately that gives us only the means. It's a step forward. But it doesn't change anything. The evidence is still circumstantial. Impossible to prove."

"For the moment."

The sheriff shook his head.

"All it took was a switch. Emptying the container of the potassium and filling it with the diuretic. Then a few drops of atropine sulfate into the tear drop bottle. In effect, poor Lucy did herself in by her own hand."

"But someone manipulated it. Someone clever. Someone with

knowledge of drugs." Flanagan said cautiously, adding: "A mite careless. One diuretic capsule must have been stuck to the inside of the container. Didn't pour out easily. But it did point out the possibility." He felt his thoughts beginning to ramble.

Despite these convincing new deductions, it was inescapable that they were not only skewered on the horns of a dilemma, they were playing with communal dynamite. Poor Sam was way out on a limb. He could not arrest. He had no hard evidence and no specific suspect. And he could not tell his findings to the newspaper for fear that the innuendo would backfire and show him to be a bumbling fool. Indeed, the newspaper was waiting for just such a denouement with bared fangs.

"Wouldn't take much for Dr. Mowbray to pull the medication switch," Sam said.

"Provided he knew the effects of atropine sulfate?"

"Wouldn't be difficult to find out about it," Sam countered, throwing Flanagan a sharp glance. "You did."

Flanagan thought about that for a moment, wondering if it was pregnant with insult. He decided to let it pass without a pugnacious response.

"Yes, I did," he acknowledged calmly. "It's an extract of night-shade, a poisonous plant. Atropine is a poison when taken in heavy doses, which could not have been the case here. Years ago it was also used for stomach upsets. Now it's used almost exclusively for the dilation of pupils."

"Not bad, Flanagan."

It seemed like an honest compliment. All part of the game. Now another question was called for.

"Who do you think?" Flanagan asked.

"You first."

Flanagan looked at the ceiling, if only to show some hesitation.

"There's a passel of possibilities," he said after the pause. "We have the obvious, of course. Shanks and Mowbray. And there is always Blatsford. We are aware of exactly how they benefit from

Lucy's death. But Amy, Kay and Tony also had access to Lucy and, most important, to her intimate habits. Especially Kay, who was closest to her. Actually, we have a motive for everyone but Kay."

"And I doubt if she knows the first thing about drugs. One doesn't think of Kay as some sinister genius."

"And she did make a great show of loving her mother," Flanagan said, surprised suddenly by his own cynical comment.

"Show? They were inseparable for years. No one could doubt that Kay loved her mother and that Lucy loved Kay. No," Sam shook his head. "Imagine if even a hint of that got out. They'd think we've gone crazy."

The buzzer rang on the sheriff's desk and soon the intercom was crackling with Peggy's voice.

"They're getting antsy," Peggy said. "They've been reading me the first amendment."

"Tell them to wait."

"How long?"

"A minute or two. No more."

"Can I promise that?"

"Promise them anything."

He clicked the intercom off angrily and looked up at Flanagan.

"I don't think I can keep that medical report secret any longer. My buddy will play ball, but only up to a point. Besides, there are ears everywhere. Even in Detroit. Especially Detroit."

Earlier in his conversation with Tony, Flanagan had borne witness to that fact. It was doubtful that Tony would ever reveal his source, even when pressed.

"Still...," Flanagan said, letting the pause create suspense. A new idea was beginning to percolate.

"Still what?"

"You do, after all, have some control over the situation. When you control information, you exercise power." The sheriff raised his eyebrows. Then lines formed on his forehead. Flanagan quickly rolled over possibilities in his mind. The situation, he knew, was delicate. What he was about to suggest required some careful tacking.

"Was there any reaction from today's story?" Flanagan asked, suddenly striking out in what he hoped would appear to be a new direction.

"Nothing concrete yet. It's still too early." He looked quizzically at Flanagan. "We both agreed it was a holding action." Obviously, Flanagan thought, Sam wanted that responsibility shared.

"The newspaper story has got to have made the killer nervous. At the least, uncomfortable."

"That was the point of it, wasn't it?" Sam sucked in a deep breath. "Keep him off balance, worried and anxious. Forcing an overreaction."

"Only so far... nothing."

"Afraid not."

"Now comes the medical report," Flanagan said.

"Even if you release the results, which you must, it has to continue to be worrisome for the killer. Right? Except that reason would begin to set in. So Lucy died of hypokalemia. So they found out. So what? Still no proof of foul play. In fact, no proof in sight. Not based on that medical report."

"No. I'd say there would be no surprises for the killer in this report."

"Except one."

The sheriff frowned. He was not following. Flanagan plunged ahead anyway.

"Think of yourself as the killer. What would send you up the wall?"

He deliberately did not offer a broader hint, letting Sam work it out in his own mind. Flanagan calculated that one more prod was needed.

"Finding hypokalemia in Lucy was, after all, the known quantity. The murderer knew that would have to come up...."

"Atropine," the sheriff snapped, sitting bolt upright. "That would be the most worrisome potential finding. Traces of atropine."

"A foreign substance. Atropine didn't belong in the body. It would be the only link to suggest foul play."

"But it wasn't found. Not even looked for."

"And probably too minute to be detected."

"Unless, of course, you suggest the possibility," Flanagan said. He held his breath, watching Sam's expression. Then he saw the frown flatten and the air of thoughtfulness take over.

"The trumpet is just outside the door. Give it a hoot."

"But it's a damned lie."

"You said the medical examiner in Detroit's an old buddy. Army?"

The sheriff nodded.

"One forges deep friendships in the Army."

Flanagan knew that Sam was considering all his options now. Mostly those that could backfire politically. There was some risk, of course. Sam got up from his chair and went to the combination lock of his file cabinet, which he proceeded to twirl, moving his lips with the numbers. Opening a drawer, he took out a file and read it over.

"I'm not keeping it here, that's for sure," Sam said, handing him the report. "I only hope that Charlie Waters, that's my Detroit buddy, has a good security system."

"Not that good," Flanagan thought.

"Chances are they'll accept your vagaries."

"You think so?"

"Doesn't mean they won't try to crack you open, Sheriff. But they'll never guess that you'd be so reckless as to embellish a medical examiner's report. Comes of establishing an exemplary reputation."

Flanagan wondered if he had gone too far. Even Sam Hazeltine, if all throttles were open, could pick up on sarcasm and ironies. Thankfully, he was too preoccupied with the risk he was about to take.

"And then?" Sam Hazeltine asked. "After we let it out, what can we expect?"

"If you were the killer, what would you do?" Flanagan asked.

"Run," the Sheriff muttered. "As fast as I could."

"No, you wouldn't," Flanagan corrected good naturedly. "You're too smart for that. You've nearly pulled off a perfect crime. You tell yourself not to panic. You calm yourself. Have a second cup of coffee. The ball, after all, is in the sheriff's court. And what has he got? Circumstantial evidence of foul play. And atropine sulfate."

"You said it was a poison."

"Not in small quantities."

"So I don't run," the sheriff said.

"You tough it out."

"Absolutely. You know that no one could possibly conclude that small traces of atropine could have killed the woman. You also suspect—not suspect—you know that atropine would not show in an autopsy. After all, to pull off this criminal masterpiece you'd have checked that out. So you're confused."

"So is the public."

"And the press."

Flanagan paused deliberately, hoping that the sheriff would present the next idea. The fact was that Flanagan wasn't sure he had one himself.

"But the killer would have to fight the panic," Flanagan said when it was apparent that no other idea was forthcoming, although a vague shape was beginning to outline itself in his mind. "And that won't be easy. Not if he—or she—or they—are convinced they had pulled off the perfect crime."

Sam began to pace the room in long strides. Flanagan knew that career fear wasn't the sheriff's only hang-up. He could dissimulate. He could play a role in the public interest. He could be brave and courageous and tough. But he had one flaw. It was hard for him to lie.

Flanagan left him to his agony, certain that he would make

what was the only logical decision. Sam hated a murderer to go unpunished even more than he hated to lie.

Conscious of being scrupulously observed by the two reporters who waited in the reception room, he hesitated momentarily, pausing before Peggy's desk. As a reflex, he patted the outside of his inner jacket pocket where the medical examiners report lay secure from prying eyes.

"Says he has more important things to worry about than a complaint about an unauthenticated antique," Flanagan said to a scowling Peggy, who quickly picked up on the ploy. He even detected the briefest outline of a smile.

"Shouldn't have troubled him with such trivial stuff," Peggy replied.

He noted how quickly the reporters lost interest. He hoped that Sam would manipulate them just as easily.

While walking home, the full weight of Sam's impending risk made a resounding impact on his conscience. The imponderables began to assail him. Surely, the eager beaver reporters would quickly determine that there could be no known reason for Lucy Farnsworth to have atropine sulfate in her body. But it would be doubtful that they would be able to piece together its significance in Lucy's death. If all went well, only the killer would get the message. But the risks for Sam would be great, perhaps too great. And this was troubling. It made him irritable. Was the risk worth taking?

Further reflection was short circuited when he arrived home. He was surprised to find the young couple who previously showed interest in the tall clock inspecting it once again.

"Mr. and Mrs. Parker are having second thoughts," Emily said with a wink.

The young couple nodded and smiled benignly.

"It's really a beauty," Flanagan said, almost by rote. He was in no mood for selling.

"It's that extra strike," Mrs. Parker said. She looked at her husband. "If we can't put it to rights, we may just use it for decoration."

"For decoration?"

The idea sounded offensive to Flanagan, who looked upon tall clocks in a more mystical connotation, a form of life created by man.

"It goes so perfectly with the decor, you see," Mr. Parker said.

"Well, that is a consideration," Emily interjected. Obviously, she had seen warning signs in Flanagan that were not to her liking.

"And you're sure it can't be fixed?" Mr. Parker asked, with what seemed to Flanagan a kind of artificial anxiety. Worse, Flanagan began to be conscious of some sinister intent on the part of the man, something deeply offensive and off-putting.

Mr. Parker backed away from the clock and looked up at its face, rubbing his chin and shaking his head. Flanagan had the distinct feeling that he was bracing himself for some inexplicable onslaught.

"We could always shut it down. It's not really the time we're after, you see. It fits so perfectly." He nodded vigorously. "I think we'll take it," Mr. Parker said, his Adam's apple working in his throat.

Emily had come up beside Flanagan, and in the rhythm of her breathing he detected a kind of ecstatic consent. Yet, somewhere deep inside himself he felt something ignite. In the distance he heard the drums of revolution, his mind's eye blinded by the fires of rebellion.

"No way," Flanagan said emphatically. "Not for triple the price."

"But that's—that's unconscionable," the man sputtered, his cheeks reddening with outrage. His wife's face puffed like a blow-fish with indignation.

Beside him, Emily's breathing sounded like a tire losing air. He was certain that her features radiated an expression of extreme alarm. The air crackled with ignitable tension. Reaching out, he touched Emily's arm. She glanced toward him, appeared to note that he was in charge of himself and offered a thin but knowing smile.

"It's a rare piece," Flanagan said. "How many tall clocks do you know that have an extra strike in their works which defies all mechanics and clockmakers? To deliberately wish to shut that down is sacrilege, a travesty."

"It's a flaw," the man grunted.

"A flaw?" Flanagan said with unabashed ridicule. "You know anything about postage stamps? Currency? Coins? You know what a flawed one of those is worth? How much the flaw enhances the price?"

"That's something else. That's irreversible."

"So is this."

Emily embraced his arm in the crook of her elbow. Years of intimacy and companionship had taught them that inner crisis often manifested itself in what outwardly seemed illogical, even bizarre. Under ordinary circumstances, he surely would have jumped at the offer. Don't ask me to explain, he begged himself, feeling emotionally offended by the couple.

"I think this is highly unethical."

"You have that right," Flanagan said pompously. He felt his cheeks flush hotly.

"It's a lemon," the woman said.

"Then why did you want it?" Flanagan snapped.

"I wouldn't touch it with a ten-foot pole," the woman shot back.

Mr. Parker was about to say something more, but his wife tugged at his elbow and they quickly went out the front door.

"You were quite ingratiating," Emily said, not without a touch of sarcasm.

Flanagan patted the tall clock.

"Needs a good home and loving care," he said. "This baby is a survivor. It has to have respect. It has to be honored. Besides, it's handicapped. It needs compassion."

"It needs to be sold," Emily said.

"Someday," Flanagan muttered. He turned and stomped through the long hall. Caesar, who had been sleeping under the kitchen table, rose, shook himself, and slobbered a hello. He resisted an unkind remark; he knew he had been cantankerous. By tomorrow he would regret his conduct and berate himself for not unloading the clock. But the beast was thrashing inside of him, the cataclysm was approaching and he was powerless to stop its effects. Emily came in and sat across the table from him.

"Talk it out," she said gently, patting his hands which lay clasped on the table.

"You think I need an exorcism?"

"Absolutely."

"I've led Sam into a patch of quicksand," he said. "The press and the public are offended by unanswered questions, especially by those charged with assuring their safety."

* * *

IT WAS, he knew, high time to fill her in on all the details, which he did. She listened calmly, patting his clasped hands from time to time.

"I see what you mean," she said when he had finished.

"All we can do is wait for the killer to react."

Emily shook her head.

"And you're not sure he will?"

"The fact is, Sam needs a confession. Knowing the identity of the killer is not enough in this case. Barring a confession, there is no indictable offense. The evidence that exists is completely circumstantial and speculative and the real damning evidence is undoubtedly destroyed."

They sat in silence for a long time. Caesar went back to sleep under the kitchen table.

"Flanagan, do you know who did it?" Emily whispered.

"I know who. But not why."

"And the two are inseparable."

Exactly, he thought. Suddenly a charge of adrenaline roared through him. The all-powerful gush moved inexorably, like a river that had crashed its dikes. The room swayed. His ears crackled. He stood up, held the edges of the kitchen table as if for support as he bent over and kissed Emily on the forehead.

"You said it."

"I did? What?"

"Wait until the debris clears."

Chapter Twenty-Two

Sometime between the hours of two and three a.m., the debris cleared. Flanagan opened his eyes and turned his head on the pillow.

"You up?"

"I've been up. How could I sleep with all that noise?"

"What noise?"

"The noise of you thinking," Emily said, moving to plant a kiss on his cheek.

"Actually, I was listening to you."

"To me?"

"I was searching for something you said, replaying the old tunes."

"And you found it?"

"In spades."

"Should I wait breathlessly?"

"No. Breathe while I talk. Besides, you'll be answering questions."

Flanagan's eyes searched the shadowless ceiling, looking for chinks in the relentless black. The metaphor, he thought, was apt. He nodded and began.

"You said that you had seen Kay Farnsworth in Dr. Blandings' office, reading a magazine."

"Yes. I did see her."

"And she was not wearing glasses?"

"Not that I remember. In fact, I don't remember ever seeing her with glasses. But then, Dr. Blandings is a specialist in contacts." He had looked deeply into Kay's Wedgwood blue eyes in the last few days. It was the way he looked at people. In both Lucy and Emily, he had observed the telltale lines of the lenses. He could remember no trace of them in Kay's eyes. But he wasn't sure, truly dead certain. Emily's words echoed his thoughts. "It would be a simple matter to find out. Just check with Dr. Blandings."

"Tell me about Dr. Blandings."

"Quite good-looking, actually. Jet black hair. Eyes a kind of royal blue in color, coal black lashes under thick eyebrows. Wonderfully white teeth." She paused. "Strong hands. Little ridges of hair over long tapering fingers. Oh yes, and the most marvelous cleft in his chin."

"You're darting around shamelessly."

"Women observe men in a special way," she said with an air of amused authority.

"Is he tall or short? Is his voice high-pitched, a deep bass, somewhere in between? Is he all business? Flirty or standoffish?"

"Doctorly," she said after some thought.

"Sexy?"

"Now there's a subjective question."

"You know what I mean. What is his aura?"

"All right. You asked for it. He is sexy. I'd say he was an attractive male animal, all in all. A bit on the solemn side. No. I'd say aloof. Someone who held himself back."

"Restrained?"

She paused for a long moment.

"Proper. That's the word. He was, after all, in a dark room at very close proximity."

Flanagan moved his hand suddenly. It came to rest on a warm haunch.

"He seemed to make every effort not to be touchy."

"Disappointed?"

"What would he want with an old bag like me?" She giggled girlishly. His hand moved laterally. She let it move, then stopped it with her own. "Besides, I'm not interested in Prince Charming. I have the frog, the real thing."

"Even to break the monogamy."

"There's got a be a point to all this."

"There is."

This time her hand moved laterally.

"I'm getting the message."

He clasped her fingers.

"An attractive man, this Dr. Blandings. Ambitious and industrious. Trying to make a good living in this little town. Comes the ugly duckling heiress...."

"You're not serious?"

"Dead. Like Lucy Farnsworth."

"A daughter to do that to her mother?"

"That could be the missing link. There is something intrinsically unnatural in an adult child whose life is defined by her mother's domination or possessiveness. Something inside could be stunted. The child cannot be free. But the child is not a child. The biological clock keeps ticking away. Dry tinder waiting for the match."

"Dr. Blandings?"

He felt her shiver and move closer to him. Her arm embraced his chest.

"There are many kinds of desperation," Flanagan sighed, wondering if his theory made sense to her. She nestled her head in the crook of his arm and he stroked her hair.

"It's so sad." In an unexpected gesture, she lifted her head. "You think it was money? He wanted her money?"

"Certainly if it wasn't all of it, it was part of it."

"And she?"

"Does it need an answer?"

She shook her head.

"You think I'm on the mark?" he asked.

"Would a woman do that because of a man?"

"I'm not a woman."

She grew quiet and he knew she was using the silence to explore the question. He waited.

"Passion, I suppose, makes fools of us all. But I suspect that a woman in the throes could lose all control, especially one who had been deprived. Yes—" He could feel her nodding her head. "A woman conditioned like her could do it. Absolutely."

"Allow herself to be aimed like a missile?"

"And enjoy it." Again she nodded.

"Enjoy?"

"In spades. The sacrifice. The proof of passion. Showing her lover absolute proof of her total commitment."

"But he'd have to be specific in what he wanted."

"Of course. How then would she be able to offer proof?"

"Show me you love me."

"You got it."

"For money?"

"For whatever. I speak only for the woman."

He followed her mental trail, trying to impress her logic onto his understanding.

"And if she were betrayed in the end? By the man."

"I'd say a woman who did that for a man would need a great deal of convincing. A great deal." She patted him deliberately. "Repetitively. For a woman deprived for years it might become— for some, not all—an addiction. Threaten its removal—" He felt her grip grow more earnest. "Earthquakes and eruptions."

"You think so?"

"For her?" She paused. "I'd have to imagine the perils of deprivation. Never been there."

"Passion's pull," he said. "Remember your lit classes. Juliet,

Emma Bovary, Anna Karenina, on and on. Like waving a magic wand.

"More powerful than do re mi."

"Maybe," she sighed, still leaving some room for speculation. Wisdom, he knew, was never absolute. Again, they both grew silent.

"Let's assume the passion was a two-way street?" she asked. He waited, knowing she was intending to answer the question herself. "And the inheritance was a means for them to be free, to go away, to live happily ever after. Something like that. Suppose he was returning the passion in kind. Not merely manipulating. Participating. After all, no one really understands the chemistry that ignites the sexes."

"And the only way he would enjoy the money would be for them to be together," Flanagan said, enlarging the chink in his own theory. It was as if he were deliberately following a completely unfamiliar path. "Suppose it was a one-way street. On his part."

"I don't understand."

"I'm not sure I do myself," he admitted. He felt himself probing deeper into his own mind. "This Dr. Blandings. Has he a girlfriend? Has he ever been seen with a woman? Is he married? What is the emmis?"

"Not a word. No family pictures."

"A handsome bachelor. Comparatively new in town. A rich heiress. Not very attractive. The old cliché. Maybe he has history."

Knowing they were onto something, he let it simmer.

"Do you think men are more rational than women about love?"

"I don't think men are more rational than women about anything."

A spark ignited in the dark tunnel of his mind. He'd have to think about that, he decided, let it lay fallow for awhile. A false accusation would be a real blow for Sam. His thoughts suddenly followed another path. He reached over and embraced Emily.

"Must be awful to be alone," he whispered, knowing that she would understand his meaning. Despite his obvious condition, he was not referring to being physically alone only. Alone had many facets.

"We come in alone and go out alone," she sighed. Stroking her arm, he felt her goose bumps.

"It's all in the in-between," he said, kissing her neck. She caught his arm and kissed his palm. It was, he was sure, beyond words now. Their lives were living proof of their commitment to each other. He felt a profound sense of peace and for the first time in days, with Emily as close to him physically as comfort would allow, he fell into a deep, dreamless sleep.

* * *

AS IF BY PREARRANGEMENT, he was up at dawn. Carefully, he slid himself away from the still-sleeping Emily and quietly dressed. Tiptoeing downstairs, he shaved in the bathroom off the den, then slipped out the back door. After the talk with Emily, he understood. To know the how and why of Lucy Farnsworth's murder was, unfortunately, not enough. An official accusation would be considered dangerously arbitrary and irresponsible. The bottom line was irrevocable. There had to be a confession.

He got into the station wagon, moved it through the alley behind the houses and parked it where he could get a clear view of Dr. Blandings' office. It was in the front parlor of another converted Victorian house, sitting far back on its lot and surrounded by evergreens which previous owners had obviously nurtured with loving care. Dr. Blandings apparently lived on the second floor of the house. Flanagan noted, too, that The Lakeside Falls Herald was lying helter-skelter in front of every door on the block.

The sun was just peeking out under a bank of clouds at the edge of the horizon. In a little while, the clouds would gain the upper hand and blot it out. To keep from attracting attention, he had shut off the motor, leaving the car unheated. He stuck his chin in the turned-up collar of his mackinaw jacket and waited. He was also sorry he had worn his Adidas. Not warm, sensible shoes. There was, he decided, an element of foolishness about his actions. Had he become the town snoop? After all, the enforcement of justice was not his business. Was he, as his mother had characterized, certain of his friends years ago, mischief-makers? He felt himself nodding affirmatively.

Then, through the rearview mirror, he saw her coming. She had just turned the corner three blocks away and was walking purposefully in his direction. He crunched down in the seat, leaving a thin sliver of watching space. He had banked on her following this scenario. She would, obviously, be the less stable of the two, and, therefore, the more anxious. Nor would she trust the phone. He would have warned her about that. He would also have warned her about staying away from him until the smoke cleared. But she would need reassurance, face to face, perhaps body to body, reassurance.

She was moving swiftly, and he noted that there was a furtive, hunted look on her face. She was pale, haggard, hunched up, frightened. Yet, there was no hesitation in her gait as she passed his car, gaining speed as she approached the front entrance of the house. After she entered, he sprang up, started the ignition, and pulled swiftly away, heading for the sheriff's house.

It did not surprise Flanagan that the sheriff was already dressed. He poured out two cups of coffee and they sat in a breakfast nook that overlooked a wide expanse of lawn, still green despite the cold.

"You see the paper?" Sam asked.

"Didn't have to," Flanagan said. "I saw the evidence." He spun out what he had seen that morning. The moment to be coy and manipulative had passed.

"Unfortunately, we can't just barrel in there and confront them," Sam said.

"Now comes the hairy part."

Sam nodded and crinkled, but it was not a smile, more a gesture of painful hesitation.

"But who will be first? The man or the woman?" Flanagan looked at him cautiously, wondering if the question were rhetorical. "Or should they be confronted together?"

Flanagan shrugged, noncommittal.

"Tough call," Sam said. From his pained expression there was no doubt he meant it.

"Especially since it looks like they conspired together this morning. Got their stories straight."

"Break him. Break her," the sheriff said, nodding to himself. Then he looked at Flanagan, obviously for affirmation. Unfortunately, in Flanagan's expression he did not get the answer he was looking for. By all rights, Flanagan thought, he should have been quick to agree. Again, he felt something nag at him, something deep inside, something obscure. The sheriff sighed, shook his head, got up from his chair and paced the room for a few moments. Then he walked to a desk in a corner of the room and took out a folded document, handing it to Flanagan.

Flanagan looked at it, then at Sam, who turned away, finding suddenly some special interest in a batch of unopened mail that was lying on an end table. Opening it, Flanagan read.

"You're deputizing me, Sam?" Flanagan asked. Was it surrender on his part or the highest form of flattery?

"Might as well be in on the kill," the sheriff muttered. Flanagan, of course, knew what he really meant, what was between them now. I need you. The message was loud and clear. Flanagan had to turn his face away to hide eyes welling up.

<h1 style="text-align:center">Chapter Twenty-Three</h1>

Although Flanagan had met him before, both at Lucy Farnsworth's funeral and at the family home after the funeral, he had preserved only the vaguest recollection. But there was no question that he was more to Kay Farnsworth than her mother's optometrist. In a town like Lakeside Falls, when a spinster heiress and an eligible newcomer are seen together at frequent intervals, at times clandestinely, tongues flap, eyes do double takes and the gossip rises like the pull of the tides by the moon.

At that moment, Flanagan sensed a kind of motivation overkill. Too many people had too many reasons to benefit from Lucy Farnsworth's demise. Worse, every motive was infected with desperation.

Dr. Blandings had obviously interrupted a rather busy schedule. His reception room was filled to capacity, but he had sent word out that he was available immediately. Sam introduced Flanagan as his deputy, which somehow rang hollow as if the sheriff had swallowed the word.

Greeting them with mechanical handshakes, Dr. Blandings led them down a corridor to an office in the rear decorated with his diplomas and two prints, one of Mount Vernon in winter and the other of George Washington's tomb. Before sitting down, Flanagan inspected them.

"Currier and Ives. Looks like the real thing."

"It is," Dr. Blandings said with a tiny hint of sarcasm.

"Are you a collector, Doctor?" Flanagan asked.

"My father was," he replied. "He collected American folk art. All kinds. Was a bit of a nut about it. Left me warehouses full."

"Ever had it appraised?" Flanagan asked.

"Some day."

"We didn't come here to discuss folk art," Sam Hazeltine said.

"At your service, Sheriff," Dr. Blandings said. "I assumed it was important."

"It's about Lucy Farnsworth," the sheriff said slowly.

Both men watched the optometrist's face. Not a sign, Flanagan thought. No odd tics. No change of expression in the eyes. Not a shade of difference in the man's skin color.

"I assumed it was," Dr. Blandings said in a businesslike tone. "I saw the papers this morning."

"She was your patient?"

"Yes, she was. I fitted her for lenses."

"You knew she was a diabetic with congestive heart failure?" the sheriff asked.

Dr. Blandings looked back at him severely.

"Of course. To understand the eye of a particular patient, you must know the medical history."

"And you knew the medications she was taking?"

"Absolutely."

The sheriff turned toward Flanagan who nodded.

"Diabinese, digitalis, hydroDIURIL, potassium," Dr. Blandings said, a recitation that seemed to Flanagan surprising in the light of all the patients he was servicing.

"You've got a good memory," Sam said.

"About Lucy Farnsworth. She was a very important patient for me. She sort of broke the ice for me in Lakeside Falls. It's not easy to start a practice in a town like this, with the natives set in their ways."

"And drops for the eyes," Flanagan interjected, hoping to catch the optometrist off guard. It didn't, but did get a reaction of annoyance from the sheriff.

"Of course. She needed constant liquefaction since she did not produce enough tears due to the use of diuretics. Nothing unusual about that."

His expression was unchanging, his answers concise and businesslike. Exactly to the point. Oddly, it was Sam who appeared on the verge of being rattled.

"Then how did the autopsy report find atropine in the eye?" the sheriff asked suddenly. It was meant to be a surprise question. Dr. Blandings showed no surprise.

"I saw that in the papers. Frankly, it was very confusing. The body absorbs it so swiftly. I can understand the hypokalemia. Obviously, she must have been losing potassium faster than it was being replaced. But finding traces of atropine baffles me."

"You know what it's used for?" the sheriff asked. Flanagan wished he would have held that one. The doctor's face registered an expression rather close to contempt.

"Are you serious? In the eye business, we could hardly exist without it. It dilates the pupils. Gives us a chance to study the retina."

"Does it have other uses?"

"I think it's used by veterinarians. Years ago it was used for stomach ailments. It's also a poison."

At that, the sheriff shot a knowing glance at Flanagan.

"We know the cause of death," Flanagan said, summoning up as much humility as he was able to muster. "She didn't die of poison."

"Didn't sound like it," Dr. Blandings said.

The sheriff paused, rubbed his chin, and studied the optometrist. It's coming, Flanagan thought.

"Have you ever treated Kay Farnsworth?" the sheriff asked, the accusation unmistakable. Dr. Blandings showed little reaction.

"I've examined her eyes. She has perfect twenty-twenty vision."

"How long since you last examined her?"

"About a year ago. When her mother first came here."

"They came together?"

"Sheriff, they went everywhere together." Flanagan noted a quickening irritation just beneath the surface.

"She was here on every visit?"

"Of course."

"Never by herself?"

There was a brief flash of uncommon expression. Panic, Flanagan wondered?

"Not for an examination," Dr. Blandings said, with obvious caution.

"A social call?"

"Not exactly. Sometimes she came to pick up her mother's drops. She used a great deal of them. When she ran out, Kay would come by."

"Often?"

"Fairly often."

"Why not go to a pharmacy? Why come by here for a refill?"

"I get lots of samples. It was more like a courtesy. And not just for the drops."

Flanagan saw the hesitation. He watched the man's lips, waiting for the telltale dab of the tongue.

"For what then?" the sheriff asked.

The dab came, a quick stabbing motion. Also there was a brief over-blinking of the eyes.

"You might call it a social call as well," Dr. Blandings muttered. "Kay and I developed a genuine friendship during Mrs. Farnsworth's frequent visits. It takes many of them to be sure a woman in her condition gets the proper results."

"How social?" the sheriff asked.

This time the reaction was clearly hostile.

"I resent the implication of that remark. We were friends. I would not want you to make anything else out of it. Also I don't quite know what you're implying here. I've agreed to be cooperative, but I frankly don't understand where these questions are going. Kay Farnsworth is my friend."

His composure was cracking.

"We could be dealing here with murder, Dr. Blandings," the sheriff said dramatically.

"I noted that fact in the paper, Sheriff. I'm an optometrist. Not a killer."

"Do you believe Lucy Farnsworth was murdered?" the sheriff snapped.

It came too late. The optometrist's equilibrium was already restored. There was a long pause.

"I haven't an opinion either way."

Flanagan detected a sense that he wanted to say more. The sheriff must have felt the same way. What followed was an awkward pose.

Was the time right to spell out their theory on how Mrs. Farnsworth died? Dr. Blandings seemed to be getting away from them. The sheriff was apparently having a simultaneous thought. He looked toward Flanagan, who shrugged and nodded.

"Our theory is this, Doctor."

The sheriff proceeded to outline the logistics of the medical theory, explaining the diabetic neuropathy, Lucy Farnsworth's inability to distinguish by touch, the substitution of the potassium, the inducement of hypokalemia. Most important, the spiking of the tear drops with atropine. The optometrist listened attentively but without any unusual reaction. He was quite obviously back in full command of himself.

"It's an ingenious theory," Dr. Blandings said calmly. "Probably medically correct."

"Especially if we put atropine into the picture."

"Yes," Dr. Blandings agreed. "That would fit nicely. Atropine would paralyze the ciliary muscle within the eye, the one responsible for changing the shape of the crystalline lens within the eye. When her lenses were out, her vision would drop off considerably." Dr. Blandings cleared his throat. "And with the diminished feeling in her fingers, she could make a mistaken identification of her capsules."

He was, Flanagan thought curiously, not showing signs of breaking down at all. It began to worry him. He had expected that the optometrist might be more rattled. A flush was beginning on the sheriff's cheeks, a sure sign of his frustration.

"With that kind of knowledge," Sam said slowly, "all a person would have to do would be to substitute the diuretic for potassium."

"You have a great deal of imagination, Sheriff."

"You don't think it's possible?" Sam said, his annoyance clearly visible.

"Of course, it's medically possible. I told you so, although I doubt that your medical examiner's results, the finding of the atropine, as I also told you before, would stand up. Besides all that, I can't conceive of why anyone would want to deliberately murder Mrs. Farnsworth."

"Money. For one thing," Sam said quickly. There was a long pause. Dr. Blandings was not following his part in the scenario. Flanagan, too, was beginning to feel a sense of galloping frustration.

"Were you and Kay Farnsworth lovers?" Sam Hazeltine asked suddenly, his voice rising. Flanagan watched as the optometrist sucked in a deep breath. Again he began to over-blink, but his hands were steady, his color unrevealing, his expression fixed.

"Good friends, Sheriff," the optometrist said calmly. Then his voice broke slightly. "Not lovers." His voice grew small, as if he had swallowed the words.

"All you did when you got together was to have conversation?"

"Yes."

He seemed to be clamming up, becoming deliberately uncom-
municative.

"No future plans discussed?"

"What we discussed was our business."

"So you did discuss future plans?"

"What exactly are you after, Sheriff?"

"Someone substituted that medication."

"That is a very serious accusation."

"Bet your life it is."

"And you're suggesting that Kay Farnsworth did it?"

"With your help," the sheriff snapped.

It was only then that the optometrist's color drained from his
face. The over-blinking went out of control. His lips curled and
trembled. At that point, though, it did not tell Flanagan much.
Few people would remain calm in the face of such an accusation.

"She visited you early this morning."

"My God, you know that, too?" The man clasped his hands
until his knuckles were almost white.

"What did you talk about?" Sam asked.

Dr. Blandings shrugged in a gesture of resignation.

"She was frightened. She needed reassurance. Those newspaper stories were abominable."

"Why come here? To you?"

"I told you we were friends, good friends. Isn't that the role of
good friends? To give comfort and reassurance?"

"Not lovers?"

"No, not lovers," Dr. Blandings sighed. "Not in the carnal
sense."

"What does that mean?"

"Our relationship was on a higher plane than that."

"She could have used the phone."

"The phone has not yet replaced human beings."

It was, Flanagan noted, starting to go around in circles. The
optometrist's wall held and was going to hold. But all was not
lost. There was a relationship between him and Kay Farnsworth,

freely admitted. Love on a higher plane, Flanagan repeated to himself. Which meant that the opportunity had not yet presented itself for a more intimate relationship. Perhaps both he and Emily had it wrong.

"Are you then denying that you and Kay Farnsworth conspired to kill Miss Farnsworth's mother? That you spiked her tear drops with atropine, caused Miss Farnsworth to substitute potassium supplements with what amounted to overdoses of diuretics...."

Dr. Blandings stood up and slapped his desk. Who could blame him at that point? Yet Flanagan could not fault the sheriff his impatience. If the optometrist was stonewalling, he had succeeded admirably. He had not cracked. He had not sold out Kay Farnsworth.

"Unless you are going to arrest me on these ridiculous charges, I demand that you leave my office immediately. There must be legal recourse for such irresponsible acts on the part of the police. I will not sit here and be badgered. And I would hope that you not confront Kay with such awful, awful accusations. Kay loved her mother with all her heart and soul. I cannot tell you how far off the mark you are, Sheriff. It is wrong, heartless. I can't believe that this is happening."

He glared at the sheriff and Flanagan from what seemed like a morally superior position. In the face of that, there was nothing for them to do but leave. They had, after all, entered the premises on a false note.

"He sure kicked out the props," Flanagan said when they had gotten back into the car.

"When he questioned the atropine being found?"

"A good fallback position. We had no defense."

The sheriff shrugged.

"I could have pulled him in on some pretext," he muttered. "Damned press has my hands tied. Would have been too much of a gamble. Be all over the front page. Probably on the phone to her right this minute, telling her how he was harassed."

After they had gone a few blocks, the sheriff braked to a halt. "Somehow I think we've blown it."

This time the use of the third person was jarring to Flanagan. It implied a joint defeat, like two boxers knocking themselves out in the ring simultaneously. It was not, Flanagan felt, a satisfying denouement. Worse, it would hurt Sam career-wise, which was not, after all, the objective of their little competition. Flanagan's thoughts spun out wildly in different directions. Something was very much awry and he could not fix it in his mind. He felt the sheriff's eyes probing him.

"Dead end?"

Flanagan could not find an adequate answer. The sheriff started the car again and headed toward his office.

"Not dead yet," Flanagan said suddenly, touching Sam's arm. Again, he braked to a halt.

"Kay?"

"Can't quit now. Besides, if the press is going to kill you anyway, they can't kill you twice."

"You think we can break her?"

"Where there's a pill, there's a way."

The sheriff turned and looked at him, his face crinkling with a wry smile. So show me, the smile said. I will, Flanagan answered. Also to himself.

Chapter Twenty-Four

"I see Tony is out," Flanagan said as they turned into the road leading to the Farnsworths' house. The sheriff's eyes darted to the rearview mirror which framed Jack's gas station.

"Looks different without that big black car," Flanagan observed.

"At least they'll keep any eye on him," Sam said. One couldn't quite call it a conspiracy, Flanagan thought. But somewhere down the line Sam must have made a conscious decision to allow the Annunzio family to track their quarry. A small sacrifice for a mob-free county, Flanagan agreed, thankful that it was not his own decision to make.

"He'll never get off their hook, I'm afraid," the sheriff said with some sadness in his tone. "Not until they get their money. In the end he'll be left with nothing."

"And yet, Lucy did try to do the best for her kids. Sometimes it just doesn't work out."

Sam's eldest son Tom had quit high school and was someplace in Montana living out a cowboy fantasy in some cattle ranch. It was a subject seldom broached by Emily or himself. He acknowledged the statement with a grunt.

"At least I know the county's clean. Don't have to be a hypocrite accepting that award." Flanagan detected an edge of apology in his tone. The Farnsworth episode was taking its toll.

A sad and somber Kay let them in. She was wearing black flannel slacks and a black turtleneck sweater, which set off her dead-white complexion. She wore no makeup and her Wedgwood blue eyes peered out at them with a tense and nervous stare. She was clearly frightened, with the look of a trapped animal.

She held herself rigidly with an obvious effort of will; it was apparent that Dr. Blandings had already spoken to her. As one would expect after such a discussion, she made no pretense of being ingratiating.

She led them into the living room and, taking a seat on the couch, clasped her hands in front of her. Contrasted against her black slacks, her hands looked like pieces of delicate white marble. Her posture was stiff, as if she had found the inner strength to brace herself upright. Flanagan had the impression that she was holding body and persona together with intense willpower and determination.

The sheriff cleared his throat, covering his mouth politely with his fist. He did not look at Flanagan, which meant that, at some point, Flanagan would have to take the lead. Not yet, he told himself. Not yet.

"I have to assume that Dr. Blandings has called you," the sheriff began.

"Of course John called me."

The muscles worked in her neck as she held back indignation and anger. Above all, control yourself. That would be the bottom line of Dr. Blandings' admonition to her. She was obviously struggling to keep up a pretense of equilibrium.

Deliberately, the sheriff stretched out his pauses, a common interrogation tactic to induce a nervous compulsion to fill in the gaps with talk. To Flanagan's surprise, Kay seemed to react to it.

"It's the most disgusting accusation I have ever heard. The idea of accusing me of murdering my mother. She was my best and closest friend. I adored her. I loved her dearly. Life without her is...." She started to lose control, but checked herself. "Terrible. Lonely."

"Nevertheless it is my job to find out," the sheriff said gently, very gently.

"What is there to find out? Can't you leave the woman in peace? No one in my family would have done a thing like that. No one. Not Dr. Mowbray either. Even old Blatsford could not have done such a thing. How could he?"

"Nevertheless she did die of hypokalemia."

"She was ill. She died a natural death," Kay said between clenched teeth. "And this idea of my tampering with her medication. The idea is beneath contempt."

"But Dr. Blandings did supply the artificial tears?" The question was offered as a hybrid, both statement and query.

"For an entire year, Dr. Blandings gave those drops. Mother used a great deal of them."

"And you always went to pick them up?"

"Sometimes with mother. Sometimes by myself."

"And you struck up quite a friendship with Dr. Blandings."

"He is a sweet and gentle man. I trust him implicitly. You've hurt him deeply by your accusations. If you only knew what a kind, decent and compassionate man he is. I'm sure he'll take some kind of legal action."

"Did he ever come to the house?"

"On occasion. Yes, he did. Both socially and professionally. And he would always look at her lenses—you know, to see if she was wearing them correctly."

"Socially, you say. To see you as well."

"And mother," she answered quickly.

"He was at the funeral and later at the house."

"Of course. He had become a dear friend."

The sheriff paused, obviously searching his thoughts for some magic lever that would instantaneously open all closed doors.

Something is missing here, Flanagan thought, not quite certain of what it was exactly.

"Did you know what drugs your mother was taking for her various ailments?"

"Of course I did."

"And exactly what each of them was supposed to do?"

"My mother suffered from diabetes for years. When you live with a diabetic, you know her medications. Most of all, she was her own expert. If you had such an affliction, you would know. I am an occasional asthma sufferer. After a while you become your own best doctor."

"So she administered her drugs to herself?"

"My mother depended on no one for that."

"Even in the last moments, as she grew weaker?"

"Her medications were always beside her."

"You didn't help her? No one helped her?"

"Even on the last night of her life, she did it herself. She died in her sleep. Thankfully."

"You noticed nothing different in her drugs? Nothing amiss?"

"No. I did not."

Her attitude seemed to be hardening. Her answers were swift and to the point. Sam's frustration seemed to increase as he searched for different ways to probe.

"All of you depended on her?"

"I did. She was the strongest one of all of us. She had to be, considering her responsibilities."

"Did that affect you? I mean...." Sam was suddenly embarrassed.

"You mean did I feel hemmed in, possessed, not my own person?" She offered a faint trembling smile. "Not in the least. I loved my position with her, loved the way we worked things out. Felt no constraints."

"You weren't sorry you never married?"

She shrugged and her smile broadened.

"Why do people always think in clichés? Why is it necessary to be married? I had her, you see. I was quite content and happy." She paused thoughtfully for a moment. "Occasionally we might get a little snappy and irritated with each other. But isn't that sometimes the way people work things out?" Her look grew vague. "I was a sick little girl myself. My asthma was really bad when I was younger. But mother was always there, always my strength...." Her voice drifted off.

Was the woman deliberately diverting the intent of the sheriff's questions? It was difficult to know.

"When did you throw away your mother's drugs?"

"When?"

She seemed suddenly confused. She scratched the back of one hand with the nails of the other, raising pink tracks on her skin.

"A day or so after the funeral, I suppose. They were of no use to anyone else in the house."

"Not before."

"Before the funeral?" She seemed surprised by the idea. "No, I think we did it a day or so later."

"We?"

"The maid. I couldn't bear to touch her things."

"But you left the clothes?"

"Someday I'll be able to go through them. Keep some of them. Something to keep her memory alive. Or don't you understand such things?"

It was a rebuke. Flanagan could not fault her for it.

"But you ordered the drugs to be removed?"

"I simply told the maid to straighten things out and throw away useless things."

"Like drugs?"

"I suppose I said something like cleaning out the medicine cabinet."

The sheriff glanced at Flanagan, who raised his eyebrows. He was probing, but getting nowhere. It was hardly the kind of questioning to produce a confession. It was obvious, too, that Dr. Blandings had urged her not to be hostile. Yet, despite her obvious effort at control, she sometimes appeared ingenuous, an innocent. Was it possible to be such a consummate actress under such tense conditions?

"When did your mother's eyes start to bother her?" Sam asked.

"I'm not sure. Maybe two weeks before she died. Maybe more."

"Did you tell Dr. Blandings about it?"

"Yes, I did."

"And what did he say?"

"She was not having any trouble when the lenses were in. Only after she took them out. He told us that when she felt better, she should come in and he would examine her. She couldn't wear the lenses all the time. The diuretic dried her eyes out, you see."

"She couldn't read very well?"

"Not without her lenses."

"Bad enough for her to make a mistake in distinguishing her medication?"

"I doubt it. Not after all these years."

"But she also had a loss of feeling in her fingers."

"She knew the containers. I can't see how she would have made a mistake."

"Were the supplements in pill form or capsules?" Flanagan suddenly interjected, his voice surprising them both.

She rubbed her chin.

"I'm really not sure. Capsules, I think. But I couldn't swear to it. You see, I never paid that much attention to it. It was a part of her life that was so personal, hers alone. She was always so thorough about these things."

"But you did get her drops?"

"On occasion. Yes, I did."

"What exactly is your relationship with Dr. Blandings?" Coming as it did, it struck Flanagan as an act of desperation.

Kay's reaction was a trembling smile.

"He said you would ask me that."

"And did he tell you what to answer?"

"Certainly not."

She paused, unclasped her hands and fluttered her fingers in front of her for a moment.

"We became very close friends," she said, shaking her head as if to validate her comment. "I've already told you that."

"Lovers?"

She shook her head.

"More clichés. We were reaching out to each other. I'm sorry to disappoint your dirty minds, gentlemen. It is quite possible to have a relationship on a higher plane than just the physical. No. We never had carnal knowledge of each other."

"Which of you was the inhibiting factor?"

"That is such an awful question to ask," she said with resignation.

The sheriff's discomfort was becoming clearly visible. A film of perspiration had begun to form on his upper lip. "Has he asked to marry him?"

"I think you're getting rather too personal now, Sheriff. I believe I have been completely cooperative up to this point. But I refuse to go beyond the bounds of propriety."

"He told you to say that?"

"No, he didn't. He told me to tell you exactly what I knew. The rest is my idea."

"It seems a pretty harmless question," the sheriff said with a glance at Flanagan.

"It is. But it's very personal to me."

"So he did ask you to marry him?"

"I won't say another word about it."

She squared her shoulders further. Interesting, Flanagan thought, his mind groping to find the real meaning behind her answers. At the same time he searched for distance, detachment, forcing himself to operate on two levels, as both observer and participator. This was the role that Sam had, whether he knew it consciously or not, chosen for him. He saw in Kay now a remarkable transformation. With the inhibiting shadow of her mother removed, she had emerged as a circumscribed entity. Forced to depend on her own resources, she revealed a strength and subtlety that had totally changed his previous understanding of her. Was it also changing his theory of the crime?

He sensed that the pause between the sheriff and the woman had stretched to another dimension. But the pause did not mean silence. The protagonists were merely squaring off, circling, pawing the ground, waiting. Flanagan wondered if the moment for his intervention had come. An idea was growing in his mind, not quite fully materialized. He urged himself to wait.

"Shall I tell you how I see it?" Sam said with slow deliberation.

"I've already heard," Kay said.

"It will stand up," Sam said. Unfortunately his tone was too tentative for credibility.

"No, it won't," the woman snapped, clasping her hands again on her lap, draining their last shades of color.

"You had access. You knew your mother's habits. Dr. Blandings had the medical expertise to understand the implications of a chemically induced imbalance. And, most important, he knew what results would be obtained by manipulating your mother's sight."

"That is totally ridiculous."

"Well then, how do you explain the finding of atropine?"

"John explained that to me. He says it can't be true."

"How can he question the medical examiner's report?"

The ice was beginning to crack under the sheriff's feet. It was, after all, his theoretical ace in the hole. Only it was a total bluff. Flanagan felt a brief stab of compassion for him. He was drowning in Flanagan's man-made pool. The revelation must have been startlingly transparent, for suddenly Kay struck out on her own.

"I don't believe we would ever have had this trouble if it wasn't for him." She gave Flanagan a frosty look. "He's made assumptions that are totally without foundation. He's intruded into our lives. And he's convinced you that something was amiss in my mother's death. Frankly, I don't understand his motive. Even this story about the dolls. A tall tale, Mr. Flanagan."

Flanagan hadn't expected the attack, but it did jog him into action.

"That day of the funeral," Flanagan said. With great effort, he was keeping, as Emily would say, his "dander" down. "We looked in your mother's medicine chest. We could not find your mother's drops. And the bottle of potassium capsules—they were capsules —contained a diuretic capsule. Only one to be sure. But how did it get there?"

"You went into my mother's medicine cabinet? You deliberately did that? How awful. How absolutely awful."

"I'll admit it does sound a bit intrusive," Flanagan said, not without feeling a slight tinge of shame.

"Nosy, you mean."

"Maybe so. But how do you explain it?" Sam asked.

"I don't have to explain it."

The fantasy of her alleged cooperation was fast disintegrating as she took ultimate refuge in indignation. Were they botching it, Flanagan wondered?

"You're not being forthright, Kay," Flanagan said, his tone as accusatory as he could make it. In his mind, he had finally settled on a strategy. He hoped Sam would get the message, although the risks to him were enormous.

"Forthright? I have absolutely nothing to hide." She paused. Her lower lip curled. "Except my rage." She patted her thighs in a gesture of finality and stood up, making it perfectly clear what she wanted them to do. Both Sam and Flanagan remained seated.

"You don't expect me to sit here and listen to your inflammatory accusations?"

"We haven't reached any conclusions yet, Kay," the sheriff said tentatively, obviously backing off.

"Well, I have. You're harassing me. John as well. We have

rights. We have legal recourse. I do not intend to be victimized." She turned toward Sam. "I think you are abusing your office, Sheriff. I say if you are so terribly convinced that I killed my mother, that John and I were, in some way, conspirators, then you should take me into custody." Pressing her wrists together, she offered her outstretched arms. "Just handcuff me and, as they say, take me downtown."

A taunting grin formed on her lips. She was definitely, Flanagan decided, not the same Kay she had been only a few days before. The sheriff glanced toward Flanagan. In his eyes, Flanagan saw defeat, the end of the line. Not yet, Sam, he urged silently.

"That's probably a very good idea," Flanagan said.

Sam's forehead wrinkled in a puzzled frown.

"Take her in?"

"I can't see how you can just let it go. Can you?"

It was a remark expressed deliberately out of character. He dared not signal with his features, since Kay was inspecting both their faces. She appeared incredulous and somewhat stunned.

"For God's sake. Have you people gone crazy?"

"We have to get to the bottom of it," the sheriff muttered. Flanagan felt a sense of relief. Sam, however reluctantly, was going along with the idea. He wondered if the parameters of his plan had become clear, knowing that if he had given it a voice, the sheriff would have rejected it out of hand.

"And suppose I refused to go?"

"Then we'd have to take you by warrant—or force."

"Do you realize how humiliating this is going to be for me— to be accused of the murder of my mother...." Her voice broke briefly, but she quickly recovered.

"I'm sorry," Sam said, avoiding her eyes.

Her indignation had turned to docility. Flanagan hid his pity as best he could.

"Just for further questioning," Sam added. Obviously, he was not sure of the tactic.

"And I suppose it will be all over the papers?"

"With a little luck, we might keep it from them for a while," the sheriff said. "But you might make it easier on all of us by telling us the truth."

She made a scoffing sound.

The sheriff stood up and Flanagan did the same. For a moment, Flanagan was sure that the woman contemplated resistance. But then she rejected it.

"May I make one call?" Kay asked.

"Make as many as you like, Kay," the sheriff said.

Flanagan lagged behind with the sheriff as Kay went upstairs, obviously to make a call far from their prying ears.

"Blandings?" Sam asked.

Flanagan shrugged noncommittally as they both waited in silence.

To the sheriff, Flanagan was sure, it probably seemed as if events were taking on a life of their own. He knew that Sam wanted a reaction from him, certainly a revised scenario. It was a silent offer steadfastly refused. As always between them, there was a departure point, the moment when the sheriff bobbed helplessly in his wake.

Kay came down the stairs, somber and deliberate, giving no hint of the results of her call, although there was in her carriage and demeanor a broad sign of self-assurance.

It was only then that Flanagan knew that their course of action was right on target.

Chapter Twenty-Five

On the way to the sheriff's office, not a word was spoken by any of them. In the rearview mirror, Flanagan could see Kay Farnsworth huddled in a corner of the back seat. Not conscious of being observed, she appeared forlorn, vulnerable, hunched in a heap, like a puppet whose strings had been cut. For Flanagan the sight became too painful to watch, although there was no avoiding thinking about it.

Yet when the car finally stopped abruptly in the parking lot of the sheriff's office, she apparently could summon enough self-possession to let herself out of the car and walk with dignity by the sheriff's side. Flanagan followed them through the lobby and into his reception room, where they were immediately accosted by the two reporters who seemed to have established a permanent camp there.

They immediately rose as he entered with Kay Farnsworth. The young woman reporter aggressively surged forward, elbowing past her male counterpart, the increasingly arrogant Harry Ketchum, who looked seedier and more ill-kempt than ever. There was no question that a frenetic competitive spirit existed between them. Both had obviously grown cocky with exposure.

"Where the hell is the damned photographer?" Ketchum muttered, looking past the shoulder of the oncoming group for the photographer. "Probably gone for a snort." He scowled and ran past them, while the Livingston woman blocked their path in front of the door to the sheriff's office.

"Can't you keep these people out of here?" Sam snorted to Peggy Bilton, who pursed her lips in obvious frustration.

"You can't keep us off county property, Sheriff," Livingston said. Somehow she had managed to keep herself perfectly groomed. She was, unlike her colleague, quite obviously on the way up the media ladder.

"Why is Miss Farnsworth here?" she asked sharply, as if in imitation of someone she had seen in a movie.

"No comment," the sheriff said. Kay stood stoically beside him, her features immobile. They began to move forward. Once again, the Livingston woman blocked their path.

"Is she a suspect?"

"No comment."

"Then she is a suspect?"

"No comment."

Flanagan observed with respect the way in which Sam kept himself under control. He had certainly learned a great deal about how to handle a hostile media. Again they started forward. Again Livingston barred their path.

"She's here. You can't deny that?" Livingston said in frustration.

"No comment."

Her face flushed. Her lips curved inward in an unmistakable expression of extreme frustration. She was, Flanagan observed with some comfort, madder than hell.

"What about the atropine?"

The sheriff turned ashen. Kay looked up at him with sudden confusion. Flanagan watched as the sheriff groped for words. He couldn't seem to muster the energy for a terse "no comment."

"What are you talking about?" he whispered, struggling to gather his wits.

"The atropine," Livingston repeated. "What you told us yesterday? We printed it. You saw it." She held up a copy of the paper. Flanagan felt his projected strategy fall apart like a house of cards.

"I stand on that," Sam said, regaining his voice.

"But it's a lie." Livingston was reveling in her power, embellishing her arrogance with sly glances at Kay and Flanagan. Obviously, she had been saving her little bombshell for the most propitious moment. She had certainly chosen correctly.

"No comment," the sheriff growled.

Thankfully, he had regained some of his poise and they once again began their march to the sheriff's office door. This time Livingston threw herself against the door and flayed out her arms.

"You lied to us, Sheriff. There was no atropine. You owe us an explanation."

Kay gasped audibly, much to Livingston's satisfaction.

"No comment," Sam said, reaching beside her to grasp the knob to the office door.

"We got a copy of the Detroit medical examiner's report, Sheriff. Would you like to see it?" She reached into her oversized bag. To do that, she had to drop her arms. The sheriff lost no time in turning the knob and shouldering the lady aside. With a quick movement, he grasped Kay by the elbow and pushed her through the open door. Flanagan slipped behind them, getting through the door just before Sam slammed it behind him, but not before Livingston got in a last lick.

"They didn't find atropine. You lied and I want to find out what that means."

In his office, Sam got behind his desk as Kay and Flanagan took seats in front of it. At first, the sheriff swiveled in his chair, showing his broad back, facing out of the window, surely seeing nothing more than the potential disaster that was facing him.

Sam Hazeltine was not, after all, a man without imagination.

He could see his career going down in flames. His carefully nurtured image as a paragon of virtue and ethical standards was on the rocky road to oblivion. Nevertheless, Flanagan reasoned, it was unlikely that he had been betrayed by his buddy in Detroit. Sam's most durable instinct was to understand the parameters of trust in human beings. No matter how deep the underlying competitive instinct between Flanagan and himself, for example, Sam knew that Flanagan would never, under any circumstances, betray him.

It seemed obvious to Flanagan that Ketchum and Livingston had somehow found a way to acquire the report through underlings in the Detroit medical examiner's office. Bribery. Theft. What did it matter? The lesson to be learned, painfully, was that the press, in search of a story, stopped at nothing.

Peripherally, as they both waited for the sheriff to face them again, he could see Kay's eyes, like lasers of hate, burning into Sam's back. Finally she could not contain herself.

"You did lie about the atropine. Just as John suspected." She sucked in a deep breath of obvious relief. "For a moment I was beginning to have my doubts."

"Doubts?" Flanagan asked.

Sam swiveled in his chair with sudden curiosity. He was still pale, but his eyes, Flanagan noted, flickered with hope. Kay glanced at the two men in sudden confusion.

"I wouldn't say doubts, exactly," Kay said defensively.

"That Dr. Blandings was telling you the truth?" Flanagan pressed. Sam's head cocked like a concentrating canine.

"About the possibility of Dr. Blandings spiking your mother's artificial tear solution with atropine?"

"It crossed my mind." She squared her shoulders. "But only briefly."

"In other words," Flanagan continued, "our odd speculations did make some sense. They had some logic."

"It did have me concerned," Kay said hesitantly, squirming in her chair. "I told you we are very close friends."

"Sweethearts?"

She shot an angry glance at the sheriff.

"Is all this necessary now?" Kay said. "It will be bad enough when we see the papers tomorrow morning. Why compound it? Frankly, I cannot understand how you ever got the idea that Mother was murdered. I think the best thing for all of us would be to forget it. Enough damage has been done already. Why tear my family apart any further? As for John Blandings, I think we should, once and for all, bury those terrible implications."

The sheriff turned toward Flanagan, who could see in his eyes the sure signs of total capitulation.

"No crime to admit you were wrong, Sheriff," Kay said, unable to resist the temptation to turn the knife. "Although I doubt that you will ever be able to fully salvage your reputation."

"We were just looking for justice, Kay," the sheriff whispered. Flanagan watched and waited.

"You do owe us all an apology, you know," Kay said with surprising gentleness. "I would prefer your not being specific. I'd hate anyone in Lakeside Falls to think that you could even entertain the idea that I caused my mother any harm." She looked down at her lap and clasped her hands tightly, obviously fighting back tears.

"Nothing more to do than to tell them out there that we simply made a mistake," Sam Hazeltine said, pulling himself up to his full height, obviously steeling himself.

"Can I just ask one question, Kay?" Flanagan asked gently.

Kay looked up at him and said nothing.

"Before I ask it, I want you to know that I feel just as awful as the sheriff. After all, it was me that brought these suspicions to his attention. In the end, you see, we men don't know as much about women as we like to think. I know I don't deserve it, but I do wish you would consider forgiveness. I do apologize."

"I'm not ready for that yet," Kay said coldly.

"Now the question. May I?"

"I suppose. If it's only one." She looked at the sheriff. "I really would like to go home, if you don't mind."

"I'll see that you're driven home," Sam said.

"How soon after your mother's death did Dr. Blandings come to your house?"

Her brow wrinkled. He could see the quick rise of agitation. She turned to the sheriff. The color was flowing back into his cheeks.

"As soon as we knew that Mother was dead, I called him. And, bless him, he came right over. It was very comforting. Knowing that you had such a friend."

Suddenly they heard loud noises outside the door. Voices shouting. A moment later, the buzzer sounded on the sheriff's desk. The sheriff pressed a button and Peggy's scratchy, grating voice filled the room.

"It's a Dr. Blandings. He's making a racket. Insists he see you now."

"John...," Kay said, swallowing whatever was coming next.

The sheriff rubbed his chin, glanced toward Flanagan and nodded.

"Send him in," the sheriff said with unmistakable authority.

Dr. Blandings burst through the door. He was far from the cool and confident figure he had cut earlier that day. His face was blotchy, his eyes were swollen and his lips trembling. Yet, despite the air of desperation, he still had a modicum of command over himself. Ignoring Kay and Flanagan, he strode toward the sheriff's desk, put shaking fingers on its ledge and hunched over it, his face directly across from Sam's.

"She knows nothing about it," he cried. "Nothing." For a moment, he lost control, bowed his head and his shoulders shook. Kay seemed to freeze in her chair, pale, immobile, her eyes moist with fright and anguish. Dr. Blandings did not turn around and look at her.

"It was all my idea." Again, he started to break down. "I loved her so. I couldn't wait forever. Until we were old. She would never have married me until her mother died. Oh God God God."

The sound of Kay's gasp, like a hysterical scream turned inward, filled the room. She seemed suddenly to hunch up in her chair, her eyes rolled up and her head fell on her shoulder.

"She's fainted," Sam said, coming round his desk and rubbing her hands.

"Nature's way of shutting it out," Flanagan muttered.

Dr. Blandings dropped to his knees on the floor before Kay's chair.

"Please forgive me, my darling. Can you forgive me? Please." He reached out, but the sheriff brushed him aside.

"I think you're asking a bit much," Flanagan said as Dr. Blandings dissolved in hysterical tears.

Chapter Twenty-Six

"How do you suppose crow tastes in the morning?" Emily said, dipping a bagel in her Queen Victoria Commemoration coffee mug and daintily biting off an end. A moist crumb dropped on a picture of Dr. Blandings handcuffed and being led to the county jail by Sam Hazeltine.

"Who would be eating that?" Flanagan asked, sipping his coffee. He had overslept, a deep, untroubled baby's sleep. When he had finally tramped downstairs in his robe, the tall clocks had already struck ten. Except, of course, for the Hoogendyk, which had struck eleven. As an award for his apparent success, she had made him flapjacks. For some reason, she always made him flapjacks as a gesture of celebration and he always ate them, drowned in maple syrup and butter, down to the last morsel.

While he ate, she had read him the story. It was quite long, taking up almost half the front page and a full page on the inside.

"Herb Braker, of course. Intrepid publisher of this rag."

"The taste of that fat and juicy crow would be sweet, indeed. And it wouldn't be crow. More like pheasant under glass in an especially delicious sauce."

"Sauce?"

"They don't reveal their sauces. I don't reveal mine."

She looked at him and shook her head.

"The objective is to get people's attention, to get them to read, to put down that quarter."

"I give no quarter," Emily muttered.

"Now don't you start. I'm the punny one here."

She blew air threw her teeth.

"Audrey's floating on air. Look at that headline. 'Sheriff Sam Cracks Farnsworth Case.' Sheriff Sam. It sounds so affectionate."

"Big ox needs to be loved," Flanagan said with heavy sarcasm. It was, perhaps secretly, meant to be sincere, but he preferred to show his competitive banner flying high in the wind. She reached across the table and squeezed his hand.

"He's also lucky. Lucky to have you."

"He doesn't have me anymore," Flanagan snapped with mock testiness. "My deputation ran out...." He looked at his watch. "Ten minutes ago."

"So now it can be told," Emily said, expectantly.

Flanagan shook his head.

"It was hairy, Emily. I was thrown off by the stereotype."

"What stereotype?"

"That a woman of a certain age who is not married necessarily pines for a man, would do anything for a man. And if she was, well, unattractive, her desperation would increase proportionately."

"Where did you ever get that idea?"

"That's just it. I don't know."

She looked at him with scolding but gentle eyes.

"I might have opined such a false premise at one of our nocturnal conventions, perfect venue for claptrap that a woman in love would do anything for a man."

"And I believed it."

"And further, I must have illustrated the canard," she said, squeezing his hand again for emphasis. "To heighten the response."

"Works every time. In this case, I simply let my insufferable male ego—I speak generically—get in the way. I did not look at the other side of the coin. Takes two to tango. A man in love is also capable of committing desperate acts to attain the consummation of his obsession."

"What a clinical way to put it."

"You put it better, sweetheart, gave me the idea. I forgot for a moment how crazy a man in love gets," he said. He picked up her hand and kissed it, then worked up to her elbow. "Crazy. Crazy. Crazy."

"But he was also clever," she said, pointing a finger of her free hand. "Pity. He was so good with contact lenses."

"Not clever. Brilliant. And we'd never have got him, either, if he hadn't flown in the transom. But he loved her so much, he couldn't bear to see her hurt or pressured in any way."

"Nasty of you fellows to use her as bait. Poor Kay."

"She stuck with him to the end. Almost...."

They were silent for a long time.

"What did it, Flanagan? What made you turn the corner?"

"Three things," he said, a trifle pompously. "He knew more about Lucy's medication than she did. He specifically referred to them as capsules. She wasn't really sure whether they were capsules or pills. They were, of course, capsules, which was essential to his plan since they—the potassium and the diuretic—had to have, more or less, the same general feel."

"And the second?"

"By then it was the frosting on the cake, of course. The wheels were already in motion. I had to find out if he had gotten to the drugs before we did. You see, he had simply substituted diuretics for potassium supplements. That was easy. He had visited them a number of times socially. Getting into Lucy's medicine cabinet was no sweat. But he had to come back and replace the potassium. Unfortunately, he missed just one little capsule. It could, of course, have got into the container by accident. But it gave me the idea just the same. I'm sure he was just in such a hurry, he was careless. The artificial tear drops, of course, had to be disposed of since they contained the atropine."

"Why didn't he replace the drops?"

"Goes to show. No one is perfect. He didn't expect an investigation in the first place. He was right, too. The medical examiner would never have found the trace of atropine. Goes to show that Dr. Grant knows his onions."

"And the third thing?"

He stretched across the table and kissed her on the lips.

"What's that for?"

"I wanted to see if your breath was bated."

"And was it?"

"I'm hooked."

She pushed him away playfully.

"The third thing, of course, was that my motive went down the tube. I thought he wanted her money. More stereotypes. Then I saw his Currier and Ives and he told me about his father's folk art collection. Warehouse full, he said. It sounded to me—especially, when he said that he had not appraised it as yet—that he was a man to whom money was of secondary interest."

"Just like you, Flanagan."

"I have other more basic priorities," Flanagan said, reaching over and caressing Emily's face. She grabbed his hand and kissed his palm.

"By the way, I donated the dolls to the hospital, including the one out for repairs. After all, the Bonnie Babe worked wonders for little Charlie. Think of what the others would do for other little girls."

"We stay in this business any longer, I figure we'll be broke by the time we're sixty."

He noted that something had changed in the room. The sound of Emily's tumbler.

"You finished it. The jewel tree."

She pointed to the windowsill. On it stood the jewel tree.

Shiny pebbles hanging from wire branches, potted in a small Meissen urn.

"The real value is in the intrinsic beauty."

"Yes it is."

When she turned, she discovered that he was not looking at the tree, but at her.

"As for me, my only interest at the moment is in dolls, live ones, one in particular."

He stood up and walked around the table, bending down to whisper in her ear. "With one exception."

He kissed her hair and went off to flip the sign.

Acclaimed author, playwright, poet, and essayist Warren Adler was best known for "The War of the Roses," his masterpiece fictionalization of a macabre divorce adapted into the BAFTA- and Golden Globe–nominated hit film starring Danny DeVito, Michael Douglas, and Kathleen Turner. Adler's internationally acclaimed stage adaptation of the novel premiered on Broadway in 2015–2016.

Adler also optioned and sold film rights for several of his works, including "Random Hearts" (starring Harrison Ford and Kristin Scott Thomas) and "The Sunset Gang" (produced by Linda Lavin for PBS's American Playhouse series starring Jerry Stiller, Uta Hagen, Harold Gould, and Doris Roberts), which garnered Doris Roberts an Emmy nomination for Best Supporting Actress in a Miniseries.

Adler's works have been translated into more than 25 languages, including his staged version of "The War of the Roses," which opened to spectacular reviews worldwide. Adler taught creative writing seminars at New York University and lectured on creative writing, film and television adaptation, and electronic publishing. He lived with his wife, Sunny, a former magazine editor, in Manhattan.

Also by Warren Adler

FICTION

Banquet Before Dawn

Beneath the Ivory Tower

Blood Ties

Cult

Empty Treasures

Funny Boys

Madeline's Miracles

Mother Nile

Mourning Glory

Natural Enemies

Private Lies

Random Hearts

Residue

The Casanova Embrace

The David Embrace

The Henderson Equation

The Housewife Blues

The Serpent's Bite

The War of the Roses

The War of the Roses: The Children

Treadmill

Twilight Child

Undertow

We Are Holding the President Hostage

CHURCHILL'S SHADOW: A HISTORICAL THRILLER SERIES

Mission Churchill - Written by Alex Abella, Inspired by Warren Adler's Target Churchill

Target Churchill - written by Warren Adler & James C Humes

FLANAGANS ANTIQUES COZY MYSTERIES SERIES

Flanagan's Dolls

Flanagan's Strings by Andrew Frothingham & Warren Adler

THE FIONA FITZGERALD MYSTERY SERIES

American Quartet

American Sextet

Death of a Washington Madame

Immaculate Deception

Senator Love

The Ties That Bind

The Witch of Watergate

Washington Masquerade

THE TRANS-SIBERIAN EXPRESS THRILLERS

Trans-Siberian Express

Trans-Mongolian Express - written by David L Robbins, inspired by Warren Adler's Trans-Siberian Express

SHORT STORY COLLECTIONS

Jackson Hole: Uneasy Eden

Never Too Late For Love

New York Echoes

New York Echoes 2

New York Echoes 3

The Sunset Gang

PLAYS

Dead in the Water

Libido

The Sunset Gang: The Musical

The War of the Roses

Windmills